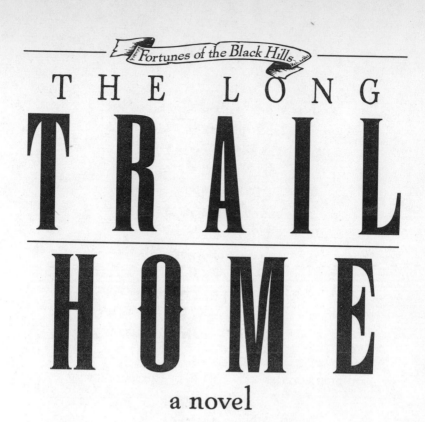

Fortunes of the Black Hills

THE LONG TRAIL HOME

a novel

There will be six books in this series
FORTUNES OF THE BLACK HILLS
by STEPHEN BLY

Book #1
Beneath a Dakota Cross
Book #2
Shadow of Legends
Book #3
The Long Trail Home

For information on other books by this author, write:
Stephen Bly
Winchester, Idaho 83555
or check out
www.blybooks.com

Fortunes of the Black Hills

THE LONG
TRAIL
HOME

a novel

STEPHEN BLY

BROADMAN
& HOLMAN
PUBLISHERS

Nashville, Tennessee

0–8054–2356–7

Published by Broadman & Holman Publishers,
Nashville, Tennessee

Dewey Decimal Classification: 813
Subject Heading: WESTERN FICTION

Library of Congress Cataloging-in-Publication Data

Bly, Stephen A., 1944–
    The long trail home : a novel / Stephen Bly.
        p.   cm. — (Fortunes of the Black Hills ; bk. #3)
    ISBN 0–8054–2356–7
    1. Black Hills (S.D. and Wyo.)—Fiction. I. Title.

PS3552.L93 L65   2001
813'.54—dc21
                                    00-060821

For
Mike
our middle son

"Have mercy upon me, O God, according to thy lovingkindness: according unto the multitude of thy tender mercies blot out my transgressions."

PSALM 51:1 (KJV)

AUTHOR'S NOTES

Sin is lawlessness.

Lawless people have sauntered across the face of the earth since the Garden of Eden. But perhaps no era has had its lawlessness so romanticized and remembered like that of the Old West. Even a hundred years later, the desperados are recalled and portrayed in movies, books, and songs.

Often, we can remember their demise.

In the early morning hours of July 14, 1881, Billy the Kid was shot and killed by Pat Garrett in Pete Maxwell's bedroom at Fort Sumner, New Mexico.

On April 3, 1882, Jesse James was shot in the back by Bob Ford in St. Joseph, Missouri.

On October 5, 1892, Grat and Bob Dalton were killed by irate citizens of Coffeyville, Kansas.

On August 19, 1895, John Wesley Hardin was shot in the back at the Acme Saloon in El Paso, Texas, by John Selman.

And of course, George Leroy Parker (Butch Cassidy) and Harry Longbaugh (the Sundance Kid) were killed in . . . well, that all depends on who you choose to believe—family or film.

However, the Old West did not have bandits hiding behind every sage and cactus. Most folks were law-abiding, but they lived in a land so new, few laws had been established. Temptation was always before them: stagecoaches, banks, and railroads provided a good supply of targets. With law enforcement stretched thin or non-existent, crime often succeeded. Lawless lifestyles needed to be supported because whiskey cost only ten cents a glass and morphine only a quarter. And sometimes, sheer desperation motivated the crime. The civil war left many homeless, shiftless, and jobless.

But not every outlaw met a violent end.

Over seventy years old, Frank James sold tours of the James brothers' farm for fifty cents a person.

In 1910, Cole Younger still toured the country, lecturing on "What Life Has Taught Me."

And some bad men turned out good.

The Lord has always been in the redemption business. He came to the earth to "save sinners." Some of whom, like Samuel Fortune, had spent many a day on the owlhoot trail. Sam Fortune finds that Jesus' work for him provides more than an eternal home.

It drastically affects life on this earth as well.

It's a lesson we all need to learn.

Because, it seems to me, all of us come into this world as spiritual outlaws. And for many, it's a long trail home.

Stephen Bly
Broken Arrow Crossing, Idaho
Fall of '00

CHAPTER ONE

Near Dry Fork, Indian Territory, June 17, 1885

You ain't got no friends left but me, Sammy. All the rest are dead or in prison. Except maybe some lady friends."

In a night too dark to see dirt, Sam Fortune stooped at the waist and tried to catch his breath. The prairie dirt radiated a stifling heat and masked the normal aroma of scattered sage. A lineup of past acquaintances paraded across his mind. *T-Bow: gunned down in a Chinese chophouse in Wichita. Grant: ambushed by a posse while trying to cross the Red River. Elmer Red: knifed in the Signal Mountains along Wildhorse Creek. Whitey and Harmon: hung by Judge Parker. And the rest . . . rotting in some jail, someplace.* Sam stood up straight. He couldn't see the man's straight, black hair that hung well past his shoulder, or his ragged duckings, or his dirty, black felt, wide-brimmed hat, but he could hear him gasp for breath.

"I can't for the life of me figure out how you lasted so long, Kiowa," Sam panted.

"Devilishly good looks and a superior brain," came the low, almost musical reply.

HOME

"Well, pick up your saddle, handsome—we need to keep hikin'."

"Do I detect white-man jealously in that sarcastic reply?"

"Right at the moment, neither of us have a horse, a home, or a meal. In the darkness behind us, six men are ridin' after us, apparently to kill us. I figure your good looks and great brain are in the same fix as mine."

"Fortune, you're a lucky man!" Kiowa called out somewhere ahead of him.

"How do you figure that?"

"Look down there."

Reaching the top of the rise, Sam peered at lantern light that flickered out the front door of a shadowy building.

"That's Dry Fork!" Sam reported.

"Yeah, well all the other folks must be in bed, 'cause only one building still has lanterns lit."

"There is only one building in Dry Fork."

"We hiked ten miles to get to a town with only one building?"

"You want to turn around and hike back?" Sam challenged.

"Well, . . . as long as we're here, we *could* survey it for possibilities."

After a short hike, they sat their saddles on the boulders across from the saloon door. "Stay here. I'll take a look inside. If you hear a ruckus, steal the best horse and ride west. No one's dumb enough to chase you out on the staked Plains."

"If I hear a ruckus, I'm comin' in to save your pitiful white skin again, and you know it."

The building pitched to the right, windblown like everything else for a hundred miles. The clouds that had covered the night sky several hours earlier made the air heavy, smelling of sulfur. It felt too hot to rain but not too hot to hail. In the distance, thunder rolled somewhere out on the Llano Estacado.

Four men with cards in their hands and wide-brimmed hats pulled low huddled around a blue-painted table in the back corner of the twenty-by-thirty-foot room. Two others leaned on the mahogany bar. One propped his massive stomach on the bar itself. To the left, a man wearing a vest embroidered with gold cord sprawled on top of a faro layout. A big woman in a straight-hanging, gray cotton dress and jowls caked with rouge rifled his pockets.

Bullet belts crisscrossed the bartender's chest. A vertical scar on his forehead forced a permanently raised eyebrow as if always asking a question. His chin was clean-shaven but his mustache was bushy and ragged.

Sam ambled slowly up to the bar. Next to the faded portrait of a rotund brown-skinned lady—draped in nearly transparent gauze—a sign read: "Whiskey—10 cents/Water—25 cents."

The bartender sponged the sweat off his forehead with a flour-sack towel. Then he used it to wipe the glass in his hand. "I didn't hear you ride up, mister. What can I get you?"

Sam studied the four at the card table. They, in turn, surveyed him. "I had a friend that said he might leave a message here for me."

"What's your friend's name?" the bartender asked.

"Lafayette Wilson," Sam said.

"He's dead." The bartender slapped the glass upside down next to several others. "Some ol' gal up in Hays City shot him twelve times in the back. Can you imagine that? Twelve shots in the middle of the back."

Sam brushed his mostly gray mustache, then slid his fingers down his narrow chin. "I reckon he didn't leave me a message, then."

HOME

The bartender, reeking of sweat, whiskey, and onions, leaned closer. "I don't know. What name do you go by?"

Sam heard shouts from upstairs. Several bullet holes punctured the unpainted, planked ceiling. The holes were old, and he couldn't tell if they'd been made by firing up or down.

"I said, what name do you go by?"

Sam stared into the man's coal black eyes. "Sam Fortune."

The bartender took a step back. "The outlaw? I heard you was in jail."

The two men at the bar eyed Sam, slapped coins on the counter, and lumbered out the front door.

"I was." Sam watched the two depart, but kept an eye on the four men in the corner. "But I'm out now."

"You escape?"

Fortune's right hand rested on the walnut grip of his Colt .44 revolver. "Why do you ask?"

The bartender again wiped the sweat off his round face with the towel, leaving a clean streak across his cheek. "You're right, ain't none of my business. But there's a woman upstairs who claims to know you. I heard her say that. Maybe she has a message."

"What's her name?"

"Ladosa."

The image of a very short, black-haired woman with long braids and riding boots up to her knees flashed in Fortune's mind. "What room is she in?"

The bartender held up a large, puffy hand. "She's busy right now, but she should be down pretty soon. You want the dime whiskey or the two-bit whiskey?"

"Neither." Sam surveyed the comely woman on the painting behind the bar. "I'd like . . . something to eat."

"It's midnight. Why would you want that?" The bartender wiped his nose on the towel.

"'Cause I'm hungry." Sam studied the worn brass rail of the bar. Half a pair of handcuffs were still fastened to it.

The bartender peered at the woodstove at the end of the bar and waved his hand. "I can give you a fried beef chop and some beans for two bits."

Fortune spied several flies buzzing around a slab of dark red, almost black meat on a chopping block by the stove. "Is the meat spoiled?"

The man shrugged. "Just a little."

"Then fry it extra done, and give me two plates full and a cup of coffee."

The bartender surveyed the open front door. "You expectin' company?"

"Either that, or I'm very hungry."

The bartender shooed the flies with a sweep of his hand and sliced the meat. Then he waved the knife toward the corner table. "You want in on that poker game?"

"No. They haven't dealt a hand since I walked in. It's too slow a game for me."

The big man leaned over toward Sam. "I reckon they cain't figure out whether to shake your hand or shoot you in the back. They ain't got a full cup of brains among the lot of 'em. You want whiskey?"

"Just that coffee."

"Help yourself, but it's gettin' a little rancid. I ought to wash that pot one of these weeks."

Fortune poured himself a tin cup of steaming, black, lumpy liquid, then strolled to the open doorway; one hand rested on the grip of his revolver.

HOME

They don't have the nerve to shoot me in the back. At least, not yet.
He pulled off his hat with his right hand and took a sip of coffee.
Without glancing out into the darkness beyond the doorway, he replaced his felt hat and meandered over to the big woman who stood
behind the faro table. The man with the black beard still sprawled
on his stomach, motionless on the green felt table. She was dealing
out a hand of solitaire on the back of the man's gold braided vest.

She looked at Sam. A soft, pleasant smile broke across her puffy
lips.

"You want to play faro, honey?" she asked.

Fortune pointed his coffee cup at the man on the table. "Is he
dead or alive?"

"Don't matter, does it?" she winked. "But, I'll throw him on the
floor if you want to play."

He stepped closer to the lady and caught a whiff of very strong,
lilac perfume. "Darlin', I'm just wonderin' if that's the way all your
customers end up."

She grabbed a handful of the man's oily, dark hair and yanked
his head up off the table then dropped it down with a thud. "Only
them that welch a bet."

Sam took another sip of hot, bitter coffee. "Leave him there.
Looks sort of picturesque, you playin' cards on his back." He turned
a one-armed wooden chair so its back was to the wall and plopped
down beside the woman.

Kiowa Fox entered the saloon and meandered to the bar. His
duckings looked even more tattered in the lantern light of the
saloon.

The large woman continued playing cards on the unconscious
man's back. "You hidin' out or just lost?"

Sam took another sip of coffee but didn't look up at her.
"Neither."

"Mister, no one comes to Dry Fork unless they're hidin' or lost. There is absolutely no other excuse for being in this place."

"Which is it for you?" he challenged.

"Hidin' from an angry husband."

"Yours? Or some other gal's?"

Her laughter rolled out like the lowest notes on a piano. "Both! Now, it's your turn."

He peered at the stairway in the back of the room. "I'm waitin' for someone."

She studied the numberless playing cards in her hand. "The half-breed you signaled at the door is over at the bar now."

"You don't miss very much."

"There ain't very much happenin'." She poked two cards in front of him. "Which one of these queens do you think I look like?"

"Neither, darlin'—they are both old and fat-faced."

She buried the queens in the deck and looked around the room. "Who are you waitin' for?"

Sam sipped the now tepid, rancid coffee. "Ladosa."

She sorted three cards in her right hand. "I should have known."

He rocked the chair back on its hind legs. "I just want to talk to her."

The woman raised her thin, dark eyebrows. "Honey, this is Dry Fork. We don't give a cow chip what you two do."

"I'm waitin' to see if she has a message for me."

"She's up visitin' with the deputy."

Fortune sat his chair back down with a thud. "Who's up there?"

She reached over with long fingers and patted his shoulder, as if patting a favorite dog's head. "You ain't much of a card player, precious. You jist tipped your hand. You on the run?"

HOME

"Let's just say I'd rather avoid a deputy U.S. marshal." He stood up and glanced at her makeshift table. "The jack of hearts will play on the queen of clubs."

"You talkin' cards?"

He grinned and squeezed her hand. "Yep."

"That's too bad." She tugged at the sleeve of his cotton shirt. "You sure you don't want to play?"

"I'm lousy at cards, remember?"

"Of course I remember, honey." Her light, girlish giggle did not match her size. "That's why I asked you."

"I think I'll check on my chops."

"The meat's rank," she warned him.

"Anybody get sick on it?"

"Not yet."

"Well, if it kills me, you can have first rights to rifle my pockets."

A big grin broke across her face. "I'll take you up on that, darlin'."

Sam Fortune headed toward the bar. The four men at the poker table followed his every step. Their cards still laid facedown on the round blue table. He backed up against the bar next to Kiowa Fox.

"Is that man on the faro table dead?"

"Nobody seems to know . . . or care," Sam reported.

"You want a whiskey, yet?" the bartender called from the frying pan.

Kiowa set down his glass. "My compadre don't believe in drinkin' alcohol. Course, he could drink this dime stuff. There ain't nothin' in it but prickly pear juice and strychnine." He leaned a little closer to Fortune, and lowered his voice. "Those four in the corner drinkin' up the nerve to start a fight?"

"Sort of looks like it."

"Spot anyone you know?"

"Not yet," Fortune whispered.

"Good, let's go steal us a horse."

"What? And miss a fine meal?"

Kiowa pointed at the woodstove. "You ain't really goin' to eat that, are you? I hear it's spoiled."

Fortune pointed at the whiskey glass. "You aren't really goin' to drink that, are you?"

Kiowa threw his head back and gulped down the amber liquid. "Maybe we ought to leave. There's only six horses left out there."

"Which direction did the first two head?"

"East."

"Good. We won't trip over them later. Did you ever know a girl over at Fort Still named Ladosa? She's not much more than four foot eight."

Kiowa raised his thick, black eyebrows. "Ladosa McKay is in Dry Fork?"

"How many other Ladosas do you know?"

"Maybe I'll wait, too," Kiowa grinned. "She may be short, but she's fully growed elsewhere."

Sam kept his eyes focused on the front door and the black Oklahoma night. "She's upstairs with a deputy U.S. marshal."

Kiowa's hand slipped down to his holstered .44. Chairs scooted from the corner table, and two men jumped to their feet. All faced the bar; hands rested on pistol grips.

"You boys aren't gettin' much poker played," Sam called out. "You seem to be a little nervous."

"We're jist waitin' for you to make your move, Fortune," a shallow-eyed man mumbled.

9

HOME

Fortune looked each of the men in the eyes. "Boys, all I'm here to do is eat a chop." *There's not a one of 'em that would draw on me face-to-face.*

"That there meat's a little spoiled." The spokesman kept his left hand buried in the pocket of his jacket.

Fortune's face returned no expression. "A man has to take a few risks in life."

"Ain't that the truth," a short, red-haired man agreed. His right hand now clutched the grip of his revolver. His finger rested on the trigger of the barely holstered gun.

"Mister, that ain't a risk you want to take," Kiowa informed him.

The men slowly pulled their hands away from their guns. The two that stood sat back down.

"Your chops is ready," the bartender interrupted. Two tin pie dishes, piled with slabs of blackened meat and smothered in pinto beans with hunks of sourdough bread plopped on top, appeared before them. "You want a fork or a knife?" the cook asked.

"Both," Kiowa instructed.

"Well, ain't you choosy?" He tossed the tinware on the counter. "That's four bits for the two suppers."

Sam Fortune paid the money. "Think we'll eat out in the dark on the porch," he announced. "That way we don't have to see how spoiled the meat is."

"How do I know you ain't goin' to steal them plates?" the bartender protested.

"Why on earth would we do that?" Kiowa picked up his plate and walked to the door.

"Tell Ladosa I want to talk to her," Fortune commanded as he scooted out into the night.

The men hiked across the dirt road, then sat on the boulders in the shadows, and faced the front of the saloon.

Kiowa took a big bite of beans and wiped his mouth with the back of his hand. "How long before they sneak up the side of the building?"

"Not until Ladosa comes out," Sam surmised. "They'll use her for a diversion." He cut off a chunk of meat, stabbed it with the knife, and plopped it into his mouth. It tasted like fried fat and burnt toast.

"The longer we sit here, the harder it will be to steal a horse," Kiowa stated. "They'll have someone at the window."

Sam swallowed a wad of half-chewed meat and felt it rub all the way down his throat. "I don't aim to steal a deputy's horse."

Kiowa mopped beans with sourdough bread. "We goin' to wait until he rides off?"

"The others will just fret and drink themselves into a stupor. Maybe we ought to wait until they all pass out." Sam scooped beans into his mouth with his knife. They tasted crusty and smothered in hot spices.

"You know what's funny, amigo?" Kiowa laughed. "That deputy is goin' to come out here looking for us carrying a lantern tryin' to cut our trail—but he'll look for horse prints, and he won't find any. The amazin' Kiowa Fox is impossible to track on horseback, especially when he doesn't have a horse!"

For several minutes the only sounds were the scraping of tin pie plates and the smacking of lips.

"Here she comes!" Fortune pointed across the dirt road to the open door of the saloon. "In the black dress."

"That ain't no dress," Kiowa whispered.

"Sure it is."

"There ain't enough of it to be a dress."

Sam took a big bite of sourdough bread. "Well, it's Ladosa, all right."

HOME

Kiowa scratched the back of his neck. "Ever'one includin' the angels in heaven can see that."

They pulled back into the deep shadows of the boulders.

"Sammy?" the lady called out staring into the June night.

Fortune pointed to both sides of the Dry Fork Saloon, where men snuck in the shadows. Kiowa Fox scooped up a rock the size of a sweet potato and chunked it fifty feet to their left.

Four shots flared almost in unison.

"What are you doin'?" Ladosa screamed. "Sammy's a friend of mine!" She yanked a broken crate off the front porch and tossed it at the shadowy gunmen. Then she spun around and stomped back into the building.

Sam watched through the saloon door. Ladosa marched across the room and up the stairs. Several men entered the saloon from the back door, then all the lights dimmed to black.

"They're layin' in for a siege," Kiowa whispered. "What are we goin' to do?"

"Finish our supper. We've got the advantage."

"How do you figure that? They've got six men and two women."

"Seven men," Sam corrected.

"Are you countin' the dead one?"

"Yep, but we got the edge. We know where they are—but they don't know where we are."

"You think they'll try to sneak out after us again?"

"Nope." Sam picked his teeth with the fingernail of his little finger. "They've got no motivation. No reward's out on me. No warrants. And they don't know you."

"Some of 'em jist want to be the one who shot Sam Fortune."

"I don't know which is sadder, Kiowa, them or us."

"I'll sneak up there and get us two horses."

"Not until I talk to Ladosa."

"She ran upstairs."

"She'll come see me."

"The old 'Sammy charm'?"

"I just treat 'em decent, that's all."

"She ain't a decent woman."

"I figure that's for the Lord to decide, not me." Fortune pointed to the side of the leaning building. "Over there! She's climbing down that escape ladder."

"I don't see nothin'," Kiowa insisted.

"Neither do I," Sam replied. "But, I hear the rustle of her petticoat."

"She wasn't wearin' a petticoat."

"She is now," Fortune assured.

"Sammy, you're crazy."

"Finish your supper. We'll be leavin' soon," Sam whispered.

"On horseback?"

"That remains to be seen."

"I ain't walkin' out on that Staked Plain," Kiowa declared.

"Maybe we'll go north."

"I ain't walkin' north either."

Fortune sat his tin plate quietly on the boulders, then crept to the edge of the road. By crouching low on his haunches, he could spy the dark silhouette of Ladosa McKay.

"Sammy?" she whispered.

He scooted far to her right, then answered softly, "Don't walk to my voice, Ladosa, keep walkin' straight."

She had crossed the road in the dark and was about to stumble into the boulders when he called out again, "Stay right there, darlin'. I'll come to you."

She flinched but didn't say a word when he slipped his hand into hers. He tugged her back into the safety of the rocks.

HOME

He could not see her face, but he smelled her rose perfume and felt her dancing brown eyes on him.

"Sammy, who's with you?" she asked.

"You remember Kiowa?"

Her voice dropped to a soft murmur, "I thought he was dead."

Kiowa's voice was low, lilting: "I am . . ."

"That ain't funny," Ladosa complained.

"His death was just a vicious rumor," Fortune added.

"Who would start a rumor like that?" she quizzed.

"Me," Kiowa chuckled. "Bounty hunters don't go after dead men."

"What are you two doin' here? Don't you know there's a deputy U.S. marshal in there?"

"Which one?" Kiowa queried.

"Roberts."

"We're out here whisperin' because of S. D. Roberts?" Kiowa groaned. "He couldn't hit a buffalo with a shotgun at ten feet."

Ladosa pressed her chest against Sam Fortune's arm, her hand still in his. "As long as you don't go near that saloon, they won't come after you. At least, not until daylight. They're all scared to death of the legendary Sam Fortune."

"We'll be out of here by daylight." Fortune released her fingers and stepped back. "How have you been, Ladosa? Why are you out here at the edge of the plains?"

"Sammy, how long has it been since you were in Fort Still?"

"Not since I got out of jail."

"Well, it's bad. The Apaches and the Comanches were knifin' each other, and the soldiers stayed drunk most of the time. Then the Ratton Boys moved up, and it was like a civil war. I hitched a ride with a drummer and got out. This is as far as he made it."

"What do you mean, 'this is as far as he made it'?"

"He got shot in a poker game. I was stuck without a penny. Well, I do have one valise of clothes, two jack mules, and a wagon half full of General Marsh's Health Restorer. Now you know why I'm here, but I don't know why you're here."

"We rode our horses down. We stopped to pick up a couple new ones," Sam announced.

Ladosa clutched onto Fortune's arm. "There ain't any horses for sale around here."

"That's OK," Kiowa laughed; "we don't have any money."

"If you steal that deputy's horse, he'll follow you for sure. Course, he might follow you, even if you don't steal the horses," she warned.

Sam sat back on a boulder and pulled her closer. Her bare arms felt soft, smooth, and warm to his calloused hands. "I served my sentence. They can't arrest me in Indian Territory."

"No one wants to arrest you, Sammy," she clarified, "they want to shoot you. Pat Garrett, Bob Ford, Jack McCall—everyone knows the names of the men who kill famous gunfighters. They're lookin' for fame and some free drinks."

"Sam Fortune doesn't rank up there with those."

"Maybe not in the states, but you certainly do in the Territory. Ain't that so, Kiowa?"

Fox scraped his tin plate with his knife. "Ladosa's right, amigo."

"You want to go for a ride, darlin'?" Sam invited.

"I thought you said you didn't have a horse?" she countered.

"We don't. But we can all ride in your wagon."

With him sitting and her standing, their heads were about the same height, though she was still unseen in the darkness. "You want me to hitch up my wagon and take you somewhere?"

"If we don't steal a horse, they got no claim on following us. We could swing over to Texas and drive up to the Washita."

HOME

"And then where?" She pulled away. "Once you two get horses, you'll leave me in some dump worse than Dry Fork."

Sam reached out and felt a satin dress at her shoulders. He began to rub her neck and back. "There is no place worse than Dry Fork."

She leaned into him. Her neck muscles relaxed.

"Where do you want to go, Ladosa darlin'?"

"Dodge City, Kansas."

"We'll take you there," Sam assured.

"No we won't! I'll get hung on sight in Dodge," Kiowa protested.

"Then, we'll take you near Dodge City," Fortune promised.

Excitement filled her voice, "Really?"

"Yep."

She stepped toward the darkened saloon. "OK, I'll do it. Let me sneak back in and pack my things. My mules are in the corral behind the saloon, and the wagon is behind the privy. But I don't know how you two will hitch it up and ride out of here without them shootin' you."

"I thought I'd tie 'em up first." Fortune took a hold of her small hand.

"How are you goin' to do that?" she asked.

He tugged her close. "I'll sneak back in with you, darlin'."

"You're crazy, Sam Fortune," she said.

He pulled her fingers up to his lips and kissed them. "You've known that for a long, long time."

☞ ☞ ☞

Overpowering the aroma of dirt and grime in Ladosa's room was the waft of a recently extinguished vanilla candle, and the sweet sickening smell of rose perfume filled the room.

16

"Can you find your things in the dark?" he whispered.

"I spent most of my life in the dark. Besides, my valise has been my dresser ever since I arrived in Dry Fork."

He cracked open her door and tried to eavesdrop on the hushed conversation in the room below. He felt Ladosa's hand touch his shoulder. "I'm ready," she whispered.

"Darlin', when you get down, help Kiowa hitch up your mules to the wagon, but don't drive it around front until you see light come on in the saloon."

"And the saddle horses?"

"Leave 'em at the rail for now. I want 'em to see that we didn't steal any horses."

"Are you sure you can handle the deputy and five men?" she worried.

"Six, countin' the dead one on the faro table. Where's the big woman goin' to be?"

"Monique went to her room, locked the door, and took her laudanum as soon as the lanterns went out. She won't wake up until afternoon."

"Monique? Her name's Monique?"

"Yeah. So what?"

"She doesn't look like a Monique, that's all." He clutched her arm. "Before you go back down, call the deputy up here."

Her lips were only an inch away from his. "You goin' to kill him?" she questioned.

"Of course not. I wouldn't have to go to all of this trouble to kill him. I'll just crease his head and let him sleep it off in your room."

"What shall I say?"

"Anythin' that'll make him hurry in here with his gun in his holster."

HOME

"What if he won't come?"

"Honey, any man that won't come when you call ain't much of a man."

She kissed his lips then scooted over to the partially open door.

"S. D.?" she sang out. "I'm scared up here by myself. Why don't you come up here and keep me company?"

A deep voice rumbled up from the room below, "We're waitin' for Fortune to make his move."

"Well, havin' one gun at the head of the stairs would be a good position, wouldn't it?" she persuaded. "I'm really, really lonesome."

Boot heels rattled across the wooden saloon floor and started up the stairs. Sam motioned toward the bed, Ladosa stepped back, and he crouched behind the now open door.

"Don't just stand in the doorway, Deputy," Ladosa cooed.

He took two steps forward.

Fortune slammed the barrel of his .44 revolver into the back of the man's head and kicked the door closed.

The deputy collapsed on the bed.

Ladosa scampered to the window and out on the ladder with her valise.

Sam opened the door slowly, grateful it didn't squeak. He sat on the stairs and slid down one step at a time, his pistol in his right hand, his head behind the handrail. The room was coal black. He listened carefully as he neared the saloon floor. The voices were muted, anxious.

"That deputy has the right idea."

"It sure beats sweatin' here in the dark."

"They's left for sure. There ain't nothin' in all of Dry Fork that Sam Fortune wants to steal."

"Our horses are still out there. I say they're out there, and they're goin' to steal our horses."

"Well, they ain't gettin' much there. We stole 'em three days ago and purty near rode 'em down. I say we're missin' out on a good poker game."

"Ain't nothin' good about it. You was cheatin', Leon, and you knowed it."

Fortune heard the hammer on a revolver click.

"You callin' me a card cheat?"

"Not in the dark, I ain't. Simmer down. Let's have another whiskey."

"Cain't—the bartender is asleep on top the bar, a pistol in each hand."

"The deputy went upstairs. The bartender's snorin'. They ain't takin' this seriously!"

"If it's so blame serious, why don't you go out there in the dark after Fortune and that half-breed?"

"I ain't goin' out there until it breaks day."

"Well, ain't this a fine sight? They probably stole our horses and rode off, and we is hidin' under our desks like schoolgirls."

"Our horses are still there," one voice reported.

"Well, if somethin' don't happen soon, I'm goin' to play poker."

Sam Fortune tugged off his boots and padded slowly toward the bar in his stocking feet. With his eyes adjusted, the room's shadows varied from dark gray to black to dark black.

His big toe stuck out of his sock and brushed along the sticky wooden floor. He slipped behind the bar and sniffed his way to the unbathed bartender. Sam pinched the man's nose closed and shoved the barrel of his .44 into his mouth. The startled man jerked up but found his head pinned to the top of the bar. Fortune yanked both revolvers out of the man's hands.

"Hey, barkeep, you awake? We want some whiskey over here—the good kind," someone demanded.

HOME

"He's still asleep," another guessed.

"He ain't snorin'."

"I'll get the whiskey."

Sam hunkered down behind the bar and listened to the man's boots.

"How am I goin' to see which is the good whiskey?"

"Light a match."

"Fortune will shoot me fer sure if he sees a light in here."

"Squat down behind the bar to light it. He can't see through walls, and you're too far from the door."

Sam held one of the bartender's revolvers in each hand. Only a few feet away, he heard the man fumble for a match. Suddenly the light flared and Sam jammed a barrel in each of the man's ears.

The man's eyes widened.

The match dropped.

"Tell them to light a lantern," Fortune hissed as he forced the man to his feet with guns in place.

"Light a lantern . . .," the man managed to choke out.

"We ain't goin' to light no lantern. Use a match."

Fortune pulled both hammers back at the same time. "I said light a lantern!" Sam's captive hollered.

"Get away from the windows, boys," one warned. "I want to see what's goin' on over there."

When the kerosene lantern began to glow, Fortune sat on the bar behind a frightened man with one gun in his ear. The other revolver pointed at the three near the front door.

"How'd you get in here?" one of them roared.

"Lay your guns on the floor," he ordered.

"What's he doin'?" one of the men pointed to the bartender, who laid on his back on the bar. Fortune's revolver stuck in his mouth like a steel sucker.

"He's lyin' real still. I've got such a hair trigger on that gun—if he even moves his head a half-inch, it will go off."

"But you ain't got your hand on it."

"Doesn't matter. You so much as stomp your foot, and it will send a lead ball through the back of his brain."

"I don't believe that," one growled.

"I doesn't matter what you believe. It's what the bartender believes that counts," Sam added.

"Do what he says, boys. You ain't got a gun stuck in your ear," the one next to Fortune blurted out.

"We ain't goin' to put down our guns and let you kill us unarmed," another insisted.

"You ever known Sam Fortune to shoot an unarmed man?" The three spun around to see the grinning face of Kiowa Fox.

The bartender mumbled something.

"What'd he say?"

"I think he said to lay down your guns," Fortune smiled. "Either that, or he wants me to uncock the pistol in his mouth."

The three dropped their revolvers on the floor of the saloon.

"Now stand up," Sam ordered.

"What are you goin' to do, Fortune?"

"I'm just goin' on down the road, boys. I don't aim for any back shooters to be followin' me. Kiowa, hunt up all the rope you can find. Let's tie these boys tight."

The man on the bar continued to sweat and stare at the pistol in his mouth while Kiowa tied the four others to their chairs around the poker table. He tied their hands in their laps and their shoulders and feet to the straight-backed wooden chairs, and then he shuffled the cards.

"What are you doin'?" one asked.

HOME

"Figured you might want to do a little bettin'." Kiowa dealt out four hands of five cards each. Then he fanned the cards and wedged them into their bound hands.

"We ain't takin' this lightly," the heaviest of the men sneered. "They hang horse thieves around here!"

"Since when?" Kiowa challenged. "You four are still alive. Besides, we aren't taking your horses," he added.

Kiowa strolled behind the bar. "How about this one?" he indicated the barkeep.

"Retrieve my gun for me."

Kiowa yanked the gun out of the barkeep's mouth. "Look at this, Sam—you had this gun clicked only once, not even at full cock. It couldn't have gone off even if you'd pulled the trigger."

Fortune grinned. "Well, I'll be!"

"That ain't funny!" The bartender raised his head straight up, and Kiowa crashed the barrel of the revolver into it. The man crumpled back onto the bar. "I ran out of rope," Kiowa shrugged. "Shall we leave the lantern on?"

"Sure, we don't want these boys to play poker in the dark."

A shot crashed into the painting behind the bar and showered Kiowa with splinters. He dove down. The man who had been passed out on the faro table now propped on one elbow and waved an old Walker Colt. Sam dropped to the floor and rolled. The man's second shot misfired in the barrel of the gun, and the recoil sent the barrel flying back into his temple. Again he collapsed on the faro table.

"I think he knocked himself out," Sam informed Kiowa, who crouched behind the bar.

Kiowa stood up and peered across the shadows. "I liked that ol' boy best when he was dead."

"Yank off his belt and tie his hands to the legs of that table before he resurrects himself again," Fortune instructed. "I'll go get the horses."

"You steal our horses, and we'll track you down!" one of the men at the poker table screamed.

"I didn't say I'm goin' to steal the horses, I said 'get the horses.'"

☞ ☞ ☞

Ladosa McKay sat in the front seat of the wagon and watched as Fox and Fortune tossed saddles into the boulders and tugged, pushed, and cajoled each of the six horses through the front door into the saloon. When they had finished they threw the bridles into the rocks with the saddles.

Kiowa stared at the darkness of the saloon, "You change your mind about the lantern?"

"Didn't want those horses kickin' it over and startin' a fire," Sam explained.

"They'll get panicky pretty soon," Kiowa reported.

"The men or the horses?"

"Both. Did you nail the doors shut?"

Sam pushed his hat back. "All the doors and windows."

"That ought to make for an interestin' evenin'."

"And who said it's boring out here on the plains?" Sam swung up in the wagon to Ladosa's side. Kiowa Fox on the other.

Sam slipped his arm around her shoulders. "All right, darlin', take us to Kansas."

The wagon lurched forward into the dark June night.

"Sam Fortune, I cain't for the life of me see how you ever stayed alive this long," she said. "It must be your mama's prayers."

HOME

Fortune's voice was soft. "Mama died thirteen years ago. But Daddy is a prayin' man."

"Good," Ladosa encouraged. "'Cause we might need them prayers tonight. If they get loose, they'll follow us. A mule wagon is mighty easy to track."

Sam hugged her shoulders. "They won't follow. We didn't steal anythin'."

"Yeah, somehow that don't seem right," Kiowa added. "At least we could have taken some food."

"You don't want anything from that kitchen," Ladosa warned. "The meat's spoiled."

☞ ☞ ☞

By sunrise they crossed into the Texas panhandle and headed north toward the Canadian River. The heavy clouds kept the air hot and humid. Kiowa slept in the back of the half-empty wagon as Ladosa continued to drive.

Her voice sounded sleepy, "We've got to buy some supplies if we're goin' all the way to Dodge."

Fortune studied the treeless horizon. "Maybe we ought to drive over to Antelope Flats and buy some food."

"I'll get arrested if I show up in Antelope," Kiowa called out.

"Is there anywhere you could go and not get arrested?" Ladosa questioned.

"Dry Fork . . .," he laughed. "But go on into Antelope Flats. I'll jist hide out back here. Besides, I could use the sleep."

"I presume you two are flat out busted, being on foot and all," Ladosa probed.

"We've got a couple dollars," Fortune confessed.

"Let me get this straight," she brushed her fingers through her long, black, uncombed hair: "You two talk me into leavin' with you, only I have to provide the rig and the grub?"

"Mighty presumptuous, ain't it?" Kiowa called out.

She wiped the back of her hand across her small, round nose. "It's sad. Course, it was the best offer I've had in months."

"Now, that's sad," Sam laughed. He glanced back at Kiowa. "We'd better buy some bullets in Antelope Flats . . . if Ladosa can afford it."

She slapped the lead lines on the mule's rump, but the animal kept to its plodding gait. "We need to go to Antelope Flats for your package, unless you've already picked it up."

Sam stretched out his arms and tried to loosen a dirty, stiff neck. "What package are you talkin' about?"

"Piney Burleson has been lookin' all over the Territory for you, because she has a package for you. Last I heard she was in Antelope Flats," Ladosa explained.

"I haven't seen Piney since I got out of prison."

"Well, she told me to tell you about a package from Deadwood, Dakota Territory."

Kiowa sat up in the back of the wagon. "You got family in Deadwood, don't you, Sam?"

"My older brother and his wife . . . Li'l sis is there with—"

"Your daddy's in Deadwood, ain't he?" Kiowa pressed.

"Last I heard," Sam mumbled.

Kiowa reached forward and slapped him on the back. "Well, they done sent you a Christmas present, boy, and you ain't picked it up."

Sam stared out across the bare panhandle plains. A stiff wind blew from the south. "It's June."

"Piney's held onto it for months," Ladosa added.

"I thought she was in Fort Smith," Fortune murmured.

HOME

"Nope. She's up at Antelope Flats. She opened up a . . . sewing business."

"Could be a trap," Kiowa warned. "Someone might jist be using the parcel to get you within shootin' distance, Sammy."

"Kiowa's got a point. It might not be smart to go where someone's expectin' me, just for a moldy fruitcake."

"It ain't a fruitcake. It's a Sharps carbine." Ladosa asserted, "And we ain't goin' to Dodge City until you pick it up."

Sam Fortune jerked around. He felt like someone had kicked him in the ribs. "A what?"

"Piney peeked at it and told me it was a converted .50-caliber Sharps, saddle-ring carbine. Now, that's worth gettin', ain't it?"

Sam yanked the lead lines out of her hands and jerked the rig to a stop. "That's Daddy's gun!" he blurted out.

"Well, it's yours now." She grabbed the lead lines away and lurched the rig forward.

"He wouldn't give that gun to anyone on the face of the earth." A cold sweat broke across Fortune's forehead. "Not while there was a breath of life in him, anyway."

CHAPTER
TWO

Antelope Flats, along the disputed
Texas/Indian Territory border

Piney ain't all here, you know." The man's narrow, straight side-
burns dropped off below his jowls and made his lower jaw look
like a locomotive piston when he spoke. He wore a dark gray, wool
suit with a matching vest, dingy white shirt, and stained gray tie.
The suit, dusty and slightly wrinkled, lacked the entire right sleeve
of the jacket, as though it had been ripped off at the shoulder.

Sam Fortune leaned against the red-spoked wagon wheel as
the two mules drank from the leaky, wooden water trough. Sam's
square, broad shoulders contrasted with his thin face.

In front of a one-story adobe building with a faded sign that read
"The Ohaysis," stretched a huge patch of prickly pear cactus like a
spiny wart on the June-dry dirt. He looked up and down the two
blocks that contained every building. Antelope Flats proved a busy
town only in the man-made shade. Sam couldn't spot a tree anywhere.

He turned to the man with one coat sleeve. "What do you
mean, 'Piney ain't here'? Where is she?"

27

HOME

"Oh, she's here—not here at the Ohaysis—but here in town. Yes sir, I seen her out walkin' just this mornin'. But she took . . . what you might call 'a bad fall' a couple months ago. She don't think too clear nowadays."

"How did she fall?" Sam asked.

"Well, you know how she liked to wrestle?" The man paused and studied Fortune.

"Are we talkin' about the same Piney?" Sam questioned as he reached under the wagon seat and pulled out a thick, black brush. "She's about six feet tall, thin as a rail, with long, straight blond hair?"

"Yep, that's Piney Burleson. Say, I didn't catch your name."

Fortune began to brush down the mules. "I'm Sam."

The round-faced man with the flat nose tugged a flour-sack towel out of his back pocket and wiped the sweat off his forehead. "And you're a friend of Piney's?" he pursued.

"Yep."

Fine yellowish dust fogged up from the dark brown backs of the mules.

"My name's Dillerd. Besides being the proprietor of the Ohaysis, I own a few lots here in town. You interested in buyin'?"

Fortune observed that the man's left boot had a heel about two inches taller than the right one. "I just want to know what happened to Piney."

Dillerd pulled a folded, worn piece of yellowed paper from his suit coat pocket and waved it to the east. "I got a corner lot right across from the undertaker's for only seven hundred and fifty dollars."

"Mister, would I be drivin' a wagon like this if I had seven hundred and fifty dollars?" Fortune patted the rump of the mule and tossed the brush back under the wagon seat.

"I reckon you wouldn't. But that price is flexible. Just between you and me, I'd settle for $500 for the lot."

Sam had a bitter alkali taste in his mouth and was tempted to scoop a palm of water from the trough. "You were tellin' me how Piney likes to wrestle," he reminded.

"Yep. Her and Cammie Woodell was puttin' on a match in back of Chet Bramer's farm wagon, right out there by the city well." His round, brown eyes danced under bushy, graying eyebrows. "Piney was jist about to whip her, but Cammie bit her on the ear, a clear violation of the rules—what there is of them—and you know how Piney hates the sight of blood, especially her own. So she let out a scream that surely could have been heard all the way down to the Mexican border. The team of horses hitched up to the wagon must've had sensitive ears, 'cause when the scream commenced, they bolted ahead. Piney tumbled off the wagon and under the back wheel that ran smack dab over her head." The man with the one-sleeved suit nodded his head as if to punctuate the conclusion of his oration.

Sam heard a rooster crow, a dog bark, a woman shout. He studied the street as he continued to talk to Dillerd. "The wheel ran over Piney's head, and it didn't break her neck?"

"Nope." Dillerd pointed a stubby finger at Fortune. "Doc said it didn't break nothin' that he could find, but she ain't exactly been the same since."

Sam rested his fingers in the empty bullet loops at the back of his belt. "Where does she live?"

"That second, little white cabin down there behind the hardware. But sometimes she don't come home for days. The boys find her wanderin' out on the plains or sleepin' behind the jailhouse."

Scanning across the swirling dust of the only street in Antelope Flats, he spotted a woman in a long white dress enter the tall narrow door of the hardware. "But you saw her this mornin'?"

HOME

"Yep." Dillerd shoved the folded papers back into his suit coat pocket. "You know I could let a fine gentleman like you have that lot for $250. Anyway none of us gets too close to Piney. She totes a .50-caliber Sharps carbine around mumbling about finding fortune."

"Fortune?"

"That's what she hollers. But like I said, she is a tad touched."

Sam Fortune studied the fine yellowish dust that hung like morning mist above the street. *I never in my life knew Piney Burleson to wrestle. All that girl ever wanted to do was dance. My-o-my how she can dance. She was queen of the ball more than once at Fort Smith.*

"You goin' to look for her?" the man pressed.

Sam rubbed his thick, sandy blond and gray mustache. "I reckon so."

"Well, if you need some place to wash down the dust, remember the Ohaysis. It's the nicest establishment in Antelope Flats."

"Thanks, Mr. Dillerd. I don't think I'll be in town very long."

The shorter man peered out at the totally barren western horizon. "You ain't headed out on the plains, are you?"

"The thought crossed my mind."

"A tornado hit out there three days ago. It picked up a grove of cottonwoods and planted them in the next county—if there were counties out there—which there ain't."

"No harm in me leavin' the rig here while I look for Piney, is there?"

"Nope. Say, is that half-breed jist goin' to hunker down in the back of the wagon, or is he gettin' out? His money is jist as good as the next man's at the Ohaysis."

Sam smiled. "I reckon that all depends on who is in town."

"We ain't got a marshal. The last one took off with Cammie Woodell after that big wrestlin' match. He's probably dead by now.

You know how Cammie is when she gets moody." Dillerd retreated toward the arched front door of the adobe building. Halfway past the prickly pear cactus, he turned back. "You boys come in and have a drink before you go out on the plains."

Sam stepped around to the back of the wagon. "I presume you heard all of that?"

Kiowa Fox continued to lay flat on his back. "How'd he know I was in here?"

"I don't know." Fortune chuckled, "Maybe he smelled you."

Kiowa propped himself up on his elbows. "That might be more true than I want to admit."

In the distance, Sam watched a man stagger out of the Armadillo Cafe, spin around, and stagger back inside. "You gettin' out now?"

"You seen any bounty men?"

"I haven't looked."

Kiowa laid back down. "I think I'll wait here for Ladosa to bring back some food."

Sam ran his fingers across the chipped gray paint on the tailgate of the paneled wagon. "Did you hear what Dillerd said about Piney?"

"Yep." Kiowa laced his hands behind his head for a temporary pillow. "I wonder if she still likes to dance?"

"I was thinkin' the same thing. When Ladosa comes back with the goods, tell her about Piney. They were close when they lived at Fort Smith. You two wait here at the wagon. It can't take me too long to find her."

"She's totin' your Sharps."

Sam tugged his black, beaver felt hat down in the front. "She's totin' Daddy's Sharps."

☞ ☞ ☞

HOME

To the west, dark clouds swirled in the hot June sky like an evil potion in a witch's cauldron. In Antelope Flats the fine alkali dust kept eyes squinted and vision limited. No one moved. All seemed to be watching and waiting to see what the weather did next.

At first, Sam avoided the saloons and searched the stores, shops, and restaurants for any sign of Piney Burleson. Everyone he talked to had seen her, but no one knew where she was. He had just stepped outside the Red Pearitt Café when he noticed a commotion across the street in the path that ran between Cranby's Saloon #1 and Cranby's Saloon #2.

Sam yanked his stampede string tight under his chin as he stepped out into the street. Dirt blasted his face and pricked his eyes. As he scooted down the narrow dirt path between the two saloons he sized up three cowboys that badgered a six-foot tall, thin woman with long, uncombed blond hair wearing an ankle-length, black dress. She waved a single-shot Sharps carbine in front of her.

"Back off, boys!" Fortune shouted from behind the men.

All three spun around, hands resting on holstered pistols. They blocked his vision of the woman.

"Who do you think you are?" A smear of fresh blood donned the cheek of the clean-shaven man.

"I want to talk to the lady. Go find yourself a nice saloon to ride out this dust storm."

"Like hades we will." The second man sported a thick mustache that hung like branches on a weeping willow tree. "You can wait your turn 'til we're through with her."

Sam stepped toward the woman with wild, blue eyes. A black-bearded man blocked his way. One glance from Fortune caused the man to slide sideways up against the unpainted board and batting of Cranby's Saloon #2.

"She's got my Sharps carbine," the man mumbled.

Without pulling it out of the holster, Sam cocked the hammer of his .44 and pressed his chest against the shorter man's shoulder. "That's not your carbine, and you know it." Sam positioned himself between the woman and the men.

The bearded one backed toward the street, as did the other two. "I paid her a cash dollar for it."

"That's right, mister . . . I seen him," one of the others concurred.

Fortune reached into his vest pocket and felt his last coin. He shoved it into the man's hand. "Here's your dollar back."

The man threw the silver coin to the dirt. "I don't want no dollar. I want the Sharps .50."

"Pick up the dollar, and get out of here," Fortune growled.

"You think you're man enough to take us all on?" the third man challenged. He wore a tattered, brown felt hat that revealed a two-inch hatband of sweat.

"It won't take a man to do that." Sam slipped the hammer down on his cocked Colt pistol. "The lady was doin' fine without me." He turned his back to the men and faced the frightened woman.

"Howdy, Piney, darlin', . . ." he tipped his hat. "Have you missed me?"

A wide, dusty grin broke across the pale, narrow face of the woman, revealing straight white teeth. "You're late, Sam Fortune!"

He ignored the men behind him. "I know, darlin'. My horse took a tumble, and I had to hitch a ride."

"It's OK, Sammy. I was waitin' for you," she explained.

He offered her his arm.

She straightened the mud-caked lace collar of her black dress and took his arm with her left hand. In her right, she still clutched the carbine by the receiver. They walked toward the three men in the alley.

"Did she call you Sam Fortune?" Sweaty Hat asked.

"Yep."

They backed up. "We didn't know it was you, Mr. Fortune. Nobody told us you was in town," Drooping Mustache explained.

"Pick up that dollar, and get out of our way."

The man with the beard scooped up the coin. "Yes sir."

"We heard you was dead," the one with the blood-smeared cheek mumbled.

Sam laced his fingers into Piney's. They felt bony, sticky, and warm. "Now who would tell you somethin' like that?"

The man stumbled, but his compadres caught him as the trio continued to back out of the alley. "Johnny Creek."

"Johnny Creek got hung last month in Choteau," Sam informed them.

"Well, I'll be . . ." Drooping Mustache muttered. They scurried into the street and into Cranby's Saloon #1.

When Sam and Piney reached the dusty street, she pushed her arms around his waist and hugged him tight. He pulled her shoulders to his chest and ran his calloused fingers through her tangled hair.

"I got hurt, Sammy." Her voice was tight, like a violin out of tune.

"That's what I heard, darlin'."

"Some days I cain't even remember my own name."

"It's OK, darlin' . . . it's OK."

He rocked her back and forth, while several faces peered at them from the saloon window.

"They took away my bullets."

"For the carbine?"

"They said I might hurt someone. All I have is this one brass casing."

Several men came out on the saloon porch and stared at them.

"Is that my daddy's carbine?" he asked.

She pulled back. Her eyes romped. "I've been savin' it for you." She shoved the Sharps into his hand.

"Did it come bundled up in a package?" he asked.

"Brown paper and ever'thing. I have it all saved for you over at my cabin."

"Was there a letter with the package?"

"Nothing. Just the carbine wrapped in brown paper. But I saved it for you."

"Well, let's just waltz over to your cabin, darlin'."

"I can dance good, you know," she bragged.

"Piney, you're the best I've ever seen."

"Do you tell that to all the girls?"

"Only you, darlin'. How about you and me dancin' down this dusty street and showin' all these boys some of your fancy steps?"

Her eyes widened. "Is this dance #5?"

"I believe it is," he nodded.

"I'll have to check my card, sir."

"Yes, ma'am. I was just takin' a chance to ask you at this late date."

She opened up the palm of her hand as if reading something written on it.

Sam could see dried blood, or jam—or both. When she threw her shoulders back straight, she was almost as tall as Fortune. "This is your lucky day, cowboy. Dance #5 is my only opening all evenin'."

He grabbed her right hand with his left and held the carbine behind her back. Piney leaned into him and he danced her out into the street.

HOME

Two men on horseback stopped to watch, and customers drifted out of the shops and saloons to squint at the swirling dust of Antelope Flats.

"You dance pretty good, cowboy," she sang out.

"With you, Piney, ever' man is a good dancer."

Across the street he spotted Kiowa and Ladosa watching them from the back of the paneled wagon. He waved down toward the row of white cabins and kept dancing.

They were in front of the Real Nice Hotel when Piney stopped dancing and began to sob. Fortune cradled her against his chest. "What's the matter, darlin'?"

"I don't know where I live, Sammy!"

"What?"

The tears cut deep tracks down her dirty cheeks. "Some days . . . I cain't remember where my cabin is. I got hurt, Sammy. I got hurt real bad, and some days I can't find my way home." She gasped for breath while he took his bandanna and wiped the corner of her eyes. "I'm too ashamed to ask. So I just wander around 'til dark."

He put his hand to the back of her head and pulled her close. "It's OK, darlin'. I know which one it is. It's the second one. Come on; you haven't finished my dance."

She drew back and raised her chin. "You're real pesky about that dance, ain't you, cowboy? I've got a whole line of other men who want to dance with me too."

"Come on, Piney. Dance with me just a little more—please?"

"I hate to see a grown man standin' around beggin' like this, but it's the only dance you get tonight. I told you, my card is full."

They danced down the dirt street to the second in a row of white one-room cabins. He led her over to an uncovered wooden porch not more than three feet by four feet. He swung her around, and they sat on the porch steps.

She dropped her chin to her flat chest. "You're goin' inside with me, ain't you?" she murmured.

"Why, look who's walkin' this way," Sam said. "It's Ladosa and Kiowa. Let's invite them to come in with us, darlin'."

"It will be like havin' company!" Piney giggled. "We ain't had company in a long time, have we, Sammy?" She rested her head on his shoulder and began to weep.

He gently rocked her back and forth.

"This ain't no way to live, Sammy. I prayed and prayed that the Lord would give me one bullet so I could end it all, if I mustered up the nerve."

If you hadn't burned all your bridges, Sam Fortune, you could at least pray for Piney. Whatever happened to your middle son, Mama? How did I get here? I'm barely a step ahead of Piney. He stood up and tugged her to her feet.

"Ladosa, how nice of you to stop by. And who is your gentleman friend?" Piney blurted out.

Ladosa had to stand on her tiptoes to give Piney a hug. "You remember Kiowa, don't you?"

"He had the fourth dance at the Harvest Ball and stepped on my corn." She addressed Kiowa, "How nice to see you, Mr. Fox, but I'm afraid my dance card is full."

☞ ☞ ☞

Ten minutes later the two men exited the small, stuffy cabin. Sam carried the carbine in one hand and a scrap of heavy, brown, folded paper in the other.

Kiowa pushed his black hat to the back of his head. "Seems strange that your daddy would send you his gun without a note explainin' it."

HOME

Sam examined his own name on the paper. "This isn't Daddy's writin': a woman wrote this. Maybe Rebekah wrote it."

"Who's she?"

"My brother Todd's wife."

"How about your sister? Maybe she wrote it," Kiowa suggested.

Sam ambled to the middle of the street where a hand-pump water well was boxed off with graying, cedar one-by-twelves. "Nah, she's just a girl . . . she wouldn't . . ." He propped the carbine against the well casing.

Kiowa surveyed up and down the street. "How old is she?"

"Dacee June is thirteen years younger than me. That would make her . . ." Sam yanked off his red bandanna and jammed it in his back pocket. Then he unbuttoned his shirt halfway down his chest.

"That would make her twenty-one, amigo. She is no little girl."

Sam stuck his head under the spout of the red pump and cranked it. "You're right. Maybe Dacee June sent this," he called out, then straightened, water streaming down his neck and shirt. "But why? Why send it to me?"

"Maybe your daddy wanted to give you a present."

Fortune tugged out his bandanna, shook the dust out of it, and wiped his face dry. "He's dead, Kiowa."

"What do you mean, 'he's dead'? They would have wrote you about that."

"Maybe they did. Maybe Piney can't remember the letter." Sam pumped some more fresh water and drenched the bandanna. "Daddy hasn't been ten feet away from this carbine since we left Brownsville. I know he's dead. What I don't know is why this didn't go to Todd. He's the oldest. Maybe . . . he's dead too."

"When's the last time you heard from 'em?"

Sam rung out the bandanna, then retied it around his neck. "I didn't exactly want them to know I was in prison."

"When's the last time you heard from them?" Kiowa pressed.

"Four or five years, I reckon."

Kiowa plucked up the gun and studied it. "It's a nice carbine, partner. When they converted them over to single-shot, .50 cartridges, they made a powerful saddle gun."

"And I don't own a horse or even a bullet for it."

"Yeah," Kiowa handed him the carbine, "but the people standin' at the other side of that barrel don't know that. Maybe we ought to rob the hardware since we don't have a dozen .44 cartridges between us."

Sam held the gun by the receiver and looped the barrel over his shoulder. "I'm not goin' to hold up anythin' with Daddy's carbine. He was a righteous man every day of his life. He was stubborn: He was wrong about the war; he was wrong about abandonin' the ranch to carpetbaggin' bankers; but he was a righteous man. It wouldn't be right to use his gun for a robbery."

"OK, that eliminates one option," Kiowa conceded. "But what are we goin' to do, amigo? We didn't do a very good job about keepin' out of sight—what, with you dancin' like a fool down the street."

"You got any money left, Kiowa?"

"Two bits. You're the one who had a dollar."

"I had to use it to get this carbine out of pawn."

Kiowa pushed his black hat back and let it dangle by the braided horsehair stampede string. "Ladosa told us we could try to sell the rest of that tonic."

"Let's pack it all into that mercantile and see what they'll give us in trade."

HOME

"It would be less work to rob a bank." Kiowa bent under the red hand-pump and cranked an uneven stream of well water over the back of his neck.

Then Sam pumped the handle while Kiowa washed his face. "Antelope Flats doesn't have a bank."

"You know what I mean," Kiowa called out from under the flow of clear water. "It don't seem right for Fortune and Fox to trade patent medicine for bullets."

"Ladosa wanted to help Piney get cleaned up and settled down. I'm not goin' to stir up town while she's doin' that."

Kiowa shook his shoulder-length, wet, black hair like a dog after a bath. He surveyed the entire length of the Antelope Flats business district. "You know, partner, some towns is so pitiful, they just ain't worth the effort to rob them."

☞ ☞ ☞

Most of the customers in the mercantile seemed to be waiting for something to happen. A store full of eyes followed Sam Fortune's every move. "We brought you six crates of that patent medicine, twelve bottles to a case, and that's all you'll give us in trade?"

The bald man with white hair above his ears and a crisp white apron forced a small smile across his narrow mouth. "Boys, I can sell one bottle to ever' family in town and still have five crates left over. There's a limit to how many bottles of General Marsh's a family needs. Two boxes of .44s, two pairs of spurs, one pair of socks, and one bandanna—that's all I can give you."

"And a box of .50s for the Sharps," Sam added.

The stocky man fanned himself with a long, narrow bill of sale. "You boys are tryin' to drive me out of business. I can't give you one thing more. I really can't. I just don't need the stuff. Maybe you can try at some other store."

Sam surveyed the mirror on the wall behind the counter. *I need a shave, a haircut, and a bath, and I'm buyin' bullets?* "How much for one of those amber bottles with the cork stoppers?" he asked.

"A nickel apiece," the man replied.

"Good, we'll take one pair of spurs and all sixteen of your amber bottles. That's the same price I believe as two pairs of spurs," Sam calculated.

"What are we goin' to do with those bottles?" Kiowa pressed.

An older woman in a gray- and yellow-flowered bonnet leaned across the yardage counter trying to hear his reply. Sam almost shouted, "Take 'em out in the street and bust 'em."

"You're not serious!" the storekeeper gasped.

"Mister, as soon as we were out that door, you were goin' to pour General Marsh's into those amber bottles and sell it as fancy liquor for five dollars each. But I just bought the bottles, so you'll have to keep it as patent medicine, won't you?"

The man reached into a glass case and pulled out a box of .50-caliber bullets. "I believe this is what you wanted."

"I think he said *two* boxes of .50s," Kiowa pressed.

The man shook his head, then pulled out another box. "I presume you have a bill of sale on this patent medicine."

"No receipt," Sam informed him, "but I can assure you that nobody will come lookin' for them. Now, have you got a bill of sale on those two pairs of used spurs?"

The man tugged on his tight black tie and started to laugh. "No, but I assure you no one will come lookin' for them. If you boys ever want a job as hagglin' clerks, I'll put you on commission."

"We ain't much at clerkin'." Kiowa plucked up one pair of spurs and flipped open a box of .44s, slowly shoving them one at a time into his bullet belt.

41

HOME

"You boys obviously need a few dollars. I know of a job, if you're tough enough," the merchant offered.

"Is it legal?" Kiowa demanded.

"It's mostly legal, all right."

Kiowa started to laugh. "Then, we ain't interested."

Sam Fortune loaded his own bullet belt. "What kind of job?"

The storekeeper stepped around from behind the counter. "A man pulled in this morning looking for help to break some horses."

Sam glanced at Kiowa, then back at the man. "What's the deal?"

"Break thirty-six horses in three weeks. It'll take the two of you."

"What's the pay?" Kiowa inquired.

"Two dollars per pony, plus you get the first two picks."

"You tired of mules, Kiowa?" Sam challenged.

"I don't even like to eat mules," the half-breed grinned.

Sam turned back to the man at the counter. "Where's the ranch?"

"That's the catch. Accordin' to this old boy, he's openin' up a ranch on San Francisco Creek."

"That's up in Public Lands," Kiowa said. "The government won't let anyone up there."

"Well, this old boy claims he has inside information that Uncle Sam is goin' to open it up for settlement, and he wants a prior claim. He said he has twelve hundred Mexican cows on the trail already. He wants this remuda broke and waitin' for his crew when they get here."

Sam plopped down on a nail barrel and tugged off his dusty brown boots. "Then, he wants someone to live up there for three weeks."

"That's the dangerous part. He doesn't even have a barn finished, just a holdin' pen and a fenced corral."

Sam peeled off his dirty, worn out socks and wiggled his toes. "Where's the man now?"

"He said he was goin' over to the Ohaysis," the shopkeeper informed. "Course, it could be he hired someone already."

Fortune slowly tugged on the new socks. "What's his name?"

"Rocklin."

Sam pulled his boots back on. "What's he look like?"

"Like west Texas: tough, dry, and windy—about like you two. You won't miss him. Must be about fifty years old."

Fox and Fortune strolled out on the boardwalk in front of the mercantile. Sam enjoyed the feel of clean cotton cradling his toes.

A wide gold-toothed grin broke across Kiowa's dark-skinned face. "You thinkin' what I'm thinkin', partner?"

Sam shook his head. "We promised to take Ladosa up to Dodge City."

"She won't mind swingin' by Public Land if it means stealin' thirty-six horses," Kiowa insisted.

"Thirty-six unbroke horses," Sam corrected.

"We can break them along the way."

"You ever done that?"

"Nope."

"Can't be done. You can't run and break horses at the same time."

"But they'd be worth fifteen dollars a head if we drove them to Denver. How much money would that be?" Kiowa tempted.

Sam rubbed his chin and studied the wild, dark clouds backing up toward Antelope Flats. "It would be over five hundred dollars, even if we kept the two best."

"Now, that sounds better. Maybe our luck is turnin'."

HOME

"I'm takin' Ladosa to Dodge, Kiowa."

"You ain't gettin' honest on me, are you, Sam Fortune?"

"I just don't feel like breakin' that promise. Lookin' at Piney today . . . I don't want to disappoint any more ladies. Maybe after we deliver her we can come back and break those ponies."

Kiowa paused at the well. Both men put one boot on the rim to strap on spurs. "I figured with that carbine in hand, you'd be in a hurry to go home to the Black Hills," Kiowa probed.

"My home was in Coryell County, Texas. You know that."

"But they took it away from you."

"Mama's buried there—bless her soul—so I guess it will always be home. I've never even been to the Black Hills. I didn't go see Daddy when he was alive; I reckon it's too late now."

"You gettin' melancholy on me, amigo?"

"Nope. We make our choices, and we pay the price. That's the way life is, Kiowa. And today I choose to take tiny little Ladosa up to Dodge City. That's all there is to it."

The strong-shouldered, dark-skinned man pushed his hat back. "Maybe I'll mosey over to the Ohaysis. No reason to hold onto this last two bits."

"You goin' to talk to Rocklin about those ponies?" Sam asked.

"I might as well find out what the story is. I didn't promise to take no one to Dodge, remember? Who's marshal up there now?"

"Does it matter?"

"I reckon not."

"I'll go see how Ladosa and Piney are doin'. Then I'll come bail you out of the ruckus you always get yourself in."

Kiowa roared, "That's good, Sammy. Because if them two women start fightin' over you, you ain't goin' to get one lick of help from me."

☞ ☞ ☞

Spurs jingled as Sam Fortune hiked to the cabins, bullet boxes in one hand, carbine in the other. The wind had suddenly stopped, and the menacing clouds from the plains crept toward Antelope Flats. The air felt as explosive as if waiting for someone to light a sulfur match.

A very short lady with long, black hair slipped out the front door as he approached. Ladosa motioned for them to sit on the steps.

"How's Piney?" he asked.

"She's clean and sleepin'. I don't think she's been home for several days."

"She can't remember where she lives, Ladosa."

"She was rememberin' pretty good awhile ago. She remembered you and her dancin'."

"Down the street?"

Ladosa slipped her arm in his. "No, at Fort Worth in the spring of '79."

"She can remember that?"

"Yes, and she remembers the men who kicked her head in."

"She didn't fall off a wagon, did she?" he asked.

Ladosa shook her head and brushed back a tear.

"They still around? I'd like to pay them a visit," he growled.

"Some say they rode out to New Mexico. One man is missin' middle fingers on both hands, and another wears gold earrings, like a pirate."

Sam's clenched knuckles turned white. "Maybe God will open up the pits of hell and drop them in."

"Do you believe in God, Sammy?"

The edge melted from his voice. "Ever'body believes in God."

HOME

"That's not what I mean. Do you believe that God has a plan for your life?"

"Ladosa, are you preachin' at me?"

"Maybe. Maybe I'm preachin' at myself."

"Where did all this come from?"

"I ain't goin' to Dodge City with you and Kiowa," she announced.

"We were only goin' up there for you."

"Well, I'm not goin'. I'm goin' to stay right here in Antelope Flats."

"Why on earth would you want to do that?" Sam quizzed.

"'Cause I think it's God's plan for me. He wants me to take care of Piney. I'll get me a job and look after her."

He hugged her shoulder. "You're bitin' off a big chew, Ladosa."

"Ever'body needs someone else to take care of, Sammy. I never had no one. Now I do. Who do you have to take care of? You goin' to take care of Kiowa? You goin' to take care of me? You'll be dead in less than a year. You're lucky to have lived this long. You told me so. If you ain't got someone to take care of, you ain't got nothin'— no matter how famous your gun is or how much money you have in your poke." She slipped an arm around Sam's waist and laid her head on his shoulder. "Ain't you goin' to say nothin'?"

He stared out across the street.

"It could have been me, Sammy. I look at Piney, and I say, 'What if it were me?' If it were me, would you stay and take care of me? Would any man want to take care of me? I'm stayin', Sammy. That's all there is to it."

He leaned over and kissed her forehead. "I'm glad you're stayin', Ladosa. Piney needs you bad. I'll rest a little easier at night knowin' that you're lookin' after her. We traded off your patent medicine, but you can sell the mules and wagon."

"What are you and Kiowa goin' to do?" she asked.

"There's an old boy who needs some horses broke. That'll give us a couple of horses and a little cash."

"Then what? Indian Territory is changin', Sammy. They're goin' to open it up, and then there will be no place left to hide."

"Maybe we'll ride down to Arizona. My little brother and his family are down there with the army at Fort Grant."

"Why don't you go up to Dakota and see who mailed you that carbine?" Ladosa challenged.

The dark, sulfur-smelling clouds crept into town, like outlaws sizing up a bank.

"Because there's no one in the Black Hills who needs me to take care of 'em."

"How do you know that?"

"Darlin', there has never been anyone in that family that needed someone to take care of 'em."

"Are they all as stubborn and reckless as you, Sam Fortune?"

"Stubborn—yes. Reckless—no. I win the prize for that one. Me and Daddy, I suppose."

"Go see 'em this year, Sam. For people like you, me, Piney, and Kiowa, there ain't no next year."

He stood up on the dirt. She stood on the porch. Even so, she remained several inches shorter than he. He leaned down and kissed her on the lips. "Good-bye, darlin'. I've got some ponies to break."

"I won't see you again, Sam Fortune. I know it in my bones."

"Then let me thank you for all the fond memories I'm goin' to have of you around some campfire on down the trail," he said.

"Thanks for dancin' down the street with Piney. She won't ever forget that," Ladosa added.

HOME

"Nor will I."

He turned and walked away.

☞ ☞ ☞

Heavy, dark clouds squatted over Antelope Flats, muting the daylight inside the building. Stagnant cigar smoke and untrimmed lanterns also dimmed the Ohaysis. Sam could barely see the other side of the building. He strained to make out the figure of Kiowa Fox, leaning with his back against the bar, glass in hand.

"You ready to pull out for Dodge City?" Kiowa tested as Fortune approached.

"There's been a change in plans. Ladosa wants to stay here and take care of Piney."

"That's good. That's real good." Kiowa picked at his gold lower teeth with his squared off fingernail. "You and me can break a few ponies, then."

"Have you talked to Rocklin yet?"

"Nope. He's in that big poker game in the corner. The bartender assured me that they don't want to be disturbed. But if we don't talk to him soon, he'll be broke. Those other three are using a marked deck, and they're fleecin' him."

Sam squinted his eyes. "How can you see through the smoke?"

"Trust me."

"Well, let's change the deck." With Kiowa still leaning his back against the bar, Sam turned to see the man with the one-sleeve suit coat.

"I see you decided to visit my establishment after all," the proprietor greeted. "I been ponderin' it, and I could sell you that lot for one hundred cash dollars."

Fortune laid the carbine on the bar, barrel pointed at the man's midsection. "No thanks, Mr. Dillerd. I'd like a cup of coffee and new deck of cards."

The man rapped his fingers on the bar, all except the stubby ones that had been cut off at the last knuckle. "The coffee's a nickel a cup, and I cain't supply cards for solitaire."

Sam nodded toward the gamblers across the room. "You'll give me the coffee for free, and the cards are for that game in the corner."

Dillerd stiffened. "They got a deck."

Sam rested his hand on the receiver of the carbine. "That deck's marked. We don't aim to see Mr. Rocklin get cheated out of his money."

"You cain't threaten me with that Sharps," Dillerd huffed.

"This gun?" Sam cocked the hammer back, leaving the barrel pointed at the trembling saloon owner. "I wouldn't think of threatenin' you. No, you'll give me the coffee and the deck of cards, because you owe me."

Dillerd didn't take his eyes off Fortune's trigger finger. "What do you mean, I owe you?"

"I had to stand out there in the street and listen to you lie about how Piney got hurt. Why would a man lie like that, Dillerd? Only because he was coverin' up for a friend . . . or for himself. Maybe you're one of 'em that kicked her in the head."

Kiowa spun around, his unsheathed knife in his right hand. "He did what?"

"No, no . . . boys . . . I didn't have anything to do with that. None of us did. It was two drifters. They've been gone for months."

Sam surveyed the room. "Then why did you lie to me?"

"Look, if all us merchants tell newcomers that women aren't safe and that they get beat up, what will that do for business? Besides, that wrestlin' story don't hurt Piney none. It gives her a

HOME

little fame and makes folks relax; that's all. Just a fib to make things easier to handle for ever'one."

"Do you believe him?" Kiowa asked.

"I don't know," Sam replied. "Ever' time I've talked to this man, he's lied to me."

Dillerd backed up until glasses rattled on the shelf behind him. "Boys, I'm tellin' the truth."

"I'd believe you a whole lot more if I had a free cup of coffee and new deck of blueback cards," Sam insisted.

Dillerd scurried into the back room and brought out a steaming black mug and a new box of cards.

"Thank you, Mr. Dillerd," Fortune said. "I do believe your story."

"Which one?" Kiowa chided.

"Well, all of 'em, I reckon." Fortune glanced into the corner. "Come on, 'pride of the Kiowa nation,' let's see if you can read those marks." They strolled over to the poker table.

Three feet from their destination, Rocklin, his back to the wall, glanced up. "This is a closed game, boys."

Fortune held his coffee cup out in front of him with one hand and scratched his ear with the other. "Jist wonderin' how close you are to finishin' up. I got me two cash dollars and wanted to play some poker."

"You're looking at the wrong table, boys." Rocklin tried to shoo them away with the wave of a hand. "Each of these chips are worth five dollars."

"Wooowee! Did you hear that, Kiowa? These boys know how to play poker." Fortune leaned over the closest man's shoulder as if to glance at the hand, but the gambler next to that man pulled a pocket pistol out of his vest and shoved it into him.

"Back off, mister!" the gambler growled.

Fortune raised his hands and jumped back, sloshing hot coffee down the back of the man in front of him. The man's cards tumbled to the table as he leaped up and spun around, gun in hand.

"Sorry, mister. . . . When he pulled a gun on me . . . like to scared me to death," Sam stammered.

"Get out of here before I shoot you both!" the scalded man bellowed.

Hands and coffee cup still in the air, Fortune backed away. "We'll leave. We don't want to play poker with you anyways. Them kind of cards ain't no fun."

Rocklin pushed his hat back and laid a tightly bunched hand face down in front of him. "What are you talking about?"

"Nothin', nothin'," Sam insisted. "I don't ever encourage a man who's holdin' a gun on me."

"Put your guns away," Rocklin told the two.

"He's drunk."

"By the looks of things, I seem to be financing this poker game tonight. Put your guns away," Rocklin repeated.

Both men hesitated, but they complied and sat back down.

"What did you mean, these cards are no fun?" Rocklin re-addressed.

"Well, me and Kiowa are out on the trail by ourselves from time to time, and we play a little poker. But the only deck we have is a marked one that belongs to my half-breed friend, here. Let me tell you, two-man poker with each of you knowin' what's in the other man's hand is about as borin' as visitin' with the moon. I ain't never tried it with four men, so maybe it's a little more fun."

This time when the man went for his gun, Fortune tossed the rest of the coffee down the man's neck and pressed his own revolver into his back before the man could rise to his feet. Kiowa covered the other two.

HOME

Rocklin shoved the table forward and leaped up. "Are you saying this deck is marked?"

"You're holdin' sixes and twos and an ace of diamonds," Kiowa reported.

"They're just guessin'," one of the gamblers groused.

"Well, they guessed right." Rocklin turned his hand over.

"We didn't know these cards was rigged. How do we know this cattleman didn't mark them?" the man to the left of Fortune whined.

"Because he's losin', that's why. But this is your lucky day," Fortune added. "I brought a fresh deck over." He slapped the blue-back cards down on the table.

"We ain't goin' to play if we're insulted like this!" The third gambler rose to his feet.

"In that case all the money goes to the man over there," Sam pointed at Rocklin. "If you refuse to play with a new deck, you forfeit all the winnin's to the man who's left. That's the rules."

"I ain't never heard that rule," the gambler beside Fortune muttered.

Kiowa shoved his revolver into the man's shoulder blade. "You heard it now. What's it goin' to be? You goin' to play fair or forfeit?"

"I don't have to put up with these insults. I'm leavin'," the third man said.

"Good choice," Kiowa answered.

The three men backed to the front door but paused by the bar. "We'll be waitin' outside for you," one declared.

"We'll be right here visitin' with Mr. Rocklin about breakin' some horses," Fortune replied.

The older man with his back against the wall surveyed them. "You know my name? I don't know yours."

"That's Kiowa Fox, and I'm Sam Fortune."

"Sam Fortune!" one of the gamblers gasped. He and the others backpedaled to the door. "You're Sam Fortune?" another exclaimed.

"Boys, we promise to see you when we come out." Fortune called out, "Now, go on."

"You ain't goin' to see me," the man with the waxed mustache mumbled. "Not if I kin help it."

Fortune and Fox scooted their chairs with backs to the wall, along each side of Rocklin.

"Are you really Sam Fortune?" he asked.

"Yes sir."

"And you two want to break some horses?"

"The man at the merc said you had thirty-five to break in three weeks and would pay us two dollars a head, plus the two top picks, and all the grub we need while we're camped up in Public Land," Sam bartered.

Rocklin stacked the worn blue chips scattered in the center of the table. "That wasn't quite the arrangement . . . but I owe you something. You've got yourselves a deal. But how do I know you aren't going to just up and steal the whole remuda?"

Kiowa took a blue chip off the table and rubbed his hands together. The chip disappeared. "You'll just have to trust us, Mr. Rocklin," he said. He reached into Rocklin's vest pocket and pulled out the blue chip.

Rocklin held out his hand. "I believe a man's only as good as his word. Mr. Fortune . . ." Rocklin offered his hand.

Sam paused—then he took Rocklin's hand and shook it. "You've got yourself a deal."

"I'll drive you up there in my wagon, but I'm not staying. I've got a herd to meet out on the Canadian River. But I am a little

HOME

concerned how we're going to get out of town without being bush-whacked. You didn't exactly make friends with those men."

"They won't be any trouble today," Fortune replied. "That type won't face you in daylight. They'll sneak up in the dark and shoot you in the back. We don't have anythin' to worry about."

"Until it gets dark," Kiowa added.

CHAPTER THREE

Along San Francisco Creek, Public Land, in the Oklahoma panhandle

The gritty, yellow dirt ground into Sam Fortune's cheek and stacked up against his closed left eye. When his chest slammed into the corral floor, his shirt ripped at the elbow. His spur hung in the stirrup for just a moment. It felt like his left leg would be jerked off at the hip. He landed full force on his shoulder. His left hand pinned back so savagely he would have screamed, but his lower lip rolled back and spooned bitter, dry dirt into his mouth.

Panicked hooves thundered in circles around him. Sam spit out the dirt and rolled to his back, trying to catch his breath.

"Are you jist goin' to lounge around all morning or are we goin' to get to work?" Kiowa Fox called out from the top rail of the fifty-by-one-hundred-foot corral.

Sam Fortune sat up and examined the blood and dirt on his elbow. "Don't you have any respect for the dead?"

Kiowa jumped off the rail and retrieved Fortune's hat. He waited for the tall bay stallion to canter by, then he strolled out to the

HOME

middle of the corral. "This sure is fun, ain't it? You want me to help you to your feet?"

"No, I thought I'd just sit here and enjoy the sunset," Sam replied.

"The sun ain't goin' down for another six hours."

"I'll wait."

Sam struggled to his feet, brushed dirt out of his sandy blond and gray hair, and then jammed his hat back on. "I reckon that bay is broke. What do you think?"

A smile swept across Kiowa's face. "You know, they say bein' an outlaw is dangerous business. But honest work can kill a man too."

They jogged over to the rail as the frightened horse with the dark mane, tail, and legs danced and snorted at the far end of the corral.

"Remind me not to choose that stallion when we finish this job."

"I don't know, Sammy, there's one good thing about the bay— no one would ever steal him from you!"

"Well, go catch him and tie him to the snub post. I'll give it another try, soon as I wash a little of this alkaline dirt out of my mouth."

"The only thing more bitter than the dirt is the water," Kiowa scoffed. "I can't believe that Rocklin actually wants to ranch out on these high plains. Nobody else wants to live out here."

"I think that's the point. It will be wide open for a long time."

Kiowa Fox stared across the thin, brown grass of the treeless plain. "Sammy, did you ever figure that maybe God made some territory jist for himself and didn't intend for it to be settled?"

"If you were the Almighty, with the power to do anythin' you please, would you create a land that looked like this just for your own backyard?"

Kiowa began to laugh. "Nope. I'd make me some tall mountains, green trees, clear lakes, big fish, abundant game, cool breezes, . . . and a dark-skinned woman with long, black hair and dancin' eyes."

Fortune examined the wound on his elbow. "Sounds like you're needin' a trip to town."

"We've been out here two weeks. That's the longest I've ever been honest in my life."

When Kiowa smiled the sun reflected off his gold teeth. "Six more horses and we're done."

"Seven, unless you don't aim to mount that bay again."

"Snub him up. Meanness can buck me off, but only death can keep me from crawlin' back up in the saddle."

"You're stubborn enough to be part Comanche. Not Kiowa, mind you, but at least Comanche."

☛ ☛ ☛

Rocklin's San Francisco Creek ranch consisted of a framed, empty barn without siding, three large wall tents with raised wooden floors, a four-rail corral, and six cottonwood trees.

One of the trees was dead.

The white tents formed a line, south of the barn. While at the ranch, Rocklin stayed in the first one. He furnished the middle one as a cookhouse, but it was too June-hot to cook indoors. The tent closest to the creek served as the bunkhouse.

But there were no bunks.

Just two bedrolls and various saddles, bits, and bridles.

With campfire flames as light, a shirtless Sam Fortune examined the wounds on his chest and arms. His lower ribcage on the right side sported a bruise the exact shape of a hoofprint. Every time he coughed, sneezed, or laughed, pain retold the incident.

HOME

Kiowa Fox peered up from the frying pan. "You're covered with dried blood and bruises. You used to look lean and tough. Now you just look beat up, like a herd of buffalo ran right over the top of you."

With a wet sack Fortune tried to dab the dirt and sand out of his elbow wound. "Kiowa, did you ever hunt buffalo?"

"When I was little, my uncle took me north. We had just crossed the Platte when we came upon a herd the size of Nebraska. It would have been easier to count the stars than to count them."

"Did you kill a few?"

"Not a one. We got chased off by the Sioux and Cheyenne. But I saw them, and I know what it feels like when they shake the ground. How 'bout you, Sam?"

"I never saw the big herds: four or five hundred is probably the extent. They make quite a rumble. I can only imagine tens of thousands of them."

Kiowa flipped the pork chunk over and set the big pan back on the coals. "It was a sight to see when they panicked and ran. Their heads were down, tongues hangin' out, puffin' the wind in and out like steam engines. And when they jumped up to run, they started spankin' themselves with their tails. Up and down, up and down . . . just as hard as you'd quirt a horse in a race. But the big herds are gone."

"Remember that time we got into a scrape with Ned Christie? I lit shuck for the north country and came across a pile of buffalo bones stacked thirty foot high by the U. P. tracks," Fortune said. "I guess they're payin' twenty dollars or better a ton for bones."

"The day will come, Sam Fortune, when kids got to go to the zoo to see a buffalo, or a mountain lion, or a wolf, . . . or a coyote."

"Oh no—coyotes will outlive us all."

Kiowa stared out across the plains into the dying daylight. "When do you reckon Rocklin will be driving that herd in here?"

"In the next five days. Depends on what condition it's in. He'll need them watered and grassed before he runs them on this dry stuff."

"You figure we'll have the horses all broke by then?" Kiowa scooped a hunk of meat and a coffee cup full of red beans onto a blue-enameled tin plate and handed it to Fortune.

Shirt still off, Sam scooped up his beans with a knife. "Depends on how the bay bucks out in the morning. If he's snuffy again, I'll have to start all over."

Kiowa stabbed his entire piece of fried pork with his hunting knife. He held it like a drumstick and gnawed off a bite. "When we pick our horses, you goin' to take the buckskin?"

"So far—he's the smartest one I've seen. You still like the big black you call One Sock?"

"He's a little rank, but he can outrun a posse."

"No fear of a posse out here." Sam set down the plate and slipped on his dirty, torn shirt.

"You should have bought yourself another shirt in Antelope Flats."

"This one isn't more than a couple of months old. Besides, I was broke, remember?"

"You live rough, Fortune."

Sam sipped his coffee then plucked up his plate. "And I'm goin' to sleep rough. That floor's goin' to be harder than ever on these old bones tonight. What I'd give for a feather mattress." He scooped more slightly gritty beans into his mouth with the knife.

Kiowa waved his pork slice, still speared to the end of his knife. "What I'd give for a feather mattress and a—"

HOME

"Forget it, Kiowa." Sam held his side and tried to keep from laughing. "There isn't a woman around for a hundred miles."

"I wonder if Rocklin's drovers know that. This might be the most isolated ranch on the plains. I can't imagine anyone wantin' to live out here. This is the kind of place where they build a prison."

Sam surveyed the first stars that had begun to flood the night sky. "I might just sleep outside tonight. That tent gets too hot, anyways."

"You complainin' about my snorin'?"

"Would it do any good if I did?"

"Nope, but I'm sleepin' in the tent. It's difficult to dream of beautiful women when scorpions and snakes are crawlin' over you all night."

"You gettin' soft, Kiowa?"

"Yeah, and you're gettin' old, Sammy. . . . Probably nothin' we can do about it, neither."

☞ ☞ ☞

With an old-style Texas, iron-horn saddle for a pillow, Fortune propped his back toward the dying embers of the campfire and stared across the dark shadows of the cottonwoods at the distant, dry lightening storm. Every two or three minutes he twisted, bent, and stretched to keep his side from cramping.

The .50-caliber carbine with twenty-two-inch barrel lay beside him. Whenever he flounced for a more comfortable position, his hand slid down to the grip and fingered the trigger.

It doesn't make any sense.

No matter what happened in the Black Hills, you just don't mail a Sharps off to Indian Territory in hopes that a wayward son will wander by and spot it.

I haven't had an address I was proud of in years.

If Daddy died, then this belongs to Todd. He's the oldest. The favorite. The one who shadowed Daddy around the ranch. The one I never could be like. Taller. Stronger. Smarter. The Coryell County ranch was going to be yours, Todd. I wonder how you ever got over losin' that.

I never did.

Or they could have sent the carbine to Robert. Why didn't they send it to him? It would have looked good on that prancing cavalry horse. It's anyway as good as a trapdoor. Robert's the perfect soldier. For every rule I broke, he kept two. Just like Mama. He was her little trooper from the day he was born. Everything was cut and dry; black and white; right and wrong. Bobby, life isn't that simple—except for you. I'm glad you're happy with your Jamie Sue, . . . and no tellin' how many children. You named the first after Big River Frank. Must be more by now. Bobby, I bet you've got their faces scrubbed and their hats on straight, and you're marchin' them around that white picket-fenced yard. You got 'em signed up to West Point yet?

Fortune picked up the carbine and held it gingerly at his shoulder. He aimed it for the southern night sky. He sighted in each flash of lightening as if it were a target. The huge Sharps hammer wasn't cocked, so he squeezed the trigger at each flash.

Daddy, no wonder you liked this old gun. It fits comfortable in the hand and packs a wallop. That's fine if you're huntin'. But if you're the one bein' hunted, . . . well, I need more than a single-shot.

. . . When Rocklin pays us off, I'm goin' home to Coryell County. Aunt Barbara and Uncle Milt will still be there. They'll tell me what happened to Daddy. I'll slip in late some night, get caught up on the news, and slip out by daylight. Maybe I'll ride by the ranch. At least I can pull some weeds from Mama's grave.

A sudden pain at the base of his back caused him to sit straight up and stretch his arms out.

HOME

I think maybe I'll retire from breaking horses. This is a job for kids. All the Fortune boys are over thirty. . . .

Dacee June's twenty-one? She could be married. Heaven help the boy she marries. She was only ten when I left home the last time. Ten, but actin' sixteen.

Fortune let out a deep sigh and tried to find a comfortable spot on his side.

That's the trouble with not sleepin': A man becomes melancholy. Maybe I ought to be like Kiowa—just think of women at night . . . instead of kin. But most of the women I've known have been like Ladosa and Piney, good-hearted women who have to live with a lifetime of bad choices.

I need to sleep.

For about a month.

☞ ☞ ☞

When he finally sat up straight, the green prairie grass around him stood a foot tall. The sun barely peeked over the western hills and the mild wind swayed the grass like gentle waves lapping the shore of a mountain lake.

The lady sitting on the blanket beside him had a wide-brimmed straw hat pulled low to shade her face. Her legs were tucked beneath her, covered by her dark blue dress. In her lap a small Bible lay open. She was reciting a verse and did not look at him.

"'Have mercy upon me, O God, according to thy lovingkindness: according unto the multitude of thy tender mercies blot out my transgressions.'"

"Mama?" he gasped.

"Well, you decided to wake up! I trust all of that watermelon didn't give you a stomachache. Sammy, go check on Daddy and your brother."

"Eh, . . . where are they?"

She waved to the north. "You know! See if they need any help. Take Daddy his carbine."

He scooped up the Sharps and meandered through the thick prairie grass toward a knoll to the north. Even before he crested the ridge, he could feel the ground begin to shake. He heard a roar like a hundred trains race straight at him.

He sprinted to the top of the hill. To the north, a fifty-mile-deep, solid mass of buffalo stampeded his direction. From his vantage on the knoll, he could look back and see his mother, still sitting on the blanket, reading. Beside her now, a little girl, no more than three or four, plucked petals off a large white daisy.

I've got to turn 'em! They're headed right for Mama and Dacee June. Where's Daddy? Why isn't he here? This is his job. I can't turn a herd this size. There's nothin' I can do!

Sam knelt on one knee and raised the carbine to his shoulder, cocking the stiff hammer. He studied the ten-mile-wide herd. Slightly in the lead, a huge bull, tongue hanging out and head down, whipped his tail excitedly against his rear end.

He sighted the .50-caliber carbine on the big bull.

But he didn't squeeze the trigger.

He waited.

Now, the buffalo pounded only a hundred yards away. The noise vibrated his eardrums. They drew close enough that he flipped down the long range sight and watched the charge from the narrow slot of the filed dime that acted as a barrel sight.

Still, he didn't pull the trigger.

HOME

He could hear them breathe. Sucking in; blowing out. He could smell the musty odor of buffalo hair. He could see the panicked big eyes of the lead bull.

Ten more steps and they would run right over the top of him.

Then he pulled the trigger.

And the sky turned dark.

Hooves thundered near him. A dead horse lay no more than five feet in front of him. A barefoot Kiowa Fox was yelling something. Yellow-red flame shot out of gun barrels from out on the prairie.

Then the shooting stopped.

Kiowa continued to shout, only this time he was yelling at the remuda, herding them back into the corral.

Sam Fortune tugged on his boots and joined him.

"Could you see who they were?" Kiowa asked.

"No . . . I was asleep, and I . . ."

"You raised up and shot the horse out from under the lead rider. I thought you'd put the second bullet through the man, but he sprinted for the plains."

"What did I do? I'm still a little confused."

"I heard them run the horses out of the corral, and I sprinted out of the tent. It looked like they would stampede right over the top of you. You waited until the last second, then you raised up and shot the lead horse. The remuda panicked at the sound of the Sharps and turned right back into the corral. The leader ran into the night to join his partners. I really thought you'd bring him down."

"I'm not used to a single-shot. I couldn't figure out what was real and what was a dream."

"Well, neither of us are goin' to do anymore dreamin' tonight. We better stand guard at the corral."

Sam stared into the dark night. "You think they were Comanches?"

Kiowa looped the wire gate latch over the corral post. "The government claims there are no bands of Comanches out here."

Sam stood on the bottom rail and peered at the dark shadows of nervous horses. "They also said they finished off Captain Bill Cole's Black Mesa gang twenty years ago, but some of them are still livin' up there stealin' horses. Ever' time the government states that a problem's solved, you can be assured it isn't."

Kiowa climbed up on the rail beside Sam. "You're a cynical Johnny Reb. But I don't think it was Comanches. They would have killed us first and then took the horses. Are all the ponies accounted for?"

In the moonlight, Sam surveyed the remuda nervously pace from one side of the corral to the other, like a trained dance troupe. He eased the hammer down on the carbine and stepped back to the dirt. "Yeah—even the bay stallion. If a horse had to die tonight, why couldn't it have been the bay?"

☛ ☛ ☛

The sun was straight above on a cloudless sky. Sam Fortune and Kiowa Fox squatted next to the dead horse at the noon campfire when Rocklin drove his wagon into the ranch. Kiowa poured him a blue-enameled, tin cup of coffee as he climbed down from the rig.

Rocklin's ever-present, black tie hung loosely around his neck, but the top button on his shirt remained fastened. His round crowned hat rested on the back of his head. "I see you got that one broke," he pointed to the dead horse.

HOME

Kiowa handed Rocklin the coffee and grinned. "Yep. It's Sammy's new method. He calls it the 'Sharps, .50-caliber approach to horse breakin'.'"

Rocklin stepped over and nudged the horse's shoulder with the tip of his dusty brown boot. "Is it one of mine?"

Fortune still squatted on his haunches next to the fire, biscuit in hand. He glanced over at the raven-black horse. "Nope."

Rocklin slowly surveyed the ranch headquarters. "You had visitors, did you?"

"Yep." When Sam stood, both thighs cramped. He hobbled around the fire trying to straighten his legs.

"Is that a new dance?" Rocklin chided.

Kiowa stared down at Fortune's boots. "Yep, it's called the 'Too Old to Hit the Dirt That Often' promenade."

Rocklin took a long swallow of coffee. "Say, were these visitors anybody I know?"

"That all depends," Kiowa commented. "Do you know any horse thieves? I mean, besides me and Sam Fortune."

Rocklin laughed and shook his head. "No, you're the lot. Hiring you two to break my ponies is sort of like hiring the James brothers to guard a bank. I heard some Apaches left the resettlement and started back to Arizona. They ended up in the Antelope Hills. It has the people of Antelope Flats scared stiff. Was it Indians that paid us a visit?"

"Couldn't even tell that," Sam replied. "This horse wasn't shod—but then, neither are yours. The saddle was a McClellan—probably stolen from cavalry—and they toted carbines and revolvers. But they backed out when we returned fire. I've never heard of Apaches backin' away from a fight. Hard to figure."

"When they heard Sammy's .50-caliber cannon, they decided they were out-gunned," Kiowa added. "We trailed them this morning. Looks like three of 'em. They went west, dropped down into that dry creek bed, and then their trail gets lost. But any decent Indian could have stolen the whole cavvy without us even knowin' it . . . or scalped us first."

Rocklin plucked up the coffeepot and refilled his cup. "I didn't expect to settle this land without a fight. We'd better drag that horse out of camp, before it stinks everything up."

"We were hopin' you'd show up today," Fortune said. "Reckon those drivin' horses on your wagon would do the job better than these mustangs."

"You're probably right. I'll hitch him up behind the wagon and drag him over to one of those barrancas."

Kiowa looped a thumb in his brown leather suspenders. "When are your twelve hundred beeves goin' to trot in here?"

"Now that, boys, has become a real mystery." Rocklin scratched the back of his leather-tough neck. "I arranged to rendezvous with the herd between the north fork of the Canadian and the Cimarron Rivers. Then, I planned to lead them over here to the ranch. I camped there five days without seeing a soul. Finally, a big herd of agency beef headed for Montana came grazing through. They claimed my crew was at least two weeks ahead of them on the trail."

"You mean they passed by and kept goin'?" Sam quizzed.

Rocklin's gray mustache drooped like a permanent frown. "My foreman has been up the trail seven times. I can't figure what he was thinking. The next morning I was about ready to head north, when several boys going home to San Antonio rode into camp. Said my whole herd and crew was in Dodge City."

"Dodge? They pushed them all the way to Kansas?" Kiowa questioned.

"I reckon. Anyhow, now I've got to hightail it up to Dodge City and figure out what's going on. I didn't want to take the wagon, so

HOME

I came back for a saddle horse. I hope I can get to Dodge before my crew breaks up and drifts back to south Texas. Every one of them agreed to work on the ranch."

Sam pulled off his hat and ran his fingers through the graying, dirty hair. "Must have been lonesome sittin' out there waitin' for a herd that didn't show up."

Rocklin stared out at the plains. The heat radiated off the fine, yellowish-orange dirt, giving the horizon a wavy look. "Reminds of one time I went all the way to Fort Worth to pick up my wife and daughter who were coming home on the train," he mumbled.

Sam glanced over at Kiowa then back to Rocklin. "What happened?"

"They never showed up. My wife decided she didn't want to live in Texas or be married to me anymore, so she stayed with her kin in Tennessee. She just didn't bother telling me about it. That's the way I felt out on the prairie—like an absolute fool." Rocklin tossed out the dregs at the bottom of his coffee cup and plunked it down on the rocks next to the cookfire.

"How about your daughter? How did she feel about all of that?" Sam pressed.

Rocklin's eyes lit up. "She's grown up now, of course. I do get to see her every so often. She's every bit as pretty as her mama. She lives up in Cheyenne City. When I have business in Denver I try to ride on up. Her husband owns the telephone company there. You boys ever use one of those telephone machines?"

Fortune shook his head. "I saw one in the warden's office at prison once, but I never used it."

"I can't figure out how they can cram a voice into that wire," Kiowa added.

"Nobody knows how they work," Rocklin declared. "It's like a talking telegraph. Anyhow, Amanda—that's my daughter—

married a man named Edgington, and they live in Cheyenne. At least, the last I heard, which was over a year ago. One of the reasons I'm pushing myself on this ranch is because I want to develop this place, and then, sometime before I cash in, I want to give it to her. What's the reason in tryin' something so foolhardy if it isn't to give it to your kid? You two will never accumulate much until you have someone to leave it to. Isn't that right?"

Fortune sipped the lukewarm coffee and eyed his ripped shirt. "Can't argue with you today, Mr. Rocklin."

Kiowa stared out across the barren, high plains. "You might want to wait a few years before you send for your daughter. This land is still raw."

"You got to have vision, boys! In my mind I can see hay fields and cattle herds, and a big ranch house, and—"

"Do you see any old horse thieves in that vision?" Kiowa interrupted.

Rocklin laughed. "You've got to find your own vision!"

Kiowa turned to Sam. "I think he means somethin' besides the end of a rope."

"Mark yourself out some of this Public Land. I tell you, in five years or less it will be open to settlement."

Fortune drug the toe of his boot across the dry, pale dirt. "It's a harsh land. It will be tough to survive out here for five years."

Rocklin pulled a neatly folded, red bandanna out of the back of his pocket and wiped the sweat off his neck and forehead. "If you got a vision for the future, boys, you can pull through all sorts of tough times."

Sam squinted his eyes in the light of the afternoon sun. "I'm afraid all I see out here is dust and alkali."

"And a few horses in the corral," Kiowa added.

HOME

Rocklin jammed his fingers into the back of his belt. "Now, tell me about my ponies. How many are ridable?"

"We've only got four left to break, but they all need to be rode," Sam reported. "We were hoping to see that crew of yours."

"I trust you didn't try to break that bay stallion," Rocklin added. "He's a mean rascal and totally unridable. Two or three times while driving him up here, I thought about shooting him. But I reckoned I could keep him around for stud."

Kiowa glanced over at Fortune. "Sammy gentled him right down."

"He didn't buck you off and try to stomp you?" Rocklin questioned. "I can't believe you climbed on that horse."

"I can't believe I climbed on him fourteen times," Sam groaned.

☞ ☞ ☞

Kiowa rode a prancing, red roan mare around the corral when the report of gunshot sounded from the north. He trotted over to Sam Fortune, who sat on the top of the corral rail.

"You surmise Rocklin found somethin' to hunt?" Kiowa asked.

The air felt hot and stagnant. Corral dust hung thick. Both men sported a yellow-dust hue.

Sam rubbed the sandy blond and gray whiskers on his unshaven chin. "He was goin' to drag that dead horse over to Stony Point. Could be he spotted an antelope over there, I suppose."

"I won't mind some fresh game. I'm a little tired of salt pork and canned meat." Kiowa circled the horse several rotations to the left.

"That's another good reason to have those beef cattle show up." Sam stretched his arms and neck.

Kiowa circled the roan several rotations to the right. Suddenly two shots fired in rapid succession. Sam leaped down from the rail and grabbed the Sharps. Kiowa plucked up his holster and gun from the corral post and slung them over his shoulder. "Open the gate."

Sam seized the cantle of Kiowa's saddle. "Is this roan ready to carry double?"

"I reckon we'll find out."

☞ ☞ ☞

Rocklin hunkered down on a pile of boulders the size of fat pumpkins not far from the wagon. His hat was pushed back, and sweat dripped off his face. He clutched his left arm.

"I went and got myself snakebit, boys. Get me a tourniquet and a knife," he hollered.

In the rocks just below him lay the headless remains of a five-foot rattlesnake. Fortune cut off a saddle string as he dismounted and yanked it tight around Rocklin's upper arm. Kiowa ripped open the white cotton shirt, then sliced a bloody X into the rancher's arm. He sucked the wound and spit half a dozen times.

"I've got a fairly clean bandanna in my back pocket," Rocklin muttered.

When Kiowa finished, Sam tied the red bandanna around Rocklin's bleeding arm. "You up to goin' back yet?"

"I ain't feeling well at all. Help me off these rocks: Ol' Mr. Snake might have relatives hiding in here."

They carried Rocklin to the wagon. "Did you bring a canteen? My mouth is drier than that alkali dirt."

Kiowa swung up on the roan. "I'll ride back to camp and fetch water. You take it easy comin' in."

Sam climbed into the wagon. "You want to lie down in back?"

"I don't want to go to sleep, that's for sure. It was stupid. I knew there could have been snakes. After I dropped that horse down into

HOME

the barranca, I figured to roll some rocks over him. I can't believe I bent over and stuck my hand in that snake hole in the boulders." He stopped a minute and held his chest. "Everything seems to be cramping up on me."

"You don't need to talk. Take it easy, Mr. Rocklin."

"When I heard you ride up I thanked the Lord for you being out here with me. It was Providence, you know."

"It'll be OK. Kiowa knows how to lance a bite and suck out the poison. You'll be sick for a day or two, but you'll pull through."

Sweat rolled off Rocklin's forehead, nose, and chin. "I kept thinking 'I can't die out here alone. There's no one who can tell my daughter what happened.'"

"Let's get you in the shade of those cottonwoods."

"Fortune, if I don't pull through this, send word to my girl in Cheyenne City."

"Mr. Rocklin, we'll get you through this and—"

"Did you hear me, boy?"

"If somethin' happens to you, I'll write to your daughter."

"And you and Kiowa keep the ponies."

"You just keep your eyes on that vision of a big, developed ranch. A wise, west Texas drover told me one time that if a man has a vision for the future, he can pull through all sorts of tough times."

"Oh yeah? Whatever happened to that old drover?"

"I heard he's got a big ol' ranch house with lots of shade trees and a wrap-around veranda. He's got a thousand long-horned bovines roamin' through green, grassy hills. Ever' summer his grandkids come and stay with him."

Rocklin's eyes lit up. He sat up a little straighter. "Say, just how many grandkids does that old, west Texas cowboy have?"

"Twelve."

"Twelve?" Rocklin gasped.

"At last count," Fortune grinned. "And ever' last one of 'em is a girl."

"Lord have mercy on that old man. You had me suckered in, Fortune, until you got to the part about twelve girls."

"You'd love it, old man."

"Yeah . . . I reckon I would. How about you? You ever been married, Sam?"

"Nope. Too wild and reckless, I suppose."

"You ever have any kids?"

"Not that I know of."

"Well, this snakebite is probably making me not think square. I'm ramblin' into areas I shouldn't—but what in the world is a man like you doing out in Indian Territory stealing horses and robbing banks? You're better than that, and you know it," the rancher challenged.

"Are you startin' to meddle, Rocklin?"

"Yep. I knew the minute you stepped into that fray in Antelope Flats. I felt it in your handshake. I knew, Sam Fortune, that there ain't no way on the face of this earth that you could steal my horses. Someplace back along the line, you were brought up right."

"Old man, you better rest up. That poison is gettin' to your brain."

"I'm sure it is. But, why do you think you're squirming around right now? It's because you know I'm right. I was over in Ames in April when Tulsa Jack Blake got killed. He deserved it. But I don't want to pick up a newspaper and read about Sam Fortune gunned down robbin' a bank for five hundred dollars or some wild-eyed Texas drifter shootin' you in the back just for fame." Rocklin wiped his forehead on the sleeve of his shirt. "Now—I'm done with my trespassin'. I don't know what made me blurt that out. We ain't knowed each other barely three weeks."

HOME

☞ ☞ ☞

Kiowa and Sam decided to post a guard at the corral at night, even though Rocklin didn't think it necessary. About midnight Fortune hiked out to relieve Fox. The night air still felt hot, so he didn't rebuild the fire.

No sounds came from the high plains west of San Francisco Creek. Fortune circled the corral a couple of times then plopped down on the dirt and propped himself against a corral post. A quarter moon hung in the eastern sky. He could see everything as dark shadows. To cover the taste of bitter, supper coffee lingering in his mouth, he chewed on the braided, rawhide stampede string.

It was salty.

I ought to stir up the fire and boil me some coffee.

Rocklin shouldn't have said those things. It's none of his business. That's why I've been in the Territory. There's no one around to preach at me.

He held the Sharps across his lap and fingered the cold, steel trigger.

Except Daddy's carbine. It preaches at me. I should just mail it back. That's what I'll do. Next time I'm in town, I'll just wrap it up and send it to . . .

I don't even know who's up there in the Black Hills. Dacee June. I'll send it to . . . twenty-one? . . . is she really? It's been ten years. She was in pigtails clutching onto Daddy's arm everywhere he went.

Far across the barren plains he heard a howl, then a duet of moaning wails. He cocked back the big hammer on the carbine. *I haven't seen a wolf or wolf track since we've been out here.* He squinted his eye to spot movement in the darkness of the night. He got up and slowly circled the corral. He noticed a lantern lit Rocklin's tent, and he spied the silhouette of the rancher sitting up on his cot. After bordering the corral once more, he hiked over to the row of tents.

"Mr. Rocklin?" he called out. "Are you all right? Can I get you something?"

The response was muted like something blurted into a pillow. Fortune opened the flap, bent over, and stuck his head inside. Rocklin sat on the edge of the cot wearing his ducking trousers and no shirt. His neck had swollen about the size of his head, his face white. He gestured for Fortune to come in.

"Isn't this somethin'?" he whispered. "I can't talk much, but I don't want to lay down."

"You want me to fetch you a drink of water or anything?"

"You tryin' to drown me? I want you to read this." He handed him a piece of stiff paper.

Sam noticed an open jar of India ink on the pork barrel that served as a table in the tent. He read through the page twice before he looked up at the man. "You want me to go to Dodge City and bring those longhorns back?" Sam asked.

Rocklin motioned for Fortune to come closer. In a barely audible hoarse whisper, he explained, "If I pull through—and I certainly aim to—it will be three or four days before I can get on the trail. I've got to find out what's going on. This gives you power of attorney to transact my business. Pay off the crew, and hire some cowboys to drive the herd out here if the others don't want to come."

"Maybe we should wait a couple days, . . . you just might be able to . . ."

"Sam, I need you to help me. I'm countin' on you." He reached out his swollen right hand.

Fortune hesitated.

HOME

"Do it for my Amanda up in Cheyenne City and those twelve girls she's going to have someday."

Sam slipped his hand into Rocklin's. The handshake was weak but sure.

"As soon as you're able, follow me into Dodge," Fortune encouraged. "I'll either be throwin' the outfit together or on the trail back"—*or in jail.*

"Don't take the wagon. It's too slow. Take two horses to trade off." Rocklin motioned for Sam to hand him his brown leather vest. He reached into the pocket and pulled out a coin.

"What's the double eagle for?"

"Expenses," Rocklin replied. "Get a bath and shave; buy yourself a new shirt and maybe a tie before you present that power of attorney."

"I don't know if I can pull this off, Mr. Rocklin."

"I don't have anyone else. It's about a hundred miles. You can make it in two days."

Fortune folded up the papers and slipped them into his shirt pocket. "I can make it by midnight, if the horses don't give out," he muttered.

☛ ☛ ☛

Rocklin's swollen neck and face subsided a little by daylight, but he was too weak to get out of bed. His arm had turned such a dark red, it looked almost black. Sam Fortune climbed up on the buckskin gelding and Kiowa handed him the lead line to the red roan mare.

"Anything I can bring you, Kiowa?"

"You've got two horses, you could always bring back—"

"You've got to find your own women," Sam replied.

"Sammy," Kiowa whooped, "you ain't much of a friend when the chips are down."

"Take care of the boss and those ponies until I get back."

"What else is there to do?"

"Watch out for the red wolves," Sam challenged.

"Wolves? There ain't any wolves up here."

"Yeah, that's what I thought. But I heard two howls from the west last night—not the yip-yip-yee of coyotes, but honest wolf howls."

Kiowa grinned. "Might be some relatives of mine."

"You got any kin that isn't lookin' to shoot you?" Sam chided.

"Nope."

"Then be careful. They'll come after these horses if they think they can get away clean."

"Bring us back those bovines and a crew. Then we can take off, and the wolves will be someone else's problem."

☞ ☞ ☞

Sam Fortune reached the Cimarron River before noon without seeing a living creature on the plains. He crossed the border into Ford County, Kansas, then swung a little to the east and followed Salt Creek straight north, looping around two large herds of longhorns that were being grazed to the railroad.

Neither belonged to Rocklin.

Both said Rocklin's bunch was farther on north.

He reached the Arkansas River and the Santa Fe Railroad several hours after dark. He followed them east to the outskirts of Dodge City.

Campfires glowed down by the river as well as lights along Front Street. He found a few unoccupied cottonwoods, picketed the

HOME

horses, and pulled the saddle. Sam slept undisturbed, even through the sounds of a passing train rolling across the river.

At 6:30 A.M. he sat at a corner table in Beatty and Kelley's Restaurant and watched each man who came in. The steaming plate of biscuits, chops, and gravy diverted his attention from the doorway.

I haven't had one sit-down meal since I left jail, not that those meals really counted. Silverware, linen napkins, and a clean coffee cup—and someone who knows how to cook! A man could get used to that.

A tall man in a black suit, with square shoulders and thick dark mustache, blustered through the front door, looked around, and left.

That man looked an awful lot like Tap Andrews. Last I heard, he got killed bustin' out of Arizona Territorial Prison when he ran across Stuart Brannon and that Yavapai posse of his. Course, if I believed rumors, I'd have to dig a grave and crawl in. No tellin' how many times folks have announced my death.

I could never live in Dodge City. Ever' shadow and shout could be someone from my past. Maybe me and Kiowa should ride out to New Mexico. I don't know many folks there.

A young lady with a long yellow dress and clean white apron filled his coffee cup.

"Darlin', you look a whole lot like my little sister. Could you tell me how old you are?" he asked.

She brushed long, light brown bangs off her eyes. "I'm going to be sixteen next week."

"Are you married?" he baited.

"Are you proposing?" she laughed.

Oh Lord, was I ever sixteen? "No, darlin'. . . I just haven't seen my li'l sis in a long time, and I'm usin' you as a substitute."

"Well, I'm not married, but I think Richard O'Brian is going to ask me by fall. He has seven hundred and ninety-two dollars, you know."

"That's nice. He's a thrifty man, I take it?"

"Yes, and he's very hardworking. He's an apprentice bootmaker for John Mueller. On weekends he works on the south side of the railroad at the Dodge City Corrals. Papa said I can't marry anyone unless he's saved up a thousand dollars."

"You have a very wise daddy. Thanks for talkin' to me, darlin'."

"You look very lonely. Where is your little sister?"

"Up in Dakota. In Deadwood, last I heard."

"I think you ought to go visit her."

"You're right, darlin'—I ought to do that. And I think you ought to hold onto that Richard. He's hardworking, thrifty, and smart. I know he's smart, because he picked you out. If I was sixteen or seventeen, I'd be saving my money too."

"You would?"

He nodded and gulped down a lukewarm swallow of coffee. "Now, where's the best place in town to get a haircut and shave? I've been on the trail too long."

"Right next door at the Centennial Barber Shop. Ask for Mr. Dieter. You can get your hair cut in the latest fashion."

"What is the latest fashion?"

"Well, for men your age, I suppose the fashions don't change much."

"You're right about that darlin'."

He watched her as she toted his dirty dishes back to the kitchen. *Kids are honest. I'm a worn-out man with mostly gray hair. I don't look thirty-four. I probably don't even look forty-four.*

☞ ☞ ☞

HOME

The immaculate man behind the barber chair almost stood at attention when he walked through the door.

"Are you Dieter?" Sam asked.

"Yes sir. Would you like a haircut today?"

"A sixteen-year-old waitress next door said you were the best barber in Kansas."

The barber used a whisk brush to wipe down the leather chair. "That's my Greta!"

"Your daughter?"

"My youngest daughter. I have six." He motioned for Sam to sit down in the chair.

"She's a jewel. You and your wife did a very good job of raisin' her."

The barber wrapped a linen cloth around Fortune's neck. "I appreciate that, mister. Her mama died when she was born. I raised those six girls by myself."

"That's a tough bronc to ride."

"The other girls are like Greta, except they are all happy and married. I am a lucky man. I figure the Lord brings sorrow to all of us, but the blessings more than make up for it. You have kids, mister?"

Fortune stared at the mirror behind the barber's chair. "Eh? No. No kids."

"Sorry, mister. I didn't mean to pry. That ain't right. Now, what can I do?"

"Shampoo; haircut; shave. Leave my mustache."

"I've got some hot towels and liniment that will lift some of the dirt out of that elbow of yours, if you'd like."

"What's this deluxe job goin' to cost me?"

"The whole works? That will be a dollar, which includes your choice of tonic water splashed on your face."

"That's what I want," Sam replied. "Now, tell me how in the world you raised six girls on your own."

☞ ☞ ☞

Sam's hat slipped down almost to his ears when he finally walked out of the Centennial Barber Shop. The first clerk who approached him at Wright, Beverley & Company ushered him to a row of Stetsons.

"You think I need a new hat?" Sam grinned.

The young man with slicked back, brown hair looked apologetic. "Most of the drovers who come up the trail want to buy a new hat."

"I need more than a hat."

"We have a trail special," the clerk reported.

"And what is that?"

"A three-piece suit, white shirt, tie, and new Stetson for eleven dollars."

"Is the suit nobby?"

"No, it's modest. But the hat is top of the line."

"Can you toss out the tie and throw in some undergarments?"

"Yep. Same price."

"What would it be if I picked up a second shirt and a new pair of ducking trousers?"

"Two dollars and seventy-five cents more."

"Well, son, let's do the whole works."

"Would you like new boots?"

"Nope. But I'd like these polished."

"Pull them off. We can do that in the back room while you're picking out your clothes."

"How long will it take you to tailor the suit?"

HOME

"We'll have it done by the time you find a bathhouse and return. That is . . . you know . . . if you were headed to the bathhouse."

Sam surveyed the dirt that coated his clothing. "I believe I'm not the first one up the trail you've waited on."

"No sir. I've been at this for almost six years. If you need a bathhouse, there's one right next door. I can bring your clothes over as soon as they're hemmed up."

Fortune studied the young man from head to toe. "Son, did you ever save up a thousand dollars?"

"Eh . . . no, sir . . . I haven't."

"Well, do it. I understand there's a lot of daddies in this town that won't let their daughters marry until the boy saves up a thousand dollars. I think that's a goal worth savin' for, don't you?"

The young man's eyes grew wide. "Yes sir, I reckon I do!"

☞ ☞ ☞

Sam Fortune studied the bathhouse mirror. The dark gray suit fit well. Though the white shirt, buttoned at the collar, did not sport a tie. The new, light gray Stetson with four-inch brim had a rounded crown, but one chop from Sam's right hand creased it down the middle.

When he stepped out on the boardwalk, he tipped his new hat to a lady in a green plaid suit made of mohair brilliantine. A double row of pearl buttons dropped down from the high collar to the skirt accenting the woman's narrow waist. Her long, curly, dark brown hair was fastened up on her head and tucked under a white straw hat with green, French silk flowers. The woman's bright blue eyes caught Fortune by surprise. She smiled slightly, and nodded as she passed by.

I doubt if that lady would have smiled at me the way I looked when I first rode to town. Although cowboys sportin' new clothes must be a fairly common event in a place like—

"Sammy?"

He looked back at the woman. She spun around to study him.

Do I know her?

It was the smile that gave her away.

"Rachel?"

"Sammy, look at you! I don't believe I've ever seen you dressed up so fine."

"Me? Rachel, darlin', you look fancy enough to be a banker's wife!"

"My husband's a doctor, actually. I'm Mrs. Hershel Sinclair."

"That's wonderful, Rachel . . ."

The flowers in her hat made her look taller than five feet three inches. "It really is, Sammy. These past seven years have been the absolutely happiest ones of my whole life."

He leaned his right hand against a porch post. It felt well-worn, slick, and a little sticky. "Seven years? It hasn't been seven years."

"It's been nine years since that night you and I got run out of Fort Worth. You went back to the Indian Territory, and I went to my sister's in Chicago, remember? It was there that the Lord decided not to give up on me."

"The Lord? Don't tell me you converted."

"You'll get no apologies from me, Sam Fortune. It's a wonderful feeling to know that God forgives you. I attended a Bible class with my sister and met Dr. Sinclair there. We've been in Dodge five years now. How have you been? From the looks of that handsome suit you're quite successful. I hear from some of the old gang from time to time. The last I heard, you were incarcerated."

HOME

Fortune scratched the back of his neck. The new hat felt very stiff. "We do have to reap what we sow."

"How true. However, we can be forgiven and start out fresh and new. I wish you could meet the children."

"How many do you have?"

"Four—and Hershel wants more. Two boys and two girls. How about you, Sam Fortune? Have you settled down yet?"

"I'm not married, if that's what you're hintin' at."

"Of course it is! I certainly like that suit on you. I'm glad you don't wear a tie. It shows a certain flair. Most men wear one because they know women find them irresistibly attractive, but being independently minded like you are, you reject such appeal and go you're own way. I like that. I always liked that in you. Now, what are you doing in Dodge, and can you stay for supper tonight? I'll have the cook set an extra plate."

"I'm reppin' for a rancher down in the Public Lands. I have to check on his cattle and get a crew to drive them out to the ranch. I'll be leavin' this afternoon, if I can."

She leaned over, stood on tiptoes, and kissed him on the cheek. "Sammy, it is wonderful to see you. I . . . I . . . well, frankly, I supposed you would be dead by now, the life you were living. I have to scoot over to a meeting at the church, but you must promise to have supper with us next time you are in town. Hershel will enjoy visiting with you. I've told him all about you and me."

"You have?"

"Well, . . ." Rachel rolled her eyes to the light blue sky. "Not exactly all . . . but you know what I mean. Say, did you ever get things settled with your daddy?"

"Why did you ask that, Rachel?" he snapped.

"Oh, my . . . I am sorry. I don't know why it popped into my head. Please forgive me, Sammy. You're right. It was uncalled for. I really must scoot. Promise me, Sam Fortune. Next time you come to Dodge you'll have supper at our house."

"I promise," he mumbled.

"Good, because Sam Fortune is a rebel and a scamp, but he always keeps his word to women."

Sam stared after her until she turned the corner and headed south.

He strolled along the shade of the covered boardwalk. *It seems like ever'one I know is either dead or reformed. Rachel Dally—you looked good, girl. Gettin' away from me was smart. Trouble is . . . I can't ever get away from me.*

Why did she ask about Daddy?

Lord, it's like you're naggin' at me! You've ignored me and let me go my way for years, and now you're nagging me!

I do believe this is my last trip to Dodge City.

☞ ☞ ☞

A big, tall man with a neatly trimmed, salt and pepper beard rested his elbows on the hitching rail in front the Chicago Meat Packing office, watching two wagons full of bleached buffalo bones, stacked sixteen feet high, roll down Front Street. "That's a lot of bones," he muttered to no one in particular.

Sam stopped beside the man. "There's a lot more out on the prairie."

"Yep, but there won't be forever. Then, everyone out here—including the Indians—will have to eat beef instead of buffalo," the man reasoned. "You just come up the trail?"

Fortune pushed his stiff Stetson with old, rawhide stampede string to the back of his head. "Hard to hide, isn't it?"

"You got cattle to sell? I'm the buyer."

HOME

Sam straightened his new black tie and brushed his thick mustache with his fingertips. "No, sir. I'm reppin' for Mr. Rocklin."

"Rocklin? Well, it's about time you showed up. Your crew pushed in here over two weeks ago."

"That's what I heard. They were supposed to rendezvous down near the Canadian in the Public Lands."

"Well, they said the trail boss took a spill and died coming across the Red Desert. So, they hunted around a little for Rocklin, but he didn't show, so they pushed them up. I bought them."

"You what?"

The man stroked his chin whiskers. "I said, 'I bought them out.'"

The suit coat suddenly felt tight across Sam's shoulders. "They weren't for sale. They were going to be foundation stock."

"Out in Public Lands?" The man spit a chaw of tobacco about ten feet out into the wide, dusty street. "Cows can't live out there. There's no water."

"That's for Rocklin to decide. How can you buy twelve hundred beef from a man who doesn't want to sell them?"

"Look, mister, that's for your boss and crew to discuss. I've been holdin' the Wells Fargo banknote for Rocklin."

"But I'm supposed to take the herd and crew out to the ranch."

"I paid them off out of his profits. Most of them went back to Texas, I reckon. As far as the herd, you can tell Rocklin to come to Dodge and pick out the ones he wants from another herd. I'll sell them for the same price per head as I bought them. These Jayhawkers are gettin' scared of Texas fever in the cattle. They won't let us bed them down north of the tracks anymore. They want them loaded in boxcars immediately and shipped east. So that's what I did. "Let's go get that draft. You do have a power of attorney on you, don't you?"

Fortune reached into his vest pocket. "Yep."

"Good, I'll draw you up a receipt and send you on your way."

"How much is that banknote worth, anyways?"

The man pulled a small notebook and stubby pencil from his suit pocket, then flipped through the pages. "Rocklin has a note for twenty-two thousand and four hundred dollars."

CHAPTER
FOUR

Dodge City, Kansas, Queen of the Cowtowns

Sam Fortune entered Big Mike Feeney's Grocery Store wearing new ducking trousers and a new white cotton shirt. The three-piece suit and tie that Rachel had chided him into buying were folded neatly in his bedroll, lashed behind the cantle of his saddle. The long-legged buckskin was hitched to the rail in front of the store.

When he left the store, Sam toted a baby loaf of yellow cheese, two dozen sticks of buffalo jerky, and a two-pound tin of salt crackers. Like a small, striped cigar, a red and white peppermint stick pinched proudly between his lips.

He tethered the grub sack in front of the fork of the saddle and tugged his new hat down in the front.

If I ride all night, I could make the ranch around noon. Providing the horses hold up and the moon's bright enough to ride . . . and I don't fall asleep and tumble off into one of those barrancas. Well, good-bye ol' paint . . . I'm leavin' . . . Dodge City.

HOME

It isn't the right words to the song, but the message fits. You've seen your day come and go, cowtown—and so have I.

Sam swung up into the saddle and untied the lead rope of the red roan. He plodded the horses west on Front Street. At the edge of town, he pivoted in the saddle and leaned on the buckskin's rump while tipping his new Stetson.

A gold reflection caught his eye.

Gold earrings.

On a man.

Like a pirate.

He and another man with full beard shoved open the tall, narrow doors of the Long Branch Saloon and disappeared inside. Sam jerked the horses around and trotted them to the rail in front of the saloon.

He left the Sharps carbine hanging on the saddle. Sam pulled his Colt out of his holster and shoved it into his sogan. He bit off the wet end of the peppermint stick and shoved the rest into his bedroll as well.

Inside the Long Branch a big, bald, black man pounded an out-of-tune piano. Sam distinguished shouts from a card game, curses from disgruntled drinkers, and an occasional giggle from one of the brightly dressed girls. Cigar and cigarette smoke drifted across the room. The floor felt gritty under his boots. An aroma of whiskey and sweat wafted from most every person and object in the room.

On the far wall, next to the back door, Fortune spotted the man with earrings. His partner had his back toward the bar.

Along with half a dozen customers, Fortune leaned against the polished wood and brass bar.

"Sam, is that you?"

Fortune stared into the friendly eyes of the tall, slender bartender with thin brown hair and hawklike nose.

"Talbert?"

"Yeah. How about this?" he pointed at the white apron he wore. "Bet you never thought you'd see me in an honest job."

Sam pushed his new hat back and grinned. "It's a long way from dodgin' bullets down on Delaware Ridge."

"Ain't that the truth." Talbert looped his thumbs through his bib apron straps. "I got me an honest woman, an honest job, and an honest little house with a picket fence around it. I like it, Sammy. It fits me."

Sam pushed his hat back even farther and scratched his neatly trimmed hair. *Is this the man who once shoved open the front door on that log cabin and dared the entire posse to come through?* "Talbert, I'm happy for you."

"You're lookin' scrubbed up and good, Sammy. Someone told me Judge Parker hung you."

"I did have a run-in with the judge, but he decided three years in prison would cure me."

"Did it?"

"Look at me, Talbert—new trousers and shirt, shaved up, and a new Stetson. What does that tell you?"

"Either you jist robbed a bank, or you got yourself a legitimate job. Did you leave the Territory?"

Glancing at the mirror behind the bar, he could see the man with the gold earrings still drinking. "I'm reppin' for a rancher out in the Public Lands."

"That's good . . . that's real good, Sam. A man has to pull out of that life before he carries too much lead. Now, you never were a drinkin' man, so what are you doing in the Long Branch?"

Fortune nodded toward the back door. "There's a couple of bushwhackers in here I wanted to . . . eh . . . visit with—but I can't remember their names."

HOME

"Who's that?"

Sam dropped his voice down a little lower. "One of 'em wears gold earrings, like a pirate. And the other has . . ."

One of the girls began a frenzied dance next to the piano. Several onlookers clapped in tune.

Talbert pointed to his own hand. "Has both middle fingers missin'?"

Sam practically shouted to be heard, "Yeah."

The piano and the clapping softened. Talbert leaned across the bar. "You ain't got your pistol in that holster, do you?"

"Nope." Sam showed him the empty holster.

"Good." The bartender shielded his lips with his hand. "'Cause it's against the law to pack in the city limits, and I don't want you gettin' in a gunfight right before my eyes."

"A gunfight? I didn't say I wanted to kill them. I just wanted to know their names."

Talbert stood straight and squared his shoulders. "Sammy, there ain't nobody that looks for McDermitt and Burns unless he's after a gunfight. They are mean and stupid. It's a dangerous combination."

Fortune watched the two men's reflections in the mirror. "Which one is which?"

"Burns has the earrings."

"Do they tote sneakguns?" Fortune investigated.

"Do you?" Talbert replied.

Sam grinned and rocked back on his heels. "Talbert, you know me better than that."

"Them is the type you can't guarantee anything, Sammy. They've been arrested a couple times this week already for carrying guns in the city limit—so, you'd think they'd learn. I'd bet anything they pack knives in their boots."

"Who are they, Talbert? I never heard of 'em until I was down in Antelope Flats."

"When they get soused up, they like to brag that they rode with Frank and Jesse James. But I don't have any reason to believe them. They seem to be in town ever' time someone gets back shot and robbed. Remember those Orval brothers down at McAllisters that sliced up that woman and her kids? These two are like that, only crazier and more brutal. Don't turn your back on them, Sammy."

"I need to have a little talk with them."

"What about?"

"They beat up a friend of mine."

"Who?"

"Piney Burleson."

"No! Piney? Is she all right?" the bartender asked.

"She won't ever be all right again, Talbert."

The bartender shook his head. "That ain't right."

"That's why I need to have a little talk with them."

The bartender rolled up the sleeves of his white shirt. "You need help?"

"Talbert, you've got a good job, a good wife, and a good little house with a picket fence. Don't jeopardize that. Take some trash out back or somethin'. Then, when you come in, tell them an old acquaintance from down in the Territory is out in the alley and needs to tell them somethin'."

Talbert glanced at the back door. "You goin' to take 'em both on?"

"You said they were dumb. Give me three minutes to get around back."

"I also said they was mean." Talbert plucked up a circular tin trash can. He also pulled a three-foot, hickory axe handle out from under the counter and jammed it into the two-foot can.

HOME

"This billy-whacker is gettin' old. Think I'll toss it out into the second barrel on the left."

Sam gazed back at the men. A heated debate brewed between them. The piano music picked up, and one of the girls sang "My Home Is on the Prairie, But My Heart Sails Off at Dawn."

Talbert leaned over the bar. "Did you hear me?"

"Axe handle, second barrel. Yeah . . . thanks, Talbert."

"What do you want me to tell them?"

"Tell them I got news from down in the Territory, and I need to talk to both of them in private."

"Are you sure you know what you're doin', Sammy?"

"I haven't known for sure what I was doin' since you and me jumped off that Missouri, Kansas, and Texas Railroad mail car five years ago."

The bartender's eyes lit up. "How did we ever live through that?"

"It was the grace of God, I reckon."

Talbert's eyes widened and his eyebrows rose. "I believe you're right, but I never thought I'd hear those words from your lips."

Fortune turned and watched three men stroll in the front door of the Long Branch. *Neither did I, Talbert Manning . . . neither did I.*

Sam slipped out of the saloon, looped his empty holster over the saddle horn. He rolled up his sleeves as he marched to the alley behind the Long Branch. The back door also worked as a loading door. It was four feet wide with a ten-foot ramp down to ground level. Several oak barrels, tucked against the back wall, served as rubbish containers. He spotted the tip end of an axe handle sticking out of the middle barrel.

The alley was half sun, half shade. Fortune stood in the shade with the brim of his hat pulled low. The afternoon sun lit up the door.

The bearded McDermitt shoved open the door and squinted as he tried to adjust to the direct sunlight.

He stretched his neck forward. "Mister, you want to see me?" he blustered.

"Where's Burns? I need to talk to both of you," Fortune called out.

The man never moved from the doorway. "What for?"

"I've got somethin' for you and him."

"Bring it to me, I'll take it to him."

"How do I know you'll share it with him?"

"Share what?"

"The reward," Fortune tempted.

"What reward?"

"I don't want to yell it all over town," Fortune baited. "It's from a lady down in Indian Nation."

The big man took several steps down the ramp. "Did Belle Star send you up here with our cut?"

"All I can say aloud is that I'm supposed to give you and Burns equal shares. I don't want to go back and tell her I only did half the job."

"I'll get Burns." The man scurried up the ramp and back into the saloon.

Within moments both men burst through the wide door. Big smiles creased dirty faces, hats rakishly tilted to the right.

Burns's earrings sparkled in the afternoon sun as he shuffled down the ramp and into the shade. "So she decided we didn't need to wait until September?"

Sam held fine, dry, alley dirt in his clenched left hand. "She figured the sooner you two got paid off, the better."

"That's exactly what I tried to tell her all along!" McDermitt added, rubbing his beard. Sam noticed the man's missing fingers.

HOME

"Did Belle send gold dust or coins?" Burns asked as he approached.

"Come here; let me show you a sample," Sam offered, holding the clenched fist in front of him.

"Where's the rest of it?" McDermitt peeked over the shorter Burns's shoulder and watched Fortune's hand.

"Don't worry. You'll get your whole share. But there is one thing you ought to know: Belle Star didn't send me up here."

"Who did?" Burns asked.

"Piney Burleson," Sam announced.

"Who in hades is Piney Burleson?" McDermitt blustered.

"Oh, you remember. She's about six foot tall, thin, with long blond hair. She lives in Antelope Flats. You about busted your toes kickin' her head in. Remember?"

Burns reached for his boot top, but the dirt in Sam's hand blasted his face. Fortune caught the man's chin with the palm of his hand and slammed his head straight back, catching McDermitt square in the forehead.

The bearded man staggered back and tumbled off the side of the ramp. He landed on his back in the alley dirt. Fortune's knee found the pit of Burns's stomach. An uppercut to the chin, followed by a resounding left jab and a right hook, sent Burns cussing and tumbling to his back.

Sam dodged McDermitt's wild roundhouse, but he couldn't escape the man's grasp. Both of them tumbled to the dirt. The full impact of Fortune's elbow slammed into the bearded man, busting the skin. The big man tried to pull away as blood dripped into his eyes, but two right crosses to the chin left McDermitt struggling to remain on his hands and knees.

Burns lunged at Sam with a one-foot blade hunting knife. Sam heard his shirt tear and felt a red-hot gouge streak across his side. Burns was off balance from the lunge, and Sam shoved him back until he tripped over his partner, sending both men to the ground.

Fortune dove for the oak barrel and snatched out the axe handle. This time when Burns came at him with the knife, Sam slammed the hickory into the man's arm, just above the wrist.

Bones broke.

The knife dropped.

Burns screamed and dropped to his knees in agony.

McDermitt, still on his hands and knees, reached down for his knife. Sam's boot caught the man right behind the ear and sent him sprawling on his back. The bearded man raised his right boot to pull his knife, but the axe handle crashed into his shin. It sounded like a dry limb cracking under the weight of a wagon wheel.

Both hands squeezing the hickory handle, Fortune lunged at Burns.

"Sammy!" A shout came from the now open back door.

Fortune raised the axe handle to strike the man's head.

"Sammy! A deputy's comin'. . . . Don't do it. He ain't worth gettin' hung over!"

Sam Fortune glanced up to see Talbert Manning and a cluster of customers gawk out at the alley.

"Give me the axe handle," Talbert insisted.

Fortune paused as two gun-toting deputy marshals trotted up to him.

☞ ☞ ☞

The jail at Dodge City had a solid brick wall between the cells. Sam couldn't see the doctor work on Burns and McDermitt, but he heard their screams and curses.

An hour later, the doctor came to examine Sam.

HOME

"Mr. Fortune, your knuckles look strong enough, and that cut in the side isn't too deep. Keep it doctored with iodine for a week, and try to keep the dirt out. When you sweat, it's going to burn like— well, you know what. You might want to get a new shirt." The doctor stood back and straightened his tie. "I understand you're a former acquaintance of my wife's."

"Are you Rachel's husband?"

"Yes. She's out in the sheriff's office wanting to talk to you. Is it all right if I send her in, since I'm through?"

"Is it all right with you, Doc?"

Dr. Hershel Sinclair studied Sam a moment. "Thanks for asking, Fortune. The truth of the matter is, Rachel's friends are my friends. I may not be the first man she ever loved, but I intend on being the last."

"She's a good woman. You're a lucky man, Doc."

"You're right, Sam Fortune, but you're lucky yourself. Most men who took on those two would have been knifed in the back. Maybe it was providential that axe handle was in the trash barrel. I'll send Rachel in." The doctor closed the jail cell door behind him.

Sam stared down the hall. *It wasn't providential . . . it was planned. I didn't plan it; it was Talbert's idea. Since when does God use a bartender to enact his will? Or help a man bent on vengeance?*

Course, I suppose he can use anyone or do anythin' he chooses.

Sam's mind drifted, and he didn't notice at first the well-dressed woman walking straight toward him.

"I really must say: This is the Sam Fortune I know and remember," Rachel began.

"I almost made it out of town a gentleman, Rachel darlin'. I should have left wearin' that suit. I don't think I'd get in a fight if I wore a suit," Sam said.

"Just what, exactly, did these men do to incur your wrath?" she interrogated.

"These are the two that beat up Piney Burleson, Rachel."

Her white-gloved hand flew to her mouth. "No!"

"She isn't well enough to testify against them. So there was no way of bringin' them to Judge Parker's court. I felt like I had to do something."

"I understand they are still alive. I'd say you've mellowed, Sam Fortune." She clutched the iron bars.

"I was ready to bash their heads in." He inched closer, but kept his hands to his side. "It was Talbert that settled me down. Did you know he works over at the Long Branch?"

"Heavens yes. He and his wife sit behind us in church. Why do you think I'm over here? Talbert sent me word of your arrest. I spoke to the marshal, Sammy. He said if you paid a ten-dollar fine and left town immediately, he'd turn you out right now."

"How about those two?" He nodded in the direction of the next cell.

"He said he would hold them until morning. They also have to pay the fine. But one has a broken leg, and the other a broken arm. He didn't think they would be trying to trail you for a while, any-ways. Do you have any money on you?"

"I got a lot of money on me, but it belongs to my boss. So no, I don't have the ten dollars," he admitted.

"That's what I thought. I'll pay the fine," she announced.

"No, you won't." He reached over and took her gloved hand. "I'm not having a married woman bail me out."

"Since when did that matter?" She squeezed his fingers, but pulled her hand back. "Sam, you really don't have a choice. If you stay in jail, you'll get out when these other two do, and they'll shoot you in the back right here in Dodge City, just as sure as the wind

HOME

blows in west Texas. Frankly, I'd like a nice, peaceful evening with my husband at home—instead of him traipsing around town patching up those left in your wake. It would be very good for us all if you left now."

"And never came back?" he added.

She raised her pointed chin and frowned. "I didn't say that."

"But you meant it."

"You are welcome at our house any day, Sam Fortune."

"But you're hoping that day won't come along for quite a spell."

She tugged off a long glove and reached into her handbag. "Perhaps, I am."

"Thanks for bailing me out, Rachel, darlin'. I'll send you back the money."

"No—I don't want you to do that. Just ride out. Don't go back to the Territory, Sam. Go someplace new. Start all over. Go up to Montana . . . or Wyoming . . . or . . ."

"Or Dakota? Go ahead and say it, Rachel."

"Sammy, I'm saying this because I care about you. Don't get yourself killed."

"I know, Rachel. Thanks for caring."

She strolled toward the door then turned. "And thank you, Sammy, for bringing a little justice for Piney Burleson."

☛ ☛ ☛

The sun hung low when Sam finally left Dodge City. It was July-hot and humid. His shirt was stitched. Sweat rolled down his side and burned into his wound.

He rode the buckskin at a slow trot; the roan mare followed behind. The road out of town had a little traffic, most of which he ignored. He surveyed the endless plains of short brown grass that had been overgrazed by the big herds moving north.

I keep tryin' to be the same, but everything's changin' around me. It's like the world is spinnin', and I'm standin' still. Rachel's settled down. Talbert's gone honest. I end up lookin' more like Burns and McDermitt than I do anyone else.

You're messin' with my mind, Lord. I know what you're doing. A month ago I would have ridden away from Dodge, regrettin' that I didn't kill those two. Now, I keep havin' regrets for whippin' 'em like that. What's wrong with me? They deserved what they got. They'll heal up. They'll still be able to find their way home. That's a lot better than Piney.

But . . . still . . . I should've had more self-control. I do believe I would have bashed their heads in, if it hadn't been for Talbert. What was that verse Mama was readin' in that dream? "Have mercy upon me, O God, according to thy lovingkindness." . . . then something about tender mercies . . .

Rachel's right. I need to go far away. Maybe California. I think some of the Dalton brothers are out there. I could go stay with them and—that's exactly what I need to get away from.

We have the horses broke. Kiowa and I will get our money and head somewhere we've never been before.

Sam planned to ride all night, but when he reached the Cimarron, he felt too tired to continue. He crossed the river and rode west along it for a couple of miles. Then he picketed the horses, rolled out his bedroll, and promptly fell asleep.

☞ ☞ ☞

When Sam woke up he saw horse lips.

Then yellowed teeth.

Coal black eyes.

And short, pointed ears.

The buckskin stood next to the bedroll, his head only inches

HOME

from Sam's. Daylight had broken. The sun cracked over the eastern plains. To his surprise, his back did not hurt, nor his ribs. The burn in his side was mild, and if it hadn't been for eight hundred and seventy-five pounds of horseflesh hovering over him, he would have gone back to sleep.

He shoved the horse's head aside and sat up. "So you pulled your picket pin, did you? You know, that's not a bad name. I'll call you Picket."

Sam carefully examined inside his boots before he pulled them on. The crown of the new Stetson was still stiff, but the brim was dirty and creased after the fight. The red roan waited where she'd been staked and seemed visibly relieved to have the buckskin return to her side.

"He went off and left you, did he? But he didn't go very far. For the life of me, I thought he'd head for the remuda. He must have smelled that tonic water the barber drowned me with."

Sam didn't bother building a campfire. He watered the horses, saddled up, and rode west. Breakfast consisted of cheese, jerky, crackers, and a few swigs from the canteen.

A good night's rest always clears my mind. A man should never make decisions when he's tired. I'm not goin' to California. I'm not going to Montana. I'm not going to Dakota. And I'm not going back into Indian Territory. I'm going to stay right out here in these public lands. I'll work for Rocklin. He'll have to hunt for a crew, now that his boys drifted back to south Texas.

This land is too barren for bounty hunters, too desolate for horse thieves, too hot for lawmen. I can see someone approach for fifty miles. Times are changin'. If this land does open up, I'll already be established. Maybe Kiowa wants to stay, too. But he'll get restless. He'll miss some action. He'll miss the women.

I'll . . . I'll miss 'em, too . . . but I'm not sure any gal is better off havin' known me. Maybe I'll stake off a little place of my own. Five, six years from now, when they move in here to take this land, some pretty, young farmer's daughter will . . . will not want to marry a forty-year-old man.

He followed the trail by the river and gazed out across the prairie.

I can't believe this. Lord, you're playin' with my mind, again. I haven't shed a tear in years. I'm not goin' to start now. But then, I haven't mentioned marriage to anyone in years either. Of course, I didn't mention it to anyone just now.

Only you, Lord.

And you don't count.

"Picket, did you know a person can spend too much time thinkin'? It's true. A person ought to keep busy doin' what they want to do, or at least what they have to do. Let's trot to the ranch and tell Rocklin the news. He can do the ponderin'."

Sam yanked the folded bank note out of his old leather vest and opened it up. *Twenty-two thousand four hundred dollars . . . I've never seen that big a sum in my life. I wonder how Rocklin saved up enough to buy that herd in the first place? Maybe he sold a ranch down in Texas. Maybe he's been savin' all his life. I've spent the better part of fifteen years wishin' I could get my hands on that much money, and now I can't wait to give it to Rocklin and get rid of the burden of it.*

What would you do, Sam Fortune, if this was yours? I'd go back to Texas and buy the home ranch. Fix it all up nice . . . then write to Dacee June . . . Robert . . . Todd—if he's still alive—and say, "Come on home."

I wonder if they buried Daddy in the Black Hills? Maybe I'd just dig up his bones and tote them all the way to Coryell County . . . that is, if I had twenty-two thousand four hundred dollars.

Which I don't.

103

HOME

It was almost noon when he saw the July sun reflect off the three white tents at Rocklin's ranch. Then the cottonwoods came up on the horizon. Then the barn frame appeared and, finally, the corrals.

The empty corrals.

"Where are all your pals, Picket? Maybe Kiowa took them all down to the creek, but I don't know why."

He spurred the buckskin into a canter and studied the horizon. There was absolutely no movement anywhere on the plains. No horses. No people. No coyotes. No birds. Even the pointed tips of the scalloped cottonwood leaves hung straight down without movement.

He had pulled out the Sharps carbine by the time he reached the corral. He tied off the horses, loosened the cinch, then walked to the tents.

"Kiowa?" he called. "Mr. Rocklin?"

He cocked the hammer on the carbine.

There was no sound of movement.

No shout of response.

No howl of wind.

Nothing but the crunch of his boot heel in the dry, yellow dirt and the jingle of his spurs.

The bunkhouse tent was completely bare.

Wherever you went, Kiowa, you took your bedroll, saddle, and gear. This isn't sittin' good. . . . I don't like the way this feels. . . .

"Mr. Rocklin?" he repeated as he stepped back out into the heat of a July noon.

Some of the supplies seemed to be missing from the cook tent.

Sam paused before he tugged open the flap on Rocklin's tent. *Lord, I know I've rebelled against you for so long, I don't even have the*

right to pray. But I'd like to ask you anyway . . . that this tent might be
empty too.

Even before he threw open the flap, he could smell the answer.
His shoulders slumped. His chin dropped. He eased the hammer
down on the carbine.

"No!" he shouted. "No, Kiowa, no!"

Rocklin's body was fully clothed and lying on top of his blanket-
covered cot. A tiny spot of dried blood marked his chest, and Sam
could see the indentions of two bullet holes. The body was stiff, but
Fortune, stunned, searched the neck for a pulse anyway.

There wasn't any.

He spun around and marched out of the tent. He sat down on
the edge of the tent's wooden platform and lowered his head between his knees.

"This is exactly what I prayed wouldn't happen, Lord! All the
way along the trail this morning I had it in my heart to change my
life around. I wanted to get a fresh start. I wanted to walk away
from the past. Now, look at this—look at this mess. Rocklin's dead.
Kiowa shot him and stole the horses. Rocklin didn't even put up a
fight. He let someone come right into the tent and pull a gun. He
was too tough to let that happen, unless it was someone he
trusted . . . like me . . . or Kiowa!"

I prayed, but I can't trust you, Lord. You've given up on me and
turned a deaf ear. I can't get out of it. I can never escape. It's like a bear
trap. It gnaws the life out of me. My God, what I am going to do? Do I
track down the only friend I have left? Do I shoot Kiowa? For what? So
that I can have the horses? I can't bring them back to Rocklin. Lord, my
life might not be very important to you, but it's the only one I have—and
right now, it's a bewilderment.

A quick hike around the perimeter of the corral revealed that
the remuda of horses had been kept bunched and driven straight

HOME

due west, even though the windswept tracks were difficult to read, at least a day old.

Sam searched the tents three times but could not locate the shovel. He stepped off a grave, anyhow, fifty feet north of the largest of the cottonwoods. He dug it with a two-by-four six feet long and a large cast-iron frying pan. He lowered Rocklin's blanket-clad body and smoothed dirt over it, blending the grave site with the high plains.

With his shirtsleeves rolled up to his elbow and sweat burning a track into his knife wound, he marched back to Rocklin's tent. In a small, black leather case he found papers, letters, and personal items that included a small, leather-bound Bible. Sam tramped back down to the camouflaged grave site. After reading aloud Psalm 23 and Revelation 21, he stared down at the dirt.

"Lord, I don't feel like praying. I don't think you want to listen to me, and I can't complain about that, because I haven't listened to you for years. But Mr. Rocklin treated me square, and I treated him square. Have mercy on his soul. In Jesus' name, amen."

And have mercy on me and Kiowa, 'cause when I catch up with him, I don't think I'm goin' to want to pray.

He spent the remaining hours sorting through supplies and re-modeling the old McClellan saddle into a packsaddle for the red roan mare. He built a small fire and cooked a little supper. He watched the stars come out, then disappear as a stiff wind whipped in from the west and storm clouds blew in.

Although he had spread his bedroll outside, the crashing thunder and vertical lightening strikes sent him to the bunkhouse tent. About midnight, the skies opened up and a deluge of rain blasted the tents and the dry, panhandle dirt. Then it hailed. For over a half-hour the roar of the storm sounded to Sam like a choir of angry knife blades dancing on the tent. When they began to slice through the canvas, he sat up, put on his hat, and wrapped the bedroll around his shoulders.

The hail turned back to rain, and—like a flash flood—the deluge melted the hail, except that inside the tent. Finally, as if taking its cue from a heavenly signal, all rain ceased at once.

The west winds picked up, and within minutes the clouds broke, the stars blinked on, and a half-moon appeared overhead. The wind died, leaving the air clean, fresh, almost cool. Sam opened both ends of the wall tent, tried to find a dry spot on his bedroll, and fell asleep with one hand on the receiver of the .50-caliber carbine.

☞ ☞ ☞

It was a bright, beautiful, refreshing morning.

Clean air, no dust, and very little mud due to the dry soil, and a steady breeze. It dawned as a panhandle summer day at its best.

And Sam Fortune was depressed.

Extremely depressed.

He packed a hundred pounds of supplies on the back of the red roan, mounted Picket, then circled the horses by the recently dug grave.

"Well, Mr. Rocklin . . . ," he tipped his still damp Stetson, "I trust the coyotes can't dig your bones, and others will let you lie in peace. I'm sorry about this place not workin' for you. I really wanted it to work. I prayed for it to work. The Bible says, 'The effectual fervent prayer of a righteous man availeth much,' but I'm afraid the prayers of an Indian Territory outlaw aren't worth much. You should have picked better friends."

Fortune looked to the west.

HOME

"I guess . . . I ought to pick better friends too. I don't know what happened here, but I'm going to find out. I pledge you that, Mr. Rocklin. I won't rest until I figure it out."

And I probably won't rest then, either.

Six miles west of the ranch, Sam lost all trace of the remuda. The combination of steady wind, followed by the deluge of summer rain and hail, returned the desertlike plains to a virgin condition.

OK, Kiowa Fox. Where did you take those ponies? Somewhere to sell them? Somewhere to sell them where you wouldn't be arrested?

That eliminates the I.T., Kansas, and most of Texas.

Black Mesa . . . they don't care where the goods come from. But, they wouldn't buy the horses. They'd shoot Kiowa in the back and take them. He knows that.

He'd go somewhere where he wouldn't get arrested . . . or shot in the back.

And someplace where the women are real friendly.

"New Mexico!"

Tramperas . . . Cimarron . . . someplace along the Santa Fe tracks . . . he'll sell the horses and chase the women until the money is gone.

Or until I catch up with him.

Someday you will have to answer to God, Kiowa Fox. But until then, you'll answer to Sam Fortune.

☞ ☞ ☞

About noon, Sam crossed Beaver Creek, not more than six feet wide and six inches deep. The water, muddied from the deluge the night before, was beginning to clear. A grassy area, no larger than twenty-five by fifty feet on the north side of the creek, had been re-

cently grazed. On the bank of the creek, up on the plains, he spotted the tracks of at least a dozen horses.

"He's still got a day on us, Picket, but he doesn't know I'm
back here." *I wonder what he thinks I'm going to do? I was supposed
to push in twelve hundred head. Wouldn't that have been a mess? No
old man. No ranch houses. No horses. We would have had to turn
around, drive them right back to Dodge City— and sell them. But you
knew that, didn't you, Lord?*

Sam figured he was straight south of Black Mesa when he
dropped down beside McNeiss Creek so the horses could drink from
a stream so narrow they could step across it. The creek flowed out of
a narrow gorge no more than ten feet across and at least that deep.

Fortune studied the eroded streambed. *From up on the plains
this little creek can't be seen, until someone rides right up to it. By ridin'
single file, you could travel along without being spotted. On the other
hand, if they spied you before you spied them, you'd be a sitting duck
down here at the bottom of this barranca.*

It's risky.

But so is ridin' straight up to a horse thief.

He turned his horses into the tiny narrow arroyo and rode up
the creek.

For the next three hours, Sam Fortune followed the barranca.
At times it rose up almost even with the flat plains. On the northern horizon, treeless mountains divided the light blue sky from the
yellowish-red soil. The dead grass grew in scattered clumps. The occasional sage grew no more than a foot off the ground. There were
no trees. No buildings. No roads. No people. No animals. And,
there was no wind.

The only sign of life on the plains was the layers of hoofprints
from the remuda being pushed along the plains north of the creek.

HOME

Late in the evening he climbed up out of the creek bed at the base of a treeless mountain range. Sam guessed he was close to the New Mexico border. Up against a rimrock, where the creek overflowed during runoff, grew a thick carpet of light green grass. He picketed the horses, pulled the saddle and pack, then inspected the treeless oasis.

At the base of the rimrock, the grass had been grazed down. On the north side of the meadow, tracks revealed the horses had galloped toward the hills.

Kiowa left here in a hurry! Maybe he spotted me. But there's not enough daylight to tell how old these tracks are. There's got to be an old campfire here someplace.

He returned to the creek, following the base of the rimrock. His boot rolled across a rock, and he stopped to retrieve a brass casing.

.45-70? Kiowa has his .44 and maybe Rocklin's '73 Winchester carbine, but that's a .44 also. This is a single-shot . . . a Trapdoor. . . . The army? Did Kiowa run across a cavalry patrol?

Fortune retrieved twelve more brass casings as he hiked along the rimrock. Near the creek he came across a shallow cave at the base of the cliff and a fire circle. The ashes were dead, but the dirt beneath them was still a little warm.

Several more .45-70 casings were scattered near the fire.

Whose camp was this? Did Kiowa come across a Trapdoor single-shot? Did someone come up on him by surprise, or did he come up on them? Someone chased someone. From the looks of the brass, there were several Trapdoor rifles.

He hiked back to the pack supplies, pulled out the block of yellow cheese, then broke off a chunk.

Nothin' ever gets any simpler. Kiowa is too Indian to stumble onto troopers by mistake. Besides, the army has never been known to camp in a discreet fashion.

Fortune set up his camp away from the cave, next to the creek where it washed down the mountainside. He led the two horses up the narrow cut and staked them out so they couldn't be seen from most parts of the meadow. He didn't build a fire, but perched himself on the Texas saddle, his back against the base of the rimrock. Cheese, crackers, and jerky lay on a rock next to him.

He folded his legs and propped the .50-caliber Sharps carbine across his lap. To the east he watched the mountain's shadow stretch for miles as the sun set behind him.

He was still in that position, his chin on his chest, stars tossed about the July sky, when Picket whinnied. Sam jumped straight up, found both of his feet sound asleep and promptly fell flat on his face in the grass and dirt. He had pushed himself up on his knees when he heard the thunder of horse hooves from the north.

The remuda . . . someone's bringing them back to the meadow.

Staying low, Sam snuck back up the barranca where his two horses pranced and strained at the picket ropes. The remuda approached the base of the rimrock, not more than fifty feet from his position. He could see their silhouettes but not who, or how many, herded them.

When Picket and the red roan settled down, he eased forward out of the barranca and hunkered down along the base of the rimrock.

If I had been chased out of this camp once before, I wouldn't go right back and build a fire in the cave. I'd . . . I'd come over here where the creek tumbles out of the mountain. If I got pinned in, I'd make a break up the mountainside and probably hold off any who tried to follow.

Fifty feet away he heard the jangle of spurs.

That eliminates Indians and the boys in blue.

A shadowy figure approached, carrying a saddle over his shoulder. Sam strained to see if there were others. The saddle blocked

HOME

any outline of the man's face. He waited, carbine at his side, finger on the trigger.

The man came within ten feet, threw down the saddle, and grabbed for his holstered revolver. This time Sam had no doubts about the silhouette.

"Don't pull it, Kiowa, I've got the Sharps pointed at your belly!" Fortune barked.

"Sammy? Oh, man, when I caught a whiff of that tonic water, I figured it was a lawman. You got yourself shaved in Dodge City, I take it."

"That was three days ago. Drop your gun belt, Kiowa."

"Well, that's strong stuff. You didn't happen to bring some gals back with you, did you? . . . What did you say?"

"You heard me."

Kiowa's holster dropped to the grass. "Sammy, this ain't funny."

"Neither is ridin' back to the ranch findin' Rocklin dead and you and the horses gone. Light a match."

The flare of the sulfur match revealed Kiowa Fox's chiseled, brown face and piercing black eyes. "You think I killed Rocklin? He died of that snakebite."

"He had two bullets pumped into his chest at close range. Sit down."

"Sammy, this is crazy."

"Do it!" Fortune snarled.

"Oh, I'll do it . . . I'll do it because I didn't kill Rocklin. We both know that I could run away in the dark and you wouldn't shoot me. We both know Sam Fortune couldn't shoot Satan in the back, especially if he were unarmed. I can't believe you'd come after me like this."

"And I can't believe you think I wouldn't come after you."

Kiowa sat down in the dark, cross-legged, and pushed his hat back. "Don't that prove I didn't do it? I knew you gave your pledge to Rocklin. That meant I would have to kill you, too, sooner or later. I wouldn't have let you sneak up on me, if I was set to kill you."

Kiowa glanced back over his shoulder. "Sammy, I've got to ask you a favor. Let me sit over there against the rimrock next to you. You can stick the carbine in my ribs if that's the way you feel, but there just might be some Black Mesa boys after these ponies, and I don't want to get shot in the back."

"Black Mesa boys? Carryin' .45-70s?"

"Yep, and that's what saved me. I could squeeze six rounds from Rocklin's carbine for every one of theirs. McClellan saddles, trap-doors . . . they must have ambushed the boys in blue."

"Start from the beginning, Kiowa, and make it believable. I've got a lousy feeling in the pit of my stomach about all of this. Tell me what happened when I was in Dodge City."

"Did you push the cattle out to the ranch already?" Kiowa asked.

"I found out that Rocklin's cattle had been sold, and the crew went back to Texas."

"You mean, there's no crew and cattle waitin' for us to bring the remuda?"

The case hardened steel trigger felt cold on Fortune's finger. "Nothin' there but a fresh grave."

"I knew you'd bury him."

"You still have told me nothin'."

"If there's no ranch to go back to, we can push these horses down to Tramperas or even La Cinta and sell them."

"Are you stallin' from tellin' me what happened, because you're tryin' to concoct a lie, Kiowa?"

HOME

"You've got a bad case of righteousness, Sammy. Didn't you tell me that Rocklin said that if he died, the horses belonged to us?"

"He said if the snakebite killed him, not if one of us shot him."

"The snakebite did kill him; that's what I'm sayin'."

"Give me the story."

"Rocklin was doin' OK the day you rode off to Dodge. In fact, he kept sitting up trying to write a few things. He couldn't eat any food, but he could swallow water if he worked at it. We both figured he was on the mend. A man can even survive a day or so without water.

"I checked on him about midnight, but he insisted I go on to bed. I left a canteen by his side so he could keep his lips wet—they were chapped somethin' bad. The next mornin' I let him sleep until I had breakfast cooked. When I went to check on him, he was dead. I saw the canteen open and tossed down on the floor, and his mouth full of water. I think he drowned, Sammy. His throat was so swollen that he drowned."

The remuda milled around nervously. Fortune studied the dark horizon. "How did a drowned man get shot?"

"I'm comin' to that. Well at first, I didn't know what to do. I figured I'd leave him right there until you returned. But I had no idea how many days you'd be gone or how long it'd take to move the herd to the ranch. I stewed around until afternoon. I hesitated to bury him, because I feared someone would accuse me of killin' him."

"The two shots in the chest are still tough to understand."

"Sammy, keep quiet until I'm done. You've got me hung for murder, and won't even listen to my story."

"I'm listenin'."

"Well, the bay stallion was kickin' other horses in the corral, so I led him down to the cottonwoods and snubbed him up tight—to drain a little meanness out of him. While I was there I decided it would be a good place to bury Rocklin. That's when I fetched the shovel and dug the grave."

"What grave?"

"You said you buried him."

"*I* dug a grave for him," Sam announced.

"Didn't you see the one I dug?" Kiowa challenged.

"No."

"Where did you find the shovel?" Kiowa asked.

"I didn't."

"It was in the bottom of the grave I dug."

"Are you tellin' me you dug a grave then didn't bury Rocklin in it?"

Kiowa rose to his feet.

"Where are you goin'?"

"The horses are gettin' snuffy. Let's slap the saddles on, just in case we need to ride."

Fortune stood beside Fox. "Who's out there?"

"No one, I hope. Can I strap the gun back on?" Kiowa asked.

"You haven't explained the bullets in Rocklin's chest. Saddle up, but leave the gun on the grass."

"Sammy, you ain't bein' very friendly like."

Fortune retrieved Picket and began to saddle the buckskin. "You were diggin' a grave in the cottonwoods, that I didn't find. Go on with your story."

"My 'story'? I'm givin' you the truth. Anyway, I was down about four feet in the grave, shoveling away, when four men came ridin' in to the ranch on three horses."

"The same that hit the corral before?"

"I figured the one's a little upset about you shootin' his horse."

"Maybe they made the fake wolf howls," Sam pondered.

HOME

"That could be. Anyways, they had the remuda out of the corral before I could leap out of the grave. They kept me pinned down in the cottonwoods with those .45-70s. I'm not sure who pumped the lead into Rocklin's dead body. I wounded one as he ran out of the cook tent with some grub. He might have been the one. I think they meant to steal all the goods, but they ran off with the horses once I started throwin' lead."

"And you saddled the bay stallion and gave chase?"

"When I went up to the tents and saw what they did to poor Rocklin, it made me so mad—I saddled him up and bucked around the yard for an hour 'til I could get him settled down to ride. Then I went after them. Wouldn't you have done the same?"

Fortune was silent for a moment. "Yeah, I reckon I would've."

"I had to follow the remuda at a distance. I dropped down into that barranca—that's the way you came up, didn't you?"

"Yep."

"I came right up that little creek and found them camped here early this morning. I stampeded the remuda north, but they had picketed their saddle horses, so they came after me. About seven miles north of here, I found an outcrop of boulders and made my stand. I killed two of them. The third one and the wounded one rode straight up into the mountains. I figured it would be a couple days before they could report to any others and come after me."

"Or they might come right back after the horses?"

"That's a possibility. I surmised to give the horses rest in this meadow for an hour, then start across the plains."

"That's your story, Kiowa?"

"That's the truth. You believe me, don't you?"

"I'll tell you what I believe for sure. Rocklin's dead. He has two bullet holes in his chest. Someone stole the horses. And I didn't see any dug grave."

"Did you go down beyond the cottonwoods?"

"No."

"Well, you got to trust me, Sammy."

Fortune pushed his hat back and ran his fingers through his hair. "Kiowa, I do trust you. Now, let's ride back and find that grave."

"Boy, that's trust all right."

"Listen, I'm not tyin' you up, disarmin' you, or coldcockin' you. I just need a little encouragement. Besides, you don't want to wait here and see if those Black Mesa boys found some pals and are coming after you."

"You're right about that. This rimrock is miserable cover, especially at night. Do you really believe my story?"

"Yep," Sam replied.

"I want to see it in your eyes. You're a lousy liar."

"Light a match."

The moment the flame blazed in Kiowa's face, a shot sounded, and limestone chips flew off the rimrock wall.

Both men dropped down to their haunches. The horses milled in a circle.

"Draw another shot, Kiowa. I'll send them one of these .50-caliber telegrams."

From a kneeling position, Kiowa Fox fired off two quick rounds with his revolver, then rolled left. As soon as Sam spotted gunfire flash from the distant barrel, he squeezed the trigger on the Sharps carbine.

In the distance, there was a scream—and a curse.

"You think they have reinforcements?" Sam called out.

"If they do, they have us pinned in."

"Let's run them through the barranca, single file. It will be easy to hold them back from down there, and they can't spot us from up on the plains until daylight."

HOME

"You want to lead the remuda or push them?" Kiowa called out.

"You lead," Fortune shouted. "Me and the .50-caliber Sharps will trail."

Two more shots exploded in the night sky. Bullets buzzed like mad bees above Sam's head. The cavvy of horses, anxious for leadership, followed Kiowa into the narrow arroyo. Sam pushed the roan ahead of him and then plunged into the darkness of the barranca. They slowed to a trot as the horses adjusted to the water and rocks under their feet.

Fifty yards into the arroyo, several shots fired over Sam's head. *They're just guessin' at the range. Two can play that game.* He turned and fired a shot straight back into the dark.

He heard the report of return fire. Two more bullets whizzed over his head only a foot or so. The little, steep-walled canyon was coal black, but the night sky outlined his course. Sam squeezed off another shot straight back between the barranca walls.

This time there was no return fire.

They kept up the pace through the canyon until they broke out on the plains at the confluence of Beaver Creek. As the eastern sky turned gray, Kiowa held up to a near dead, cottonwood stump, and Sam circled the remuda.

Kiowa, draped forward over the horse's neck, coughed out each word: "Did we lose 'em, Sammy?"

"I think so, but I'm not sure why. Maybe I didn't hit him but shot his horse in the bottom of that barranca. Lots of bullets were fired, but we didn't make much of a target in the dark. If I clipped a horse, it ought to slow them down. I reckon we can stay up on the plains now and make better time. We got away easier than I thought."

"It wasn't all that easy, partner," Kiowa groaned.

Sam rode near. There was just enough to light to see the pain in Fox's face. "Kiowa?"

Dark red blood oozed down the back of Fox's shirt. "Ain't this somethin', Sammy? After all the gunfights we been in and then to take a random bullet in the back. It's just my time. You'll be next, I reckon. Bury me in that grave I dug. I didn't kill Rocklin, Sammy . . . you got to believe me on that."

Kiowa's head slumped forward, and then his body tumbled to the ground.

CHAPTER
FIVE

Cheyenne City,
Wyoming Territory

The short man behind the register wore a black bow tie tilted in the opposite direction as his head while he attempted to read the name on the register upside down. "Yes . . . Mr. Fortune . . . will you be staying at the Inter-Ocean more than one night?" His gold-frame spectacles slid far down his nose.

Sam Fortune straightened his own tie and tugged his Stetson lower across his forehead. A gold-tipped fountain pen in his right hand. "I'm not sure. It all depends."

The man's smile looked forced, making his face seem even wider. "Are you passing through or planning to move here?"

Sam's eyes narrowed. He hesitated to respond.

The clerk rocked back on his heels, as if longing to exit but not wanting to offend.

"If I knew that," Sam replied, "then I'd know if I wanted the room another night, wouldn't I?"

HOME

The man tugged at his shirt collar, then straightened his vest. "Yes, sir, Mr. Fortune . . . didn't mean to pry. Say, are you related to them Fortunes up in the Black Hills?"

Sam rubbed the bridge of his nose, then put his hands on his hips, revealing his holstered revolver. "You ask a lot of questions for a hotel clerk."

"Sorry, sir." The clerk put both hands on top the counter and tapped his fingers across the polished oak.

Sam surveyed the uncrowded lobby. "I've got some gear at the IXL Livery. Could you send someone down to pick it up and put it in my room? I need to find some folks here in town before I settle in."

"Yes, sir. We'll take care of it." The clerk rested his elbows on the counter. "Who are you lookin' for?"

Sam stuffed the cold, brass room key into his vest pocket. "I'm lookin' for a hotel that doesn't pry into my business."

A big smile quickly replaced the chagrin. "You came to the right place. The Inter-Ocean is Cheyenne City's best and most discreet. What I was askin' is, if you need an address or help to locate someone in this town, I'm at your service. We've even got a telephone, you know. You can stand in one place and talk to folks all over town. At least, we'll have one for a few more weeks."

Fortune studied the oak and black metal box on the wall behind the counter. "What do you mean?"

The clerk dismissed the matter with the flip of hand. "Oh, it's that trouble with the bank."

"What are you talkin' about?" Sam unfastened the top button on his white shirt and loosened his tie.

"Cyrus Edgington—he owns the C.T.E., the Cheyenne Telephone Exchange—well, he pushed on borrowing money to make telephones available to most of the homes in town. Only, folks aren't too sure they want them. Two dollars a month is steep for some folks. So, Edgington couldn't meet the deadline on his big loan from First National Bank. Old man Converse at the bank decided to foreclose on the telephone company."

"The company's going out of business?" Sam probed.

The clerk's voice lowered as if revealing a secret. "Edgington asked for an extension, but Converse said no. Frankly, I figure the bank wants to own the phone company. Anyways, Edgington and that firecracker wife of his refused to surrender the assets to the bank."

Fortune brushed back his sandy blond and gray mustache with his fingertips. "Is his wife named Amanda?"

"Say, do you know the Edgingtons?"

"Her father was a friend of mine."

"You don't say? He was up here early last year to visit and stayed right here at the Inter-Ocean. In Room 208, if I remember correctly. I never forget a room."

"What's the status on the telephone exchange?"

"The bank sued for payment, the phone company countersued for obstruction, and the court will have to decide the matter. Judge is goin' to rule this morning. Edgington could go to jail if they rule against him. They won't send her to jail, being great with child like she is. It's her second one, you know. Say, were you lookin' for Edgington's house?"

"That's one of the stops."

"Twentieth and Ferguson. They got electric lightbulbs right in the house and two telephones. Can you imagine that? They have one upstairs and one downstairs. But I reckon the bank will get the house too. They're nice folks. Course, they are young. They can start all over . . . providin' he don't go to jail."

HOME

☞ ☞ ☞

A wide, wrap-around veranda surrounded the two-story, Victorian home with circular limestone turret in the northeast corner. The black iron fence encircled a yard of mostly grass with two, large elm trees in the front. Rose bushes hugged the white house with green trim.

Sam climbed the six wooden stairs to the front door. White lace curtains covered the glass front door, so he couldn't see inside. Using the glass for a mirror, Sam straightened his tie, tugged on his suit coat cuffs, and reset his Stetson. He brushed down his mustache, then stared at his clean but calloused and tanned hands.

My fingernails haven't been this clean since that winter I spent with the twins.

He rapped on the door.

The floor creaked. Shadows fell on the lace curtains, but no one came to the door.

He knocked again.

This time, no noise inside. No movement. No one appeared.

He rapped even harder.

The lace door curtains parted, and two bright blue eyes on a curly headed toddler appeared. The little girl stuck her thumb in her mouth.

With the door still locked and the curtain pulled back, a round-faced young woman—with long, curly black hair, tear-worn eyes, and quite a round stomach pushing out the front of her burgundy dress—appeared. She held a short-barreled shotgun.

"Who are you?" she called out through the glass.

He pulled off his hat. "I'm Sam Fortune, ma'am, and I'd like to speak to you about—"

"Are you a constable?"

"No, ma'am, I'm up from—"

"The bank?"

"No, I'm up from the Indian Territory, and I need to—"

"Go away. My husband's not home, and I don't want to talk to you." The curtain flopped back down. The woman disappeared.

Sam jammed his hat on the back of his head. "Amanda, I need to talk to you!"

The door swung open a couple inches and the barrel of the shotgun peeked out. "How did you know my name?"

He leaned toward the crack in the door but couldn't see her at all. "I worked for your father."

"In Indian Territory?"

"Yes, out in the Public Lands."

Her answer was definitely as the breaking of a dry stick. "My father's in Texas. You have the wrong person." She slammed the door.

Sam stepped up to the door and cupped his hand around his mouth. "I've just got one question for you, Amanda. How come your mama stayed in Tennessee and didn't even tell your daddy she wasn't comin' home? It doesn't seem right to leave a man waitin' like that at the Fort Worth station."

The door swung completely open. A scent of vanilla drifted out the door. The very pregnant woman still carried the shotgun. The little, blue-eyed toddler hid behind her mother's floor-length skirt. "How did you know that?"

Fortune held his gray Stetson in his hand. "Mrs. Edgington, can we talk for a moment? This is important."

"My husband's not home and could be in jail before the day's out. They will foreclose on this house within days and think nothing of turning me and my daughter out on the street. As you can see, sir, I'm not really in the mood to visit. I've let the hired help

HOME

go, and I do not entertain gentlemen in my home when I'm by my-self. I apologize if this sounds un-Christian, but I would rather you talk to my husband."

He motioned toward a wooden porch swing. "Would it be ap-propriate to visit out here on the veranda? I promise to keep it short."

With one hand on the shotgun and the other on the curly head of the little girl, she stepped to the doorway. "How do I know you aren't trying to evict me from my home by deceit?"

He swept his hat across the veranda. "Bring the shotgun with you, and let me have it with both barrels if I try anything deceitful or improper."

A shy smile broke across the trouble woman's face. "I don't even have a shell in the chamber," she murmured.

Sam returned his hat to the back of his head. "Ma'am, don't ever pick up a gun if you don't intend to use it."

She set the gun down inside the parlor and stepped out on the porch, leading the toddler. "You really sound like my father."

"I suppose I do. . . ." He motioned toward the oak swing. "Would you two ladies like to sit down? I'll stand."

The toddler laced her fingers and rested both hands on top of her dark brown hair.

The woman patted the girl on the shoulder. "This is my daugh-ter, Rocklin."

"Rocklin? Just like your daddy's last name?"

"It was my last name, as well. My father doesn't have any sons. I wanted to make sure the family name wasn't forgotten. Of course, Mother absolutely detests the name and calls her Missy, instead. But we like it, don't we, Rocklin?"

The toddler stuck out her tongue and nodded up and down.

Sam wanted to reach out and touch the child but pulled his hand back. "I think it's a wonderful name."

The woman eased down on the bench slowly, then tugged the little, wide-eyed girl up beside her. Fortune stood and leaned his back against the porch railing. Both ladies watched him intently.

"I don't think I heard your name," she inquired.

"Sam Fortune."

"Is Daddy dead, Mr. Fortune?" Amanda Edgington asked.

He looked away from her and the girl. For a moment, he said nothing. Then, he looked back at her. Amanda stared down at her hands clasped in her lap. Tears rolled down the perfectly smooth, pale cheeks. She took a deep breath. "I knew it in my heart a week ago. I'm afraid I've already shed my quota of tears for the day. I'm almost empty now. Isn't that sad? To receive such news and be already cried out?"

Sam rubbed his chin. Though it was freshly shaved, it felt rough. "He died around the first of July. How did you know?"

Little Rocklin reached up with chubby fingers and touched her mother's teary cheeks. Amanda reached down and hugged the girl. "Every year since Mother and I left Texas, Daddy sent me a long letter and a twenty-dollar gold coin on my birthday. Twenty years, without fail. Last week was my birthday, and no letter came. I knew that he had died. Only death could keep him from remembering me. How did he die, Mr. Fortune?"

"He got snakebit, Mrs. Edgington. We were way out in the Public Land, like I said, and couldn't do much for him. Kiowa— that's the other man that was workin' for him at the time—tried to suck out the poison, but I guess it wasn't enough. Rocklin was a good man, and I've been grievin' over his loss."

She pulled a small linen handkerchief from the sleeve of her burgundy dress. "Were you with him when he died?"

HOME

The porch railing felt hard, pressed up against his backside. The air stiffled Sam, and sweat soaked his entire white shirt under his suit coat and vest. "After the snakebite, he seemed to be doin' fair, so he sent me to Dodge City on some business. Kiowa Fox stayed with him. I was gone only a couple days, but when I came back he had passed on. I buried him along San Francisco Creek and read the Bible over him." He turned his head from her and brushed the corner of his eyes. "That reminds me, I have his Bible and some personal belongin's in a satchel at the hotel. I'll bring 'em over later. Actually, his Bible is in my bedroll. I've been readin' it at night. I wasn't tryin' to intrude. Hope you forgive me for that."

"Mr. Fortune, I'm sure my father would be delighted that one of his friends wanted to read the Bible." She took a deep breath and let the air out slowly. Her shoulders seemed to relax. "Tell me, what was Father doing out in Public Land anyways?"

"Your daddy had big dreams, Amanda. He figured they would open up Public Land soon, and he wanted a jump on securing a ranch. He said he was buildin' it up to leave to you. He talked about you a lot, ma'am."

Tears trickled from her steel gray eyes. She brushed them with the linen hankie. "Excuse me for my emotions. Perhaps I do have a fear or two left. Do you and your wife have any children, Mr. Fortune?"

Sam felt blushed. "No, ma'am—I'm not married."

She attempted, unsuccessfully, to smooth her skirt down over her protruding stomach, "Well, let me warn you, women who are about to give birth can be very emotional."

Sam felt flustered watching her stroke her stomach. He faced the yard. "I heard about the trouble with the telephone company, ma'am. I reckon you have plenty to be emotional about."

"It has not been a good summer, Mr. Fortune. Now, tell me, were you a partner with my father?"

He turned back toward her. "No, ma'am, just a hired hand. My friend Kiowa Fox and I were breakin' horses and helpin' him build up the place."

"You're a bronco buster?" She examined him closely. "You look more like a mine owner."

Sam pushed his hat back and grinned. "You flatter me, Amanda Edgington. I scrub up good."

Little Rocklin continued to lean against her mother and suck her thumb, never taking her eyes off Sam Fortune.

"Well, Mr. Fortune, I very much appreciate your coming all the way up to Cheyenne to give me this report. A letter would have sufficed, but a personal visit is much, much better. I do wish I had some money to cover your expenses."

"Your daddy already did that. He wanted me and my partner to have the horses we broke if anything happened to him. I sold the horses in Sidney, Nebraska, a few days ago. I would have brought that money to you, but he had somethin' else in mind for you."

"What do you mean?"

"The main reason I trailed up here from the Indian Nation was to give you this." He reached inside his suit coat pocket and pulled out the banknote.

She looked him in the eyes. "What is it?"

"Take a look, Mrs. Edgington. I think you'll find it good news. Just might be your luck is changin'." He handed it to her.

She unfolded the paper and stared at the words. Her mouth dropped open, and her hand flew up to her lips. "I . . . I don't understand. . . ."

HOME

He stepped closer and pointed to the note. "Your daddy sold some cattle, about twelve hundred head. This is the profit off them. The banker down in Dodge City said any Wells Fargo office could handle it, or your local banker can telegraph the bank in Dodge to transfer the funds."

She put her left hand to her chest and took deep breaths. "Are you telling me this is for real?"

Fortune's grin stretched his cheeks. "I'm tellin' you your daddy left you $22,400."

The banknote fluttered out of her hands. She clutched her stomach with both hands and let out a scream that sent chills down Sam's back and caused the hair on his neck to bristle.

Little Rocklin started to cry.

Sweat popped out on her forehead and face.

"Ma'am?" Fortune called out. "Do you always shout when—"

"When I'm about to have a baby?" she screamed. "I certainly do!"

"A baby? Oh, no . . . no," he cautioned. "You don't want to do that!"

"Mr. Fortune . . . I have no choice in the matter. . . . Help me to my feet."

"Maybe you shouldn't move."

"I am not going to have this baby on my front porch. Help me into my bed." Her hot, sweaty palm clutched his hand.

"Oh, I couldn't do that. . . . I . . ."

"Mr. Fortune, if you don't help me, I'll pull that revolver out of your holster and shoot your head off. Do I make myself clear?" She accented the sentence with another heart-stopping scream.

"Yes . . . ma'am." He took her arm and gently helped her shuffle to the door.

"Get the banknote!" she yelled.

He ran back, snatched up the slip of paper, and scurried to her side.

"Get the baby!" she hollered.

His eyes widened as he froze in place. The little girl sat on the porch swing, sobbing.

"Rocklin. Carry Rocklin for me!" Amanda instructed.

"Me? I . . . OK." He clutched up the near hysterical child. The baby laid her head against his wide shoulder and immediately quit crying.

Sam scooted over and held the door open for Amanda Edgington, then trailed her into the parlor.

"I'll make it to bed." She was doubled over, holding her side. "You telephone for Dr. Morton."

"Me? Telephone? I don't know how to use them. I've never even seen one work."

Another scream brought him to her side. "Help me lie down," she sobbed.

"Yes, ma'am. . . ." He cradled the toddler in his left arm as she watched her mother with wide eyes.

When they reached the bedroom decorated with lace and gingham, she motioned at the bed. "Pull the covers back!"

"Eh, Amanda . . . this is . . . this is embarrassin' me," he mumbled.

"Not nearly as embarrassing as it will be if I have this baby on the floor at your feet. Help me to bed for heaven's sake."

He jerked the covers back, and she turned around, sat down, and laid her head on the big feather pillow. "Lift my feet up onto the bed, please."

The sweat poured off Sam's face and cascaded down his neck.

HOME

"Leave Rocklin on the bed with me. I can watch her. Call Dr. Morton first, and then call the courthouse and send word to my husband."

When he started to put the toddler down, she clung to his neck and wailed. He stood back up with the baby still in his arms, and she instantly stopped crying.

"She doesn't like a cranky mama," Mrs. Edgington grimaced, then screamed. When she caught her breath, she pointed at Rocklin. "Do you mind keeping her?"

"If she can put up with me, I reckon I'll put up with her."

"Go make the phone calls," she panted.

"I really have never used a—"

"Hurry," she cried out, then gritted her teeth. "This baby is coming quick. The directions are on the shelf under the telephone. Anyone can use it. Trust me."

He found the telephone mounted to the wall in the kitchen and studied the box. He could hear Amanda Edgington groan from the other room. He stared at the telephone and then at the toddler in his arms. "Li'l darlin', do you know how to make this thing work?"

Rocklin reached over, plucked up the hand telephone, and put it to her little ear. She began to chatter in monosyllables.

"OK . . . OK . . . I listen there . . . and I must talk in this piece." He leaned closer to the other circular part of the phone. "Hello, the telephone?" he shouted. "Is anyone in there? Hello?" He stared at the toddler. "I want Dr. Morton!"

There was no reply.

"It's not working. It must be broken!" He continued to hold the hand piece to his ear. "What's the matter with this? No wonder they're in financial difficulty. The thing doesn't work!"

Rocklin Edgington leaned over and tugged on the crank handle that made a bell ring. "Don't do that . . . ," Fortune protested. "I can't hear anything!"

A man's voice demanded. "Number?"

Fortune stepped back, "What? Who is this?" he shouted.

"What number are you calling, please?"

Fortune stared at the receiver, then shouted. "Where are you?"

"This is Central Office," the man replied. "What number are you calling?"

"Number? I only need one—one doctor. She's havin' a baby! Send a doctor quick!" He put the hand unit back on the hook. *I was supposed to telephone Mr. Edgington. Maybe the doctor will tell him.*

Immediately the phone rang and Sam Fortune jumped, the baby still in his arms. He picked up the hand piece again and brought it to his ear. "What do you want?" he hollered. "You scared Rocklin half to death."

In the back bedroom, Amanda Edgington screamed.

"What was that?" the man on the telephone probed.

"It's a woman having a baby! If you don't send Dr. Morton over here right away, I'll personally come down there and run you up the flag pole on the top of the Inter-Ocean Hotel."

"Sir, have you ever used a telephone before?"

"No, and I don't intend on usin' it again!"

"What doctor do you want?"

"Dr. Morton, . . . and tell her husband to come right home."

"Whose husband?"

"The woman havin' the baby," he shouted. "Are you a dunce?"

"What is the woman's name?"

"Mrs. Edgington—don't you know anything?"

"Amanda's having her baby?"

"Yes, won't you hurry?"

HOME

"With whom am I speaking?"

"The one who will hang you up the flag pole if you don't hurry!" Fortune slammed the telephone down on the hook.

"You better learn a trade, darlin', because your mama and daddy are whippin' a dead horse with this telephone thing. They are just a hassle, and you don't know for sure if they even got your message."

When he returned to the bedroom carrying the toddler, Mrs. Edgington was on her back and had her knees up in the air and spread wide, though the covers were pulled up to her chin. "Get me some clean towels," she barked out.

"Now, ma'am . . . you just hold on. . . . Don't do anything until the doctor gets here."

"Get the towels!" she demanded.

"Yes, ma'am." He ran to the dresser, grabbed up two cotton towels, and ran back, the toddler clinging to his neck. *Lord . . . I'm not supposed to be here. . . . This isn't right. This isn't my place. Her husband should be here. Or a doctor. I can't watch this. I can't do this. It . . . it isn't proper. You've got to get me out of this. Quick!*

Amanda screamed twice and began to yell, "It's coming! It's coming!"

"No, ma'am!" he screamed back. "You can't do this to me!"

The front door banged open, and a man about Sam's age sprinted into the bedroom.

"Hallelujah!" Sam shouted. "Are you the doctor?"

"I'm Mr. Edgington. Who in blazes are you?"

"I'm . . . I'm . . . a friend of your wife's daddy. . . . I'll be outside if you need me!"

"That's my daughter you're carrying."

"You take her."

Little Rocklin clutched Fortune tightly when her father reached for her.

"Eh . . . I'll watch her. . . . You take care of your wife."

A thin, gray-haired man burst through the front door as Fortune approached it from the parlor.

"Are you the doctor?"

"Yes. Who are you?"

"A mighty, mighty happy man. Amanda and the Mr. are in the bedroom."

Fortune staggered out to the front porch and plopped down on the wooden porch swing on the veranda. The toddler sat up on his lap. "That was close, little darlin' . . . very close. I think the Lord had mercy on us accordin' to his loving-kindness, don't you?"

The two of them rocked back and forth amidst screams and shouts from the back room. His coat collar was wringing wet. The toddler rested her head on his chest, and Sam laid his head on the back of the oak swing. He closed his eyes and felt his racing heart begin to slow.

The stifling heat had turned to a pleasant breeze when he opened his eyes. It dried the sweat on his face and chest, cooling him. The sun sat lower on the western horizon. Scattered, dark gray clouds rolled across Cheyenne City. The sweaty-faced little girl was asleep in his arms.

The gray-haired man tapped on his shoulder. "Mr. Fortune?"

Sam sat up straight. "Yes, sir?" Little Rocklin blinked her eyes open.

"Everything is taken care of inside. Mr. and Mrs. Edgington would like for you to bring Rocklin in to meet her brother."

"Her brother? Doc—you mean it's a boy?"

"That's normally what a brother means."

HOME

He hugged the sleepy little girl. "Did you hear that, li'l punkin? You got yourself a brother!"

☞ ☞ ☞

A tiny, round, red face slept on the feather pillow beside an exhausted woman with tangled hair and chapped lips. His tie and jacket tossed across a chair and white shirt rolled up to his elbows, Mr. Edgington paced the room.

He stopped right next to Sam. "Mr. Fortune! How can I ever thank you?"

"I just . . . just happened to . . . I'm glad. . . . Those telephones really work, don't they?"

Mrs. Edgington held out her arms to Rocklin and Sam placed the toddler on the bed. "Come see your little brother Samuel," she murmured.

"Samuel?" Fortune gasped. "You named him Samuel?"

Amanda looked up through tired eyes. "We named him after you—Samuel Gabriel Edgington—because you showed up like the angel Gabriel when we needed help most. I'm afraid we can never repay you."

"I told you, ma'am, you don't me owe anythin'. Your daddy was a good man and treated me square. I only tried to do the same for you. It was just a coincidence that I—"

"Mr. Fortune, I do not believe in coincidences," Mr. Edgington asserted. "The Lord brought you here, whether you believe it or not."

Rocklin curled up at her mother's other side.

"I think perhaps we all need a little more sleep," Mrs. Edgington declared. "Mr. Fortune, would you please call on us tomorrow about noon? We would like you to join us for lunch. I want to talk with you, but I don't think I'll have the energy until then."

Sam pulled on his hat and nodded. "Yes, ma'am. I'll call on you."

"Could I talk to you in private, Mr. Fortune?" Mr. Edgington asked.

The men strolled out onto the porch.

"Did your wife get a chance to tell you about her daddy and the funds he sent?" Sam asked.

"Yes, and I don't know how much of it was reality and how much was delirium and pain talking."

"Mr. Rocklin died by a snakebite down in the Indian Territory. I buried him there. And this," he pulled out the folded banknote, "is his inheritance that he wanted you and Amanda to have." He handed the man the paper.

Edgington gaped at the note, then looked up. "If I were an emotional man, I'd cry, Mr. Fortune. You cannot imagine the joy this brings to our lives. Surely my cup is full and runneth over."

"Mr. Edgington, I want to be honest. I haven't exactly spent my entire life doin' things I'm proud of. But seein' the joy of this day for you and Amanda and little punkin . . . well, it makes a man enjoy doin' the right thing. It might not be too bad a habit to continue."

"Mr. Fortune, forgive me if I sound presumptuous. But do you need a job or a place to stay? We would be happy to put you up with us until you find what you're looking for."

I spent most of the past three years in prison, and most of my life on the other side of the law . . . I'm not at all sure what I'm lookin' for. "Thank you, Mr. Edgington, but I'll be travelin' on in a day or so. Like I said, I'm not exactly the type that's comfortable on this side of town. I'll probably look for some ranch job. I have a friend who's up in Johnson County. And I'm still wrestlin' demons from the past."

HOME

"That can change, you know."

"You may be right. But probably I won't change overnight."

"The Lord is full of constant surprises, Sam. Look at me and Amanda today. Promise to join us for lunch tomorrow?"

"Yes, sir. I'll be here. You've got a fine family, Mr. Edgington—a mighty fine family."

☞ ☞ ☞

The yellow-haired waitress at Leighton Hotel Restaurant lingered next to Sam Fortune's table. Her long, white bib apron was starched stiff and bleached white. The high collar on her dress was unbuttoned to the top of the apron. "Do you live here in Cheyenne?" she asked.

Sam popped the last bite of biscuit into his mouth as he glanced up. He attempted to smile and chew while he replied. "No, ma'am. I'm just passin' through."

"I know what you mean." Her finger traced the back of his oak chair. "I'm just passin' through too. I'm on my way to San Francisco, but I only had enough funds for a ticket to Cheyenne City, so I took this job to save up for a through ticket."

He sliced into a thick beef chop, then stabbed a bite with his knife and held it over his plate. "How long you been here?"

"Since Christmas . . . ," she sighed. She put her hands on the small of her back and stretched, drawing her shoulders back and her chest forward, then relaxed. "I can't seem to get ahead. But I'm ready to leave, that's for sure. The rich folks don't give me the time of day in this town, and the drifters and bums . . . well, they don't know how to treat a girl decent. Say, what direction are you headed?"

"I'm not sure. Probably west." He plopped a bite of gravy drenched chop into his mouth. The gravy tasted a tad too salty, but rich.

She circled to the far side of the table and faced him. "Have you ever been to San Francisco?"

"No, ma'am."

She leaned forward, with her arms on the edge of the round table. "Some people say it's even more wonderful than Paris. How about you, mister? Would you like to go to San Francisco?"

He picked meat out of his lower teeth with his thumbnail then whacked off another bite. "I hadn't given it much thought."

Part of her blond hair came out of the combs and flopped over her eye. "Say, are you goin' out to that dance at Fort Russell?"

He surveyed the mound of potatoes on his plate. "When is that?"

She stood up straight. "Tonight, from eight o'clock until mid-night."

"I'm in town alone, so I haven't considered a dance," Sam replied.

"I bet I was asked to go to that dance a dozen times, but most of 'em were too drunk to remember me the next day. I like to dance, but not that much. If a gentleman like you asked me to the dance— well, that's one thing—but not some whiskey bum."

She scooted over so her hips were within inches of his elbow. "Say, neither of us got someone to go to the dance with. We ought to jist partner up for the dance. You interested, Mr. . . . Mr.—"

He looked up at her anxious brown eyes. "Call me Sam."

She smiled, revealing a slight overbite. "My name's Delphia. Everyone calls me Delfy."

He reached up and shook her hand. "Pleased to meet you."

HOME

"And I'm pleased to meet you." She refused to let go of his hand. "What do you say? Shall we go to the dance?"

He studied her eyes until she looked away. "Delfy, I'm not kiddin' when I say that's the best offer I've had in years. But I had a tough day, and I'm so tired I'd embarrass you on the dance floor." He tugged his hand from hers.

She laid her hand on his shoulder. "We don't have to go to the dance, Sam. The Atlantic-Pacific Club has a six-piece orchestra and some quiet tables that have fancy dividers jist like them deluxe houses in Denver."

"You're tryin' too hard, Delfy."

"What do you mean?"

"Darlin', I'm wrestlin' with some big problems in my mind. I've got to get them settled before I do anythin' else. Any other night in my life, I'd probably be carryin' you right up the stairs . . . but you found me at a tough moment."

"You got someone else in town?"

"Nope. I'll make you a pledge, Delfy. If I dance with anyone in Cheyenne, it will be with you. And if I nuzzle up in a back table at the Atlantic-Pacific, it will be with you, darlin'."

"You promise?"

"Yep."

"Do you keep your promises?"

"Always."

"OK." She stepped back from the table. "I'll quit pesterin' you. I've got to tell you, Sam, you are a smooth talker. I've been turned down before. Not often, but ever' once in a while. But I ain't never had someone make me feel good about myself when he turned me down."

☞ ☞ ☞

Sam had just taken a second helping of boiled red beets when the well-dressed man with a badge walked over to his table. Sam noticed a twitch in his right eye.

"Are you Sam Fortune from the Indian Nation?" the man demanded in a voice too loud to be completely in control.

Sam skidded a slice of beet into the gravy with his fork and plopped the bite into his mouth. "I reckon I am."

The man spoke so rapidly that all the words ran together. "I want you out of town within an hour."

Sam thought about reaching for his Colt but locked his fingers around a fork instead. "I can't do that, deputy."

The lawman's hand lingered on the walnut grip of his revolver. "I ain't askin' you, Fortune, I'm tellin' you. We don't need your kind in Cheyenne City. I had a brother-in-law down in Fort Smith, Arkansas. He sent me the newspapers all about you, the Kiowa half-breed, and them others. I want all of you out of town today."

Sam felt the blood rush to his head. He clenched his fist around the fork until his knuckles turned white. "Mister, I am not leavin' town, because I have not committed a crime and I promised to meet with some of Cheyenne's solid citizens tomorrow. As far as Kiowa and the others are concerned—they are all dead."

"Well, now, that was mighty thoughtful of them." The lines on the stocky, dark-haired man began to soften. "You ought to consider doin' likewise."

Mister, you want to step out on the street and try your hand at it? Sam stabbed a bite of potato and lukewarm, thick brown gravy.

"Did you hear me, Fortune? As soon as you are through eatin', I want you ridin' out of town."

Fortune shoved away from the table, and the man jumped back a foot. "Mister, what's your gripe?" Sam challenged. "I haven't committed a crime in Wyoming, and there are no warrants out for me.

HOME

I've served my time in prison. I'm a law-abidin' man eatin' supper. Go torment someone else."

"It ain't right," the deputy growled.

Sam draped his hand across the arm of the oak chair, only inches from the grip of his pistol. "What isn't right?"

"You killin' my brother-in-law and then walkin' around free." The man spoke so loud other customers got up and scurried out of the room.

"The one in Fort Smith? What was his name?"

"Skitter Waddle," the deputy spat out.

Fortune scooted his chair back up to the table, sipped coffee, and let out a long, slow breath before he spoke. "Waddle hid in an alley beside the Magnolia Saloon and tried to shoot me in the back with a shotgun. To my benefit, he was too drunk to shoot straight."

"And you weren't?"

"That's one of the reasons I don't drink."

"You murdered him."

Sam could feel his face and neck flush. He replied through clenched teeth, "Didn't you ever wonder why Judge Parker refused to even hear the case?"

"You ain't listenin' to me, Fortune." The man poked his finger into Fortune's shoulder. "I said you had to be out of town in an hour or else."

"And you didn't hear me." Sam quickly grabbed the finger and bent it straight back. "I said I'm stayin'. I got to meet with the Edgingtons tomorrow."

He released the finger, and the deputy clutched it with his free hand. "You're lyin' to me. You don't know them folks!"

Sam could see Delfy, the cook, and two customers watching from the doorway. "I'll tell you what." He spoke loud enough for everyone to hear. "You go right in there to the hotel lobby and call the Edgingtons on the telephone. I presume you know how to use one. Now, you can't talk to Amanda, because she's flat in bed. She just had a beautiful baby boy. But talk to Cyrus Edgington. Tell him you're tryin' to throw Sam Fortune out of town."

"I could call your bluff."

"That's exactly what I'm suggestin'. And while you are talkin' to him on the telephone, ask Mr. Edgington what they named his new little son and who they named him after."

The lawman stormed out of the restaurant into the hotel lobby. As soon as he left, the blond waitress, Delphia, came over to his table to refill his china coffee cup. "What did the deputy want with you?"

Fortune held the cup to his mouth and blew the steam off the top. "He wanted me to leave town."

Her thin eyebrows rose, but her eyes still danced. "Are you wanted by the law?"

"Not at the moment." He glanced around the room. Most of the folks filtered back to their tables.

"You surprise me." Delfy fussed with the yellow daises in the green, glass vase in the middle of the table. "I figured you for one of them rich Texas ranchers." When she arose, her hand lingered on his shoulder.

He reached up and patted her hand. "Now aren't you glad I didn't agree to take you to the dance?"

"No, I'm not. What you used to be don't matter to me. I ain't exactly spent my whole life servin' tables in a restaurant. Your past don't matter. Even that gray hair don't matter."

Sam Fortune began to laugh.

"Are you pokin' fun at me?" she quizzed.

He squeezed her hand. "No, ma'am. I like you Delfy. You're straightforward and refreshin'."

"Does that mean you changed your mind about the dance?"

HOME

"Nope, but I just might have an important favor to ask of you a bit later."

"Fortune!" the deputy constable boomed as he stomped back across the room. "I don't know how you weaseled an invitation to the Edgingtons, but you ain't stayin' in town one hour later than your lunch's through tomorrow."

"Did you ask about the baby?" Sam challenged.

"Mrs. Edgington had her baby?" Delfy interrupted.

Sam sliced a bit of now cold meat. "Yep."

"A girl or a boy?" she pressed.

He slid the bite off his knife with his teeth, chewed, then swallowed. "A boy."

Delfy ran her finger down Fortune's shirtsleeve. "What's his name?"

Sam waved the gravy-stained knife in the direction of the constable. "Why don't you tell her, deputy?"

"I ain't concerned with a baby's name, but I am concerned that you keep the law while you're in town, Sam Fortune. You better watch yourself at all times. One wrong move, and we don't intend to lock you up, if you get my drift."

Delfy pulled her hand away from his arm. "Are you really Sam Fortune?"

"Yeah, that's me, darlin'." Fortune took another sip of coffee.

"Did you hear me, Fortune?" the deputy blustered.

"What do you plan on doin', deputy? Hidin' in the alley with a shotgun, so you can shoot me in the back?"

Several restaurant patrons again exited the room.

"I heard it took fourteen U.S. marshals and six Indian scouts to capture you," she blurted out.

"The story was exaggerated," Sam grinned. "It was only twelve U.S. marshals and five Baltimore Indian scouts."

The deputy's face flushed. He waved his finger in front of Fortune. "Only the presence of this . . . this woman . . . keeps me from tellin' you how I really feel."

"For that, I am grateful. However, she isn't 'this woman'—her name's Delphia. And she's not merely a woman, but a lady. And I agree with you completely. We should not carry on this conversation in her presence. Good day, Mr. Deputy."

The deputy stormed across the room then spun around and hollered, "You watch yourself, Fortune."

"I will, Deputy. And I'm sure you will as well."

The lawman tramped out of the restaurant.

"He don't have no right to treat you that way, even if you are Sam Fortune." She folded her arms across her chest. "What kind of favor do you want?"

His voice lowered. "Would you escort me back to my hotel room?"

She tried to suppress a giggle by covering her mouth with her hand. "You want me to walk with you?"

"Yes, ma'am. That deputy will have pals hiding around town to spy on me and take a shot if they get a chance. But none of them will dare try anything with a beautiful, young woman on my arm."

"I ain't really all that young. I ain't in my forties, like you, but I ain't young."

Forty? Do I really look that old? "You are a young lady, Delfy. Trust me."

"Do I get to stay in your room for a while?"

"No. Delfy . . . *ladies* don't make requests like that."

"That's because *ladies* are married long before they reach my age. Do I have to be a lady?" She kept her arms folded.

"Of course not. But it's your God-given privilege. It doesn't make good sense to toss that privilege away."

HOME

"Well . . . since you put it that way. You're a complicated man, Sam Fortune."

☛ ☛ ☛

The pillow was fluffy.

The mattress soft.

The sheets clean.

The room dark.

The neighbors quiet.

The room at the Inter-Ocean was exactly what Sam Fortune expected from a first class hotel.

But he couldn't get to sleep.

He lit the lantern, pulled Rocklin's Bible out of the black, leather valise, and read Psalm 51.

Again.

Then he paced the room, checked the chamber of the Sharps carbine for a cartridge, and laid the gun back down on the bed. He shut off the lantern and continued to pace the room, wearing only an old pair of longhandles that he had cut off at the knees and elbows.

He stopped by the window and pulled back the drapes. The electricity street lamps gave the town a dreamy glow. Very few people were on the street. The two shadowy figures that followed him and Delfy to the hotel had disappeared.

He thought about the blond waitress. *I have no idea if I'm gettin' old . . . or wise . . . or foolish . . . or moral . . . or tired . . . or biblical. It just wasn't right to let her stay. She deserves better. She should have someone take her to that dance at Fort Russell, then on a slow carriage ride home and be given a kiss at the door.*

That's all.

I can't figure out why I'm thinkin' this. She's only another woman . . . another lady. It's like . . . like I'm seein' myself different. Seein' my whole life different. I don't know if it was the prison term . . . or Piney . . . or Rocklin . . . or Kiowa . . . or Rachel in Dodge City . . . or this servin' girl I've never met before in my life.

I can't believe I didn't call that loudmouth deputy out. He would have gone for his gun first: strictly self-defense. He wasn't worth it. It's like somethin' decent dies inside of me at every gunfight.

I don't have any more left to give.

If there's any redemption, I can't get worse. There will be no soul left to save.

"According unto the multitude of thy tender mercies blot out my transgressions."

Do you have limits on that multitude of mercies, Lord?

I reckon I used up my share years ago.

He flopped down on top of the comforter and stared up at the high, dark ceiling.

If I had to live it all over again, I would have stayed at the ranch when Mama died and insisted that we fight off the carpetbaggers. Daddy didn't have his heart in it after that. All he needed to do was admit he was wrong about the war, just say that it was good that Texas seceded, and ask me to stay and help out. That's all he needed to do, but he was too stubborn.

The cotton sheets were already damp from sweat. Sam felt no movement of air, even though the window was partially open. The room had a slight aroma of ammonia cleanser and rose tonic water.

And all I needed to do was to admit I was wrong about the war— that it hurt Texas more than it helped. But I was much too stubborn to admit that.

I still am.

And it's too late to tell him anyways.

HOME

It's been fifteen years since I took off. I'm the son that disappeared.

Lord, I'm so tired of this. Let me start all over. At least with Dacee June . . . or with Robert and Jamie Sue . . . or with whoever's left.

Jesus, I think I want to go home now.

But I don't even have a home.

Have mercy on me, O God. Have mercy on my sinful soul.

☛ ☛ ☛

Tall, dark-haired Cyrus Edgington met him at the door. "Sam, good to see you!"

The men shook hands. Then Fortune pulled off his gray Stetson. "How's the new baby and his mama?"

"He's sleeping, and she's sore. But not nearly as sore as when Rocklin was born. Amanda intends to take lunch with us at the table."

"She's Texas tough."

"And Tennessee sweet." Edgington ushered Fortune into the parlor.

"I hope she didn't try to get up and cook."

"Listen, Sam," Edgington put his arm around Fortune's shoulder as they strolled through the room, "because of you, lots of things are different around here since last night."

"I hope that's good."

"Good? It's miraculous! The bank's paid off. The lawsuit's dropped. I rehired our housekeeper. It was providential that you came to this house at the exact hour you did."

"I always supposed the Lord has good timin'."

"Precisely what Amanda said this morning. I'm sorry that new deputy constable hassled you at the restaurant."

148

"I've been through that sort of thing before. It happens in most ever' town. He has a personal grudge. I had a run-in with a relative of his."

"Yes, so I heard," Edgington continued. "I talked to the mayor, and the man was dismissed this morning."

"They fired him?"

"Personal vendettas have no place in the constable business."

The men paused under a stained glass, electric chandelier.

"Now, he'll have twice the reason to come lookin' for me," Sam bemoaned.

Edgington's hand waved in front of him. "You didn't have anything to do with his dismissal."

Sam reached under his black tie and unfastened the top button of his white shirt. "I'm not sure he'll see it that way."

"The fact remains, we can't have people using the office for personal revenge." Cyrus Edgington motioned toward the wide, arched doorway. "I believe the ladies are waiting in the dining room."

Propped up on two feather pillows, Amanda Edgington wore a green, satin robe, and sat at one end of the long, narrow table. In a wicker bassinet next to her, the red-faced Samuel Gabriel Edgington slept with only his head peeking out of the neatly folded covers. The captain's chair at the other end was for Mr. Edgington. Young Rocklin sat in a wooden chair straight across the table from an empty chair.

"Mr. Fortune, would you please sit there," Amanda motioned to the chair on her right.

"Thank you, ma'am. You're looking a little stronger than yesterday evening."

"I was a sight, wasn't I."

"You were a bit busy."

HOME

"I can't believe I allowed a man other than my husband to see me like that. And I cannot understand why I'm not totally embarrassed to see you today. It's as if you're part of the family. We will either have to remain very good friends, or I will have to have you shot," she said with a wide, easy grin.

Sam laughed and sat down. "I reckon I'll choose bein' friends. But don't worry about what I did or didn't see. I was so stunned I can't remember a thing." He surveyed the squirming, dark-haired toddler. "Good mornin', little darlin'."

Rocklin squirreled out of her chair and toddled around the table, lifting her arms to Sam Fortune. "Carry me!" she squealed.

Amanda Edgington tried to stop her daughter's advance. "Punkin, don't bother—"

Sam plucked up the smiling toddler. "Oh, me and her are pals. Aren't we, little darlin'."

She threw her arms around his neck and planted a very slobbery kiss on his cheek.

"Oh my, you get a kiss this morning, Mr. Fortune," Amanda smiled.

"It's a privilege and an honor. But call me Sam. I still think of my father as Mr. Fortune."

"Is he still living?" she asked.

Sam stared across the room at a white lace curtains in the window. "No. I don't believe he is. But, I haven't seen him in years."

"Well, we should eat before I say something else dumb." She looked over at her husband. "Cyrus, you can tell Rose that she may serve lunch, now."

☞ ☞ ☞

The fried chicken tasted crisp, yet flaky; done to the bone, yet moist. The mashed potatoes, almost whipped, yielded no hard lumps or bitter surprises. The corn, still on the cob, held small and perfectly even light yellow kernels. With each bite, hot, sweet juices delighted the tongue. The diced peaches proved ripe, but not woody or stringy. And the plum pudding, darker than mud, richer than chocolate, was covered in thick, fresh cream—ice-chilled cream.

Sam Fortune could not remember ever tasting a better meal.

At least, not since his mama died.

The conversation ranged from somber reflections of Amanda growing up without her father to the incredible future of the telephone business.

The subject that was never discussed was Sam Fortune's past.

Rocklin spent most of the meal in his lap.

"You are a natural with young children, just like my Cyrus," Amanda insisted. "It is not every man who has such patience."

Sam attempted to keep Rocklin bouncing on his knee while he sipped the coffee. "Well, ma'am, I've always been an easy mark for beautiful ladies with stunning smiles. Besides, I could count on one hand the number of times I've ever been allowed to hold a little one."

"It would be a sin to waste your God-given gift. I pray you'll have a huge family someday."

"I'm afraid I've passed up a lot of good family-raisin' years, Amanda."

"Nonsense. No man is controlled solely by his past. He is merely limited by his fascination with it. Turn it loose, and you can do anything you want. That's what I say."

"Tell me, Cyrus," Sam said. "Do all women become philosophers immediately after childbirth?"

HOME

"This lady has had big thoughts all her life, Sam. It was her idea to enter into the telephone business."

"Do you regret it?" she asked her husband.

"Never. I'll tell you straight up, Sam. This is the business of the future. You think it's in gold mines? Where are these mines going to be a hundred years from now? They'll be tapped out, every last one of them. But the telephone exchanges? Why, the day is coming when every home will have one or two, and people in Denver can pick it up and talk to someone in New York City."

"Cyrus is quite the telephone booster," Sam grinned.

"Daddy thought the whole thing was fascinating. He'd stare for an hour at the telephone wire, trying to figure out how they put a voice in that thing." Amanda sighed and smiled down at little Samuel. "I do wish my father had lived long enough to see the children. It's sad for a man never to know his grandchildren."

"That reminds me." Sam gently put down his china cup. "I left your daddy's black leather suitcase in the parlor. I didn't go through it, so I have no idea how important the things are. I did read his Bible some, but I think I already confessed to that."

"I want you to have it," Amanda announced.

"Oh no, ma'am, I couldn't do that. It should be yours or the children's."

"Sam, we have several Bibles. And one thing I know about my father is that if he knew you wanted to read it, he would have given it to you himself. It would be like him getting to help a man out, even after he was gone. He'd like that, don't you think?"

Sam rubbed his clean-shaven chin. "I reckon he would."

"Then you'll take it?"

"Yes, ma'am, and I do appreciate it. It has been more and more useful during these last weeks. That's very generous of you. I'll take good care of it."

"I do believe Cyrus has something else to talk to you about," she announced.

Cyrus Edgington pushed his empty plate back and rapped his fingers on the lace tablecloth. "Sam, I think we have both expressed how grateful we are for your faithfulness in carrying out the wishes of Amanda's father. I checked with my attorney today and asked what a lawyer would have charged to settle Mr. Rocklin's estate."

"A lawyer?" Sam asked.

"Say he had lived to a ripe old age and had a lawyer draw things up," Edgington continued. "Well, my attorney figured a lawyer would have charged around ten percent." He reached into his suit coat pocket and pulled out a slip of stiff, white paper. "So we want you to have this bank check for two thousand two hundred and forty dollars."

Sam put up his hand. "No, sir. That's mighty generous. I don't think I've ever had that much money legally in my life. I did this because Mr. Rocklin and I were friends. If I took that money, it would cloud my memory of that friendship. I could never do that."

Cyrus Edgington winked at his wife. "Amanda told me you'd say exactly that."

"I thought about what Daddy would have said in the same situation. I wasn't around him very often, but he was, like you, an easy man to predict. We understand and respect your feelings," Amanda asserted

"Now, that we've dispensed with formalities . . . I have a serious business proposition to discuss," Cyrus Edgington insisted. "Please hear me out to the conclusion. Amanda and I sat up most the night, lookin' at little Samuel Gabriel and praying about what the Lord wanted us to do next with this windfall of money you brought."

HOME

"You two wouldn't be plottin' my future?" Sam replied.

"Hear me out. You know how I feel about the telephone business. It's a struggle to establish it, but the day is coming when it will be a more secure business than the railroads or the banks. And now is the time to break in."

"You don't intend on offerin' me a job in Cheyenne? I've already made enemies, and I haven't even been here much more than a day."

"Let Cyrus continue," Amanda requested.

"Yes, ma'am."

"Sam, I want to expand my business. Yesterday, I thought I was going to lose it all. But the only way to make it really work is to expand. That means I need to develop telephone systems in other towns. But I have no intention of traveling and leaving Amanda and the children here without me. So, I don't need another employee—I need a partner. It seems like you just might be between jobs, so . . . I want you to consider taking this two thousand two hundred and forty dollars as capital if you can secure us a franchise in another town. I'll put up the seed money, you put in the work, and we're partners. We could call that venture the Edgington and Fortune Telephone Exchange."

Sam Fortune cleared his throat, glanced at Amanda and then Cyrus. Then he started bouncing the toddler on his knee again. "I can't believe anyone treatin' me this good who has known me such a short time. It's a very temptin' offer. But I see some drawbacks. First of all, I don't know one blessed thing about a telephone, except that it got the doctor and you here in a hurry yesterday."

"That's about all you need to know," Amanda suggested. "Gather a few families together, and tell them your story. I guarantee every woman present will make her husband subscribe."

"I'll give you a couple of weeks exposure to the business here," Cyrus promised. "At least you'd learn enough to know if this is a good deal."

"You'll have to eat all your meals with us during those two weeks," Amanda insisted.

"Now, that is a convincin' argument, providin' I get to hold little dumplin' on my knee," Sam said. "But I might be a big flop at this. I'm not a suit and tie man. I lived most of my life on the ground next to a campfire and a horse saddled and ready to ride."

"But you scrub up good," Amanda added. "You told me that yourself."

"Look, folks. You don't know me. A man wanted to kill me just last night."

"Did he have a good reason?" she asked.

"No, ma'am, he didn't."

"Sam, do you believe Jesus died for your sins?" she asked.

"I suppose so . . . ," he mumbled. "Why do you ask me that?"

"Because I believe you ought to start living like you believe it. Of course you've had failures in the past. Sinners are the only kind of folks the Lord has to work with. Leave your sins at the cross, and get on with your life."

Fortune shook his head at Cyrus Edgington. "Your wife is quiet an exhorter."

A wide grin crept across Edgington's face. "Actually, she's rather subdued today. I suppose she's a little tired from yesterday's ordeal."

Rocklin rested against Sam's chest, and he leaned over and kissed her forehead before looking up. "Let me get this straight: I ride into some town, get the mayor and city government to sell us telephone rights, and gather people to start takin' subscriptions?"

HOME

Cyrus Edgington's arms waved like an orchestra conductor's. "Yes, and once you have fifty subscribers, we can install the equipment. I can contract that work out, but you would need to supervise it. Once you have a hundred signed up, I guarantee you, we will make money. We'll put up the capital, you'll run the business, and we'll split the profits. It's hard work, but it'll be worth it, Sam."

Fortune shook his head. "This might be like tryin' to teach a cat to swim. I don't know if I can pull it off."

"All you would be out is your time. I'm going to expand my business. This two thousand two hundred and forty dollars is the seed money to do that. If you don't want the partnership, I'll have to find someone else up there who does. But it's not just a business, Sam—it's a public service. We're helping people: helping people telephone the doctor, the sheriff, their sick mothers. It's a good business, Sam."

Fortune looked at Amanda and then at Cyrus. "You two could get arrested for ambushin' a man like this. But up where? Did you have a target city in mind?"

"I've got the perfect place in mind: the northern Black Hills of Dakota Territory. I want to establish a telephone exchange in Deadwood and Lead. It will be one company. Then we'll move down to Rapid City, Hill City, and Custer City. Eventually we'll tie them together, all the way down here to Cheyenne. Can you imagine that? Someday we'll pick up our telephone and talk to folks in the Black Hills."

Fortune stared at Cyrus Edgington. *Lord, you're doin' this to me, aren't you? You've been pushin' and proddin' me for weeks to go up there and see what happened to Daddy.*

"Sam? Is everything all right?" Amanda pressed.

Ever since I got Daddy's carbine, you've been pushin' me. You just won't let up, will you?

"Did I say something wrong?" Cyrus Edgington asked.

"I just can't believe you said Deadwood," Sam mumbled.

"Oh, my!" Amanda exclaimed. "Do you have friends or enemies there?"

"I don't know, Amanda . . . I really don't know. I've never been there, and I've spent most of the past ten years avoidin' goin' there."

"That sounds like Jonah avoiding Nineveh, doesn't it?" Amanda said.

"So what do you think of the idea?" Cyrus challenged.

"I think it's got me by the throat and won't turn me loose unless I agree."

"Splendid. That means you'll give it a try?"

Sam leaned back in the chair and closed his eyes. "I reckon I'll have to. But I have no idea if it will turn out to be heaven . . . or hell."

CHAPTER SIX

The northern Black Hills of Dakota Territory, 289 miles north of Cheyenne City

Samuel Fortune paused at the top of Whitewood Gulch. Traffic on the road had increased as he approached Deadwood, so he rode his buckskin, Picket, up the hill to the east to a thick grove of new-growth ponderosa pines. The sun hid behind a thin veneer of gray clouds, but he knew it was about noon.

He tied up the horses then pulled a brown leather satchel off the red roan mare. The dark gray suit was still neatly folded inside. He set it gingerly on a flat rock and began to pull off his boiled white shirt, leather vest, and ducking trousers.

To the west he could hear the giant stamp mills of the Homestake Mine pound out their rhythm of success. He watched the roadway as he tied his black tie tight under the crisp collar of his laundered, white shirt.

Three more miles.

I still want to turn around and ride back to Indian Territory.

Lord, you and me settled up along the trail. At least, I stopped runnin' long enough for you to catch up and give me a good shakin'. But this

159

HOME

*is different. I don't know how to do this. I don't even know what to say.
"Excuse me, I'm Samuel Fortune, the son that didn't show up for his father's funeral. I'm lookin' for a twenty-one-year-old lady, my little sister
whom I haven't seen in twelve or thirteen years."*

He pulled on the light wool suit trousers and buttoned the
matching vest.

*I don't even know if she's still here. And Todd? What happened to my
brother?*

With his suit coat still lying on the rock he walked over to the
saddled buckskin and pulled the Sharps carbine from the scabbard.
He fingered the receiver and stock, raised it to his shoulder, then
followed an imaginary target across the cloudy sky.

*Why didn't this go to Todd? Lord, I don't know what scares me more:
ridin' into Deadwood and findin' all my family . . . or ridin' into
Deadwood and findin' none of them.*

*Of course, I could just swing around to Spearfish, send the money
back to Cyrus and Amanda Edgington, then keep ridin' up to
Montana . . . or Idaho. Idaho's the place! No one goes to Idaho except
old Californian outlaws and saints from Salt Lake City.*

Sam slipped the gun back into the basket-stamped, leather scabbard and pulled on his suit coat. He straightened the collar and adjusted a silver watch chain. He tried to whack road dust off his gray
Stetson, before he shoved it on the back of his head. He brushed his
sandy blond and gray, freshly trimmed mustache with his fingertips.

*Sam Fortune, businessman, future partner of the Edgington and
Fortune Telephone Exchange. This scene is like a dream—like someone
else's dream, not mine. I don't know what I'm doin' here, Lord. I got a
feelin' this was your idea, not mine. I surmise it's a way to chastise me.
Heaven knows I need it.*

Sam pulled a small journal out of his saddle bags and studied his
recent entries. *Chugwater . . . Eagles Nest . . . Brackenridge . . .*

Government Farms . . . Rawhide Buttes . . . Alum Springs . . . Red Cañon . . . Custer City . . . Twelve Mile . . . Mountain City . . . Rapid Creek . . . I've got three more miles to go. Have mercy on me, Lord.

Sam yanked the cinch tight on Picket then climbed up into the saddle.

I spent two weeks tryin' to learn all about a business I'd never heard of until a month ago. I'll make you a deal, Lord. If this whole telephone idea is as crazy as I think it is, laugh me out of town in the first couple of days.

"Well, ponies, let's see what's three miles down the gulch. You two will never know what great lives you live. You eat, drink, pack a saddle, and watch out for spooky demons that hide behind every sage. That's about all you have to worry about. Enjoy it."

Cabins were scattered haphazardly along the tiny creek as he rode deeper into the gulch. The hillsides stretched out and were littered with dig holes and tailing piles. When he reached a bend in Whitewood Creek, the hillside leveled. Several blocks of houses stretched before him. He stopped to watch the activity in the yards of two Victorian homes.

What if one of those was Todd's? What if that's his Rebekah in the yard? What if those are his children? Does he have children? They've been married six . . . no, eight years, I think. There's got to be kids.

Fortune followed the creek into Deadwood, but avoided Main Street. Instead, he rode straight to the Montana Livery.

A teenage boy with a floppy, felt hat that drooped to his big ears greeted him as he dismounted. "Howdy, mister, can I board your horses for you?"

There was very little air movement, and Sam felt sweat soaking into the tight shirt collar. "Thanks, son. Grain them at night and in the mornin' with whole oats, not rolled. The buckskin gets two tablespoons of molasses straight on his tongue at night."

HOME

"Molasses?"

Fortune climbed down and stretched his arms. "It helps him sleep better. Have you ever tried it?"

The teenager stared at Sam. "Are you joshin' me?"

"About sleepin'? Yep. But not about the molasses." He handed the boy the leather reins.

"You come to town for the convention or the weddin'?"

He walked with the lad toward the huge, unpainted barn. There was a strong aroma of horse sweat, fresh hay, and stale manure. "None of them, but it sounds like a busy weekend."

"Yes, sir, it surely is. There's that big weddin' up at the church, plus the Dakota Stockman's Convention. Say, what name you want me to board these horses under?"

"List them as C.T.E. for Cheyenne Telephone Exchange."

"I heard about them telephones." The boy rubbed his dirty, hairless chin. "You goin' to start a company here in Deadwood?"

Sam wiped the dirt and grime out of the corner of the horses' eyes with his thumbs. "I just might."

"Well, I'll be. Ain't that something? We need one right here at the livery. Say a man's stayin' at the hotel and wants a carriage to go sparkin' in. He can telephone us, and we'll have it ready to roll before he and his little darlin' ever show up to fetch it. Wouldn't that be somethin'?"

"It's an amazin' device, all right." Sam asked Picket for a foot and inspected the horse's left hock.

"How does it work, mister? Someone said that if you climb a pole and put your ear to the wire, you can hear all them voices just a jabberin' about. It that true?" The boy slipped off Picket's bridle and bit then replaced them with a braided headstall and lead rope.

"Nope. You can't 'cipher a thing without a receiver." Sam released Picket's leg and untied his saddlebags.

The boy turned his attention to the red roan. "How do they get a man's voice to go down a wire like that?"

"I have no idea in the world . . . ," Sam replied, pulling the Sharps carbine from the scabbard.

"You work for the telephone company, and you don't know how it works?" The boy grabbed the roan's lips and forced her mouth open, surveying her teeth.

Sam reached into his bedroll and pulled out his holster and revolver. "Son, did you ever turn a switch and have one of those electricity bulbs come on?"

"Yes, sir . . . ," the boy seemed distracted by Sam's well-worn holster, "one time in Cheyenne City."

Sam strapped the gun under his suit coat. "Did you enjoy the light?"

"Yep." The boy nodded at the gun, "You expectin' trouble?"

"Nope. Just a habit, son." Sam straightened his coat over the holster. "Do you know what electricity is and how it lights that bulb?"

"No, sir, I don't."

"You see, it's possible to enjoy somethin' without being able to explain everything about it."

"I guess you're right."

"It's like knowin' the Lord, ain't it? We can enjoy the benefits without understandin' everythin' about him."

The boy shrugged. "I, eh, never thought of it that way. Now you're beginnin' to sound like a sky pilot."

"That's somethin' I've never been accused of," Sam grinned. "Do I look like a preacher?"

"Nope, but you don't look like a businessman, neither. I figured you for one of the stock growers. I mean no offense." The boy tugged off Sam's saddle and looped it over the top rail of the corral.

HOME

"Son, I consider that a compliment."

"Where are you stayin'?" The boy pointed to Main Street, "I'll deliver your bags."

Sam peered inside his saddlebags but didn't remove anything. "I haven't decided on a place. Where would you recommend?"

The boy pulled off his hat and fanned his forehead, which sported a tan line straight across it. "You ain't got a room yet?"

"No, is that a problem?" Sam looked down at the dirt and dried mud on his boots and tried stomping them clean.

The boy pointed to the barn. "We've four men sleepin' in the loft already. There ain't a room in town this week. I bet you'd have to ride clear to Spearfish to find a room."

Sam glanced out at the dirt road where a stagecoach, drawn by six white horses, rumbled north. "I'll just leave my things here, for now. If nothing turns up, I'll check back later."

The boy plucked up a large brush with black bristles worn to the nubs. "There might be a chance you can catch a room at Miss Abby's."

Sam looped the leather saddlebags over his shoulder and clutched the carbine in his right hand. "Is that a rooming house?"

"No, it's a dress shop." The boy's blue eyes danced. "One of the finest in town. You ever heard of Miss Abby O'Neill, the actress?"

"No, I can't say I have."

The boy rocked forward on his toes, making him only a couple of inches shorter than Sam. "She retired right here in Deadwood and opened a dress shop. Only, she goes by the name Mrs. Abigail Gordon. She's got a room or two above the store. She usually rents them by the week or the month, but you could check and see."

☞ ☞ ☞

Abby's Paris Fashion Shoppe was a narrow, two-story brick building between a drugstore and a tiny Italian cafe. A brick propped open the eight-foot-tall, green and gold front door. Inside, among bolts of cloth and racks of ready-made clothing, Sam could smell a cinnamon candle burning. A young girl about ten or eleven strolled straight up to him.

She's about the size of Dacee June, the last time I saw her.

"Welcome to Abby's Fine Paris Fashions. May I assist you, mister?" the young girl announced, eyeing his Sharps carbine.

Sam shifted the gun, then held out his hand. "Very pleased to meet you, Mrs. Gordon. I just rode into town from Cheyenne City. You have a very fine shop."

The curly, light brown-haired girl wrinkled her nose and giggled. "I am not Mrs. Gordon."

Sam surveyed the room in mock surprise. "You aren't?"

"No. I'm Amber Gordon, her daughter."

Sam rubbed his chin to conceal his grin. "No!"

"Yes, really—I'm the daughter," Amber lectured like a school teacher needing to repeat an assignment.

Sam squatted down on his haunches and looked the girl in the eye. "Amber, you mean you aren't married yet?"

The girl's eyes widened. "To a boy?" she gasped.

"That's usually the way it works."

"I'm definitely not married."

Suddenly, an attractive woman with long, black hair stacked on her head, wide mouth, and full, dark lips strolled down the aisle toward them. Her deep purple dress with delicate, black lace trim on the collar, cuffs, and hem swayed gracefully. Her polished leather,

HOME

lace-up boots tapped on the wooden floor. Her green eyes left no question as to who was boss.

"This man thought I was you, Mama," young Amber giggled.

He stood up as the lady closely examined him, as if inspecting a watermelon or a new pair of boots. "Oh, he did, did he?"

"Don't tell me this is your mother?" Sam grinned. "Why, I thought she was your sister."

"You see this man, Amber?" Mrs. Gordon pointed at Sam. "This is the type I warned you to watch out for: smooth-talking and good-looking. You just can't believe a word they say."

Amber grinned at Sam. "My mother's very good at chastising."

"I can see that," he concurred.

Amber folded her dress sleeve-covered arms across her chest. "Some say she might be the best chastiser in town."

"I hope there aren't too many others," Sam laughed. Then he turned to Mrs. Gordon. "I trust I didn't offend you, ma'am. I didn't mean to say anything improper. Your daughter is as precocious as she is pretty."

"Does precocious mean bright, gifted, and intelligent?" Amber asked.

Mrs. Gordon raised her eyebrows. They, along with all her other facial features were strong, dramatic. "I think it also means a bit arrogant and prideful."

"I love it. I've always enjoyed a gal who doesn't mind speakin' her mind," Sam replied.

"Then you came to the right store," Mrs. Gordon said. "Let me guess, since you're uncomfortable in a suit, and are toting saddle-bags and carbine, I'd say you're in town for the stockman's convention and want to buy your wife a present before you ride back out to the ranch?"

"No, ma'am . . ."

"Call me Abby."

"I don't want Mr. Gordon to take offense."

She folded her arms across her thin chest. "You see, Amber, this man won't call me Abby because he's trying to sneak around the brush and find out if I'm still married or not."

The girl's brown eyes sparkled. "He is?"

"What?" Sam fumed as he felt his neck redden. "That's absurd! Why would you say that?"

"Oh . . . Amber, perhaps he really doesn't enjoy it when a woman speaks her mind, after all," Abby challenged.

Sam glanced down at Amber. "Do you gang up on all the men that come into the store?"

Amber scrunched her nose. "We don't get many men customers."

"Yes, I can see why," he laughed. "Actually, contrary to several people's opinion, I'm not a stockman. I'm a businessman. My partner and I are considerin' a business venture in Deadwood. I just rode up to survey the potential."

"I didn't mean to offend you by that analysis," Abby apologized. "I usually can place a man better than that."

"No offense. I've spent most of my life around cattle and horses. You're right; I'm not the suit and tie kind."

"You don't have any manure on your boots," Amber declared.

Sam shook his head at the girl. "Darlin', if I closed my eyes, you could be my little sister."

The young girl raised her chin and struck a pose. "I take it she's beautiful and quite talented."

"Amber!" her mother protested.

"I've got a feelin' I'll regret askin' this," Sam continued, "but the reason I stopped by is because I need a room to rent. The boy at the livery said you might have one available."

HOME

Abigail pointed to the second story of the building. "I do. It became vacant just this morning, but I only rent by the week or the month."

"I'd like two weeks . . . at least," he replied.

"It's ten dollars."

"That's steep."

"It's a good room."

"I'll take it."

"And your name?"

"Sam."

"Sam what?" the little girl pressed.

Mrs. Gordon rested her hand on her daughter's shoulder. "Amber! We don't pressure a man about his name."

He tipped his hat to Abby. "Thank you, ma'am."

"Are you married?" the girl asked.

"Amber!"

"Well, he asked me if I was married."

"No, Miss Amber, I'm not married," Sam answered. "Is that a proposal? Did you want to marry me?"

"Heavens no!" the girl's chin dropped open. "I believe I can do better."

Her mother grabbed her shoulder. "Amber Gordon!"

"No offense, ma'am. This might be the smartest young woman in captivity. You're absolutely right, honey. You can do better than me."

Abigail shook her head. "I'm not sure why she's talking to you this way. She can be quite shy at times."

"How old's your sister?" Amber asked.

"I'd guess about twice your age. She's grown up now, but I remember when she was about your size."

Abigail laced her fingers together and held her hands in front of her waist. "Would you like to see the room?"

"With you two ladies approvin' it, I'll take it, sight unseen."

"Amber and I live in the upstairs apartment across the hall," Abigail reported.

Sam smiled at the girl, who folded her arms across her chest in perfect imitation of her mother. "I reckon we'll be neighbors."

Amber studied his carbine. "We have a shotgun," she announced.

"OK, we'll be neighbors, but not close neighbors," Sam chuckled.

"Amber, why don't you go on upstairs and get ready for the wedding?" her mother suggested.

"You can't get married, you promised to wait for me," Sam challenged the young girl.

"I did no such thing! Anyways, I'm only the flower girl. I should have been the maid of honor, but I got stuck in the little girl's role." She curled her lip. "Irene Seltzmann got to be maid of honor."

"Amber, go upstairs," her mother ordered.

The girl took a couple of steps, then turned back. "I wanted to sing a song, too, but no one asked me."

"Amber!" her mother's voice rose in harmony with her thick black eyebrows.

Amber dropped her head. "No one will probably even ask me to dance."

"If I was there, Miss Amber, I'd surely ask you to dance," Sam offered.

The round-cheeked girl looked up with a wide smile. "You would?"

"Yes, but I'm not goin' to be there," Sam said.

HOME

Amber pointed at her mother. "You can go with Mama. She doesn't have anyone to sit with her. I have to stand up front. She gets lonely all by herself at things like that."

Mrs. Gordon grabbed her daughter by the arm. "Excuse me, Sam, I need to have a talk with this young lady. I'll be right back."

He tipped his hat. "Yes, ma'am."

Sam wandered along a rack of ready-made dresses. He stopped to read the neatly lettered tags pinned to each garment.

"Very handsome suit, made of French twilled cloth, in tan and brown combination. Waist and skirt embroidered in barrel cactus design. $22.50"

"Handsome suit, made of cashmere, comes in a variety of colors. Notice the elaborate embroidery on the waist and skirt. $10.50"

"Handsome suit, made of fine quality française, with choice quality of passementerie ornaments on waist and skirt. $30.00"

"Black Cashmere Suit; with plaited skirt, revers, collar, and cuffs, and panel on skirt, of faille française. $11.00"

"I really must apologize for my daughter," Mrs. Gordon announced as she returned. "I've raised her on my own for so long, she doesn't exactly know how to relate to men."

Sam watched the woman's flashing eyes. *This lady could charm a crowd of a thousand. She was, undoubtedly, a very popular actress.*

"My husband divorced me, then years later was shot and killed near here in a stagecoach holdup."

"Yes, ma'am. . . . I didn't ask. . . ."

He studied her smile and decided her mouth was wider than most women's. Her eyelashes seemed thicker and longer than any he could remember.

"I know what you are thinking," she asserted.

I certainly hope not! "Actually, I was lookin' at your goods . . . eh, the ready-made dresses."

"Would you like to buy something?" she asked.

"Yes ma'am, I would. But it's a rather strange purchase. I'd like to buy somethin' for my li'l sis, but I haven't seen her in so long, I wouldn't know what to buy."

"How old did you say she was?"

"Around twenty-one, I think," Sam mumbled.

"Is she small, medium, or large?"

Sam stepped over by a bolt of blue satin and fingered the material. "I'm ashamed to say this, but I haven't seen her in a number of years. This is a pretty color."

Mrs. Gordon stepped up next to him. Sam could smell a dainty rose perfume. "Yes, it is," she agreed. "But, it would be hard to select something without knowing your sister's size."

"Why don't you just surmise what your Amber would be like when she's twenty-one? What size do you reckon she'd be, and what present would she like? I haven't spent much time in a ladies' store."

"Sam, have you ever in your life been in a ladies' wear store?"

"No, ma'am, this is my first time. I've spent a lot of my life down in the Indian Territory. Stores of any kind are mighty rare."

"I'll tell you what piece seems to be catching attention here at the shop. No one has bought it, mind you, but most of the young ladies in the wedding today have coveted it." She led him to several silk gowns at the back of the store. "Now, I don't know if you're a brother that is embarrassed by such gowns. But this one is the most talked about garment in Deadwood."

"A nightgown?" he gasped.

"Not just any nightgown." The tone of Abigail's voice sounded as if she were giving announcements at a church potluck. "It's a Japanese silk Peignoir, with rows of shirred tucks in the front and back of the waist holding in place the Grecian drapery. The neck, sleeves, and sash are made of ribbon, and the bottom of the skirt is covered with black Chantilly lace inserts. Notice the bottom is trimmed with silk plaiting. And it is lined with soft flannel to the waist. All I have is the white, but I can order it in other colors."

He shook his head and felt his face blush. His throat grew tight, and he could hardly swallow. "That's about the fanciest thing I've ever seen in my life."

Abigail pulled the gown off the wooden hanger and held it up for him to inspect. "That's what Dacee June says," she commented.

It was like a bolt of lightening hit his toes and slowly worked it's way up, stiffening every bone in his body. "Who?" The word popped out of his mouth like a wad of meat that was caught in the throat and expelled only after the face turned blue.

"Dacee June Fortune. She's the young woman getting married today."

"Today?" he choked, then turned away.

"Yes, that's the wedding where Amber is the flower girl."

Getting married? But . . . but . . . she . . . today? Lord, you led me all the way to Deadwood to be at li'l sis's wedding?

"This Dacee June is the most adventuresome, good girl in the Black Hills. She loves this, and it is rather loose fitting, since you didn't know your sister's size. I know it's rather exotic . . . and expensive . . . but I thought . . ."

Sam Fortune did not move a muscle. Or even blink. "How much is it?"

"Thirty-five dollars."

"What time's the wedding?"

"Oh, it's not for an hour. I have plenty of time to finish waiting on you before we need to be there."

"And you said this bride named Dacee June likes the gown?"

"She adores it. I think she was a little nervous to spend that much money on herself."

"Then I reckon my li'l sis will like it too. I'll take it." He let out a deep breath before he faced her again.

"Oh, splendid. May I box it for you?"

"Definitely. I don't think I have the nerve to carry it on a hanger."

He followed her to the counter of the store. She began to neatly fold the gown. "You're a very generous big brother. This will certainly be a lifetime treasure."

"I've missed a lot of birthdays. I reckon I have a lot to catch up on. Say, this wedding today—this Dacee June—is she marryin' a local boy?" Sam propped the carbine and saddlebags against the counter.

Abigail paused and studied his eyes until he looked away. "Oh, yes. After she graduated from college she came back and—"

"College? She's a college girl?" He pulled off his Stetson and brushed his fingers through his hair.

"She went to Chicago and studied history. We're all quite proud of her. Anyways, when she returned, she told Carty it was time to get married."

"Carty?" he asked.

"Carty Toluca . . . they've know each other for years. But she's tormented him something awful. I don't know how he's withstood it. Anyways, after four years in Chicago, she came home and told him they were getting married. For a formerly gangly and awkward boy, he grew into quite a handsome young man."

I can't imagine li'l sis marryin' any other type.

"My goodness, I'm rambling on and on about perfect strangers. I'm beginning to sound like my daughter. I'm sure this is all very boring to you." She held the wrapped bundle in front of him. "How does this look?"

"Very nice, thank you."

"I'm not trying to pry, Sam. But what kind of business are you and your partner going to establish? I hope it's not another brewery or saloon."

"No, ma'am. We want to install a telephone exchange."

Abigail's green eyes widened. "A telephone company? How exciting! I used one in Denver just this spring. They are marvelous!"

"We're just speculating. My partner owns the exchange in Cheyenne City. I have to talk to lots of folks around town then approach the city fathers."

"Then, you really should go to this wedding with me," she beamed. "Every important official in Lawrence County and Deadwood will be there."

"Oh, I shouldn't intrude. . . ."

"Nonsense. In that crowd, no one will care. You come with me, and I'll introduce you around," Abby insisted.

He stared across the store and out at the dirt street. "That's an extremely nice gesture. I might take you up on it."

"Marvelous." She handed him the package tied with a white ribbon. "Does your li'l sis live here in Deadwood?"

"Yes, ma'am, I believe she still does."

"I won't be like my daughter and ask her name, but do tell her if she needs any alterations to please come and see me."

"I'll do that."

"I need to close the store now. Why don't I show you your room. Then, when Amber and I finish getting ready, we'll rap on the door. You can walk with us."

☞ ☞ ☞

The room was small, but immaculate. The bed was covered with a thick, dark blue, quilt comforter. A lion-foot, oak dresser. Framed mirror. Gas lamp. Small woodstove. A portrait of a long-legged, black trotting horse at a racetrack with well-dressed spectators hung above the bed. The lace curtains shielded the clouded daylight of Main Street.

Sam set the present and saddlebags on the bed, propped the carbine at the doorway, and left the door open to the narrow hallway.

Standing at the window, he looked up Main Street. He spotted a large, two-story brick building on the west side of the street. The name on the front riveted his attention.

"Fortune & Son Hardware, since 1876."

There it is. Robert wrote to me about it years ago. You ran a hardware store, Daddy? I can't believe it. You were a Texas drover—a cattleman of the old school. You signed up with Sam Houston when you were twelve. We all heard the stories, over and over. You rode with the Rangers; chased Comanche raidin' parties. You fought the Mexican army, the gulf shore pirates, and drought. Texas was in your blood.

Then the war came, and you wouldn't fight.

Said it was bad for Texas.

But you dragged us all down to Brownsville so that you and Captain King could sneak food and supplies to hungry, needy Texas families. That's where it started to fall apart, didn't it?

Veronica and Patricia took sick.

Sam Fortune wiped a pool of tears from the corner of his eyes.

Oh Lord, how we all cried and cried the day they both died.

Mama could never get over that. She must have cried ever'day, until the sickness took her too.

HOME

Then we went home to find someone else livin' in our house.

I couldn't take it, Daddy.

You just wouldn't fight 'em.

We buried mama on that land, and you wouldn't fight 'em for it. I didn't understand. I had to leave. All we did was argue and fight. Lord, how I said hateful things!

Sam Fortune, you've never been noted for being very smart.

What a great life you chose.

Go up the Indian Territory and join the Confederate raiders.

Confederate raiders? We were horse thieves, cattle rustlers, and hold-up men—that's all we ever were.

But you, Daddy—you left Texas. You came to a pine-covered mountain range and camped in the gulch. You made your mark in the mines— and in a store. You ran away and made it rich.

I ran away, too, Daddy.

And I ended up without a horse or a meal, down to my last ten bullets, with men no better than me tryin' to shoot me in the back.

But the Lord pulled me out of that, Daddy.

I don't know why. I don't know how heaven works—maybe you and Mama are up there talkin' to the Boss—but kickin' and screamin', he drug me all the way up here.

Things will be different for your middle son now.

But it grieves my heart that you didn't live long enough to see it.

He wiped his eyes on the cuffs of his white shirt.

"Fortune & Son . . . ," he mumbled. *It doesn't say "Fortune & Sons," does it. Todd's the right one. He always liked making all the decisions. Big brother followed Daddy. Little brother joined the army. Li'l sis . . . well, she's the only gal Daddy had left. He clutched onto her like she was a porcelain doll. So she waited to get married until after Daddy was gone.*

Mr. Carty Toluca, that's mighty fortunate for you. I can't believe Daddy would let her go.

"Is the room satisfactory?" a faint voice queried.

Mr. Toluca, you had better treat sis right. She's got three older brothers who . . . I hope she still has three older brothers. Why did she send me the carbine? The last two months have been like a puzzle where none of the pieces make sense. Maybe I'll wake up from a dream and still be in prison. Now, that's a melancholy ponder.

"Sam, I asked is the room all right?"

He spun around. Mrs. Abigail Gordon stood in the doorway wearing a deep blue, satin dress with white lace at the collar and cuffs.

"You . . . you . . ." He wiped his eyes on the sleeves of his suit coat.

"Yes? I'm sorry, did you expect someone else?"

"No, it's just I was daydreamin' and thinkin' about . . . say, you look quite fetching," he mumbled.

She waved a long, slender, pale finger at him. "Now don't start that charm on me. I spent many a year as an actress, and I've heard every line you can imagine—and some you couldn't think up in a thousand years."

His shirt collar pinched his neck, his tie unforgiving. "Then you should be able to tell if a man is just readin' a script or not."

"Point made." She dropped her hand to her side. "Thank you for the sincere compliment. But you didn't answer my question: Is the room all right?"

"It is very nice. . . ." Again he wiped his eyes on his coat sleeve.

She strolled over to him, and he could hear the rustle of her dress. "Are you all right?"

He smelled a strong aroma of violet perfume as she approached. "There's just a little dust in the air," he managed to murmur.

HOME

"In one of my rooms?" She stood next to him and looked out the window at the hardware store. "I'll have to talk to my ten-year-old housekeeper. She was supposed to dust in here."

"Oh, no—the room's immaculate. It must have been road dust." He cleared his throat. "Are you ready to go to the wedding?"

"Yes, Amber's waiting in the hall. Are you ready?"

That, Mrs. Abigail Gordon, is a question that will soon be answered. "Do I look presentable?"

"For a man with a good smattering of prematurely gray hair, you look quite presentable."

"Every gray strand was rightly earned, Mrs. Gordon. Would you care to guess my age?"

She studied him from head to foot. "I'd say . . . thirty-four."

"How did you know that?"

"Just a lucky guess. As an actress, I've played that game before. Would you like to guess my age?"

"Twenty-one?" he replied quickly.

"Oh, you are a charmer, Sam. Of course, you missed it by more than ten years, but I do appreciate a man with discretion." She pointed to the package on the bed. "Would you like to take that gown?"

"To the wedding?"

"I thought perhaps you wanted to go see your sister afterward."

He led her to the doorway. "I'll come back for it. It would be a little awkward to show up with a present, then tote it off."

At the bottom of the stairs he offered his arm, which she accepted. Amber ran ahead of them, holding the hem of her long, white dress above the boardwalk.

"I'm delighted you are escorting me to the wedding," Abigail thanked.

"It's my pleasure," he replied. "But I have to admit, I'm rather amazed that on my first trip to Deadwood, the people are so friendly to me. A little over an hour ago, we had never met. Now I'm walking you down the street, arm in arm. I've had that happen in a dance hall or a saloon, but never in the good part of town."

She paused and spun him toward her. "If you're embarrassed, I won't hold your arm."

"No, no, that's not it. But, if you knew all about me, you might not want to be seen with me."

"Oh my, a man of mystery," her songlike voice expressed. The song wasn't high or piercing but a low, smooth one like the call of a mourning dove. "Besides," she added, "if you knew all about me, you might not want to walk with me."

He stopped to stare at her.

"What are you doing? You're embarrassing me," she murmured.

He resumed their stroll. "Well, you're wrong," he asserted.

"About what?"

"No matter what you've done, I'm proud to walk with you."

"Just how long have you been out on the plains with no women around?" she laughed.

"Most of my life. Does it show?"

"It certainly does. And I certainly like it."

☞ ☞ ☞

The simple, pine-paneled sanctuary of the church at the foot of McGovern Hill was almost full when they arrived. Sam lingered outside near the street while Mrs. Gordon ushered Amber to where the wedding party huddled in the kitchen. She rejoined him. Even with a nearly filled sanctuary, Abigail found them room on the center aisle, near the front, on the bride's side.

Several people turned and greeted her as they sat down.

179

HOME

"You seem to know everyone in town," he whispered above the pump organ music.

Her head almost on his shoulder, she whispered back, "Well, this is my church. And I sold most of these ladies their dresses."

"So, you are a church woman?" he asked.

"I don't know what you mean by that, but Jesus saved me from my sins. And you?" she prodded.

"Yes, ma'am, indeed he did." He stared across the crowded pews. "Who are those folks up front?"

She leaned closer to him and resumed whispering, "Friends of the family. The man in the wheelchair is named Quiet Jim. I have no idea what his last name is."

Sam Fortune stared at the thin, gray-haired man with the thick mustache. *Quiet Jim Trooper, Coryell County, Texas.*

"Next to him, with the beautiful black hair, is his wife Columbia. They have five children: Quint, Fern, Sarah, Jimmy, and Brett." She continued, "The man with that outlandish plaid suit is Professor Edwards, and that's his wife Louise."

A smile crept across Sam's face. *Mr. Edwards is a professor and married to one of the March sisters?*

"Next is Louise's sister, Thelma Speaker. She's been a friend of the family for years and years."

Sam could only see the back of Mrs. Speaker's head. *Her hair style and color hasn't changed in twenty years. I wonder if she ever forgave Mama for stealin' Daddy from her?*

"It's rather strange to see those men without Yapper Jim."

"Whatever happened to Mr. Haywood?" Sam asked.

Abigail looked surprised. "Who?"

"I mean, this Yapper Jim fellow."

"What a tragedy. He was in his room at the Merchant's Hotel and a drunk miner started hurrahing the cafe below. A bullet must

180

have come through the ceiling and struck him in bed. They didn't find him until the next day. They buried him up on Mount Moriah in the pioneer section."

"I'd like to go up there," Sam remarked.

"Why is that?" She tried to look him in the eye, but he avoided her probe.

"Eh . . . you know . . .," he babbled, "isn't Wild Bill Hickok buried up there?"

"Yes, he is."

"Would you go up there with me?" he queried.

"How about after the wedding?"

"That would be nice. Can we walk up there from here?" Sam asked.

"Not dressed like this. We will need a carriage."

Holding his hat in his lap, Sam curled the brim as he talked. "How about those folks in the very front row? Is there anyone there I should get to know?"

"We can't see them that well since their backs are to us," Abigail explained. "The tall man with light, thin hair near the aisle is Dacee June's eldest brother, Todd. You will definitely want to talk to him about your telephone exchange. He's one of the leading businessmen in the northern Black Hills."

Sam observed the woman next to Todd lean over and whisper in his ear. "And next to him, the lady with light brown hair and narrow chin?"

"That's his wife Rebekah. That lady is pure gold. She's probably the best friend I've ever had in my life. She led me to the Lord."

"Next to her?"

"That's Little Hank, named after his granddaddy."

"How old is he?"

"He's four. Camilla's three, Nettie's two, and Stuart is one."

HOME

"My goodness, that's quite a family."

Abigail hushed her whisper and directed it in his ear. "She's expecting another, but she hasn't even told Todd yet."

I have an entire family that doesn't even know I exist. "And the man in the uniform?"

"That's Captain Robert Fortune, another of Dacee June's brothers."

Captain? Bobby made captain? I didn't even know he went to officer's school!

"The woman with the long, shiny hair is his Jamie Sue. The nine-year-old is Little Frank. You might find this interesting. He was named after the first man buried on Mount Moriah, Big River Frank, but that was way before I moved here."

Sam leaned back until the polished wood pew straightened his back. *The cemetery is full of old Texans. No wonder Daddy could never leave.*

"Next are the twins, almost seven years old. Patricia and Veronica are identical in looks only."

Like a levee that suddenly burst after years of relentless pressure, tears streamed down Sam's cheeks. *Good for you, Bobby. You named your girls after our sisters. I like that.*

"You know, I always cry at weddings, too." Abigail Gordon handed Sam a neatly folded, white linen handkerchief that she had pulled from the sleeve of her dress.

He refused the dainty handkerchief and dabbed his eyes on the back of his hand. "Eh, no . . . it's the dust again. I've had alkali in my eyes ever since Cheyenne," he muttered.

"You know what seems funny to me, Sam?"

"What's that?"

She reached over and put her hand on his. It felt warm, soft. "It is so strange for me to sit here and introduce your own family to you."

"What?" The word blurted out like a wrong note in a slow waltz. The people in front glared back at him.

"Samuel Fortune, when are you going to walk up and tell them you're here?"

"How did you . . . you knew . . . ?"

She reached up, slipped her arm in his, and whispered, "I trust you don't think I'd latch onto any drifting stranger and drag them to a wedding. Your sister has said for six months that all three of her brothers would be at her wedding, and here you are."

"But . . . but . . . I didn't even know there was a wedding. Honest."

"And the story about the telephone exchange?"

"It's all true! I had no idea in the world about the wedding until you told me."

"Well, it's true that Rebekah Fortune is my best friend. There hasn't been a holiday in five years that Amber and I haven't spent with your family. And, I might add, there hasn't been a holiday that your name wasn't mentioned and prayers said on your behalf."

"Then you know about me?"

"Yes, I do. But you have no idea about me," she replied. "Are you going to tell your sister you're here?"

"Did you tell her I'm here when you took Amber to meet with the others?"

"I told no one. I wasn't absolutely positive about your identity until I saw your tears over the twin's names. No one but family would shed a tear over that."

HOME

Just then the processional began. "I don't want to spoil the wedding. I'll wait until later," he said.

Sam didn't look back as the bridesmaids came down the aisle. He studied the face of the grinning young man in the black suit standing next to the preacher at the front of the church. "Is that the groom?" he whispered.

"Yes, that's Carty," Abigail replied.

"How old is he: Sixteen?"

She poked him in the ribs. "He's twenty-one."

"Twenty-one? He can't be twenty-one!"

She put a warm finger on his lips to silence him. "Yes he is, and he's an assistant store manager."

"At that age? Who would be foolish enough to do that?"

"Your brother, Todd."

"He's the assistant manager at Fortune & Son?"

"Yes, and he's quite a good worker, I hear."

Sam was still taking it all in when Rebekah Fortune stood up at the change of processional tunes. The congregation stood, too, and gazed back up the aisle. Sam stood, but he stared forward at the faces of Todd and Robert. *You've gotten a lot older, boys. Haven't we all. But if you're both up there, who's givin' the bride away?*

Sam spun around and was startled to see a beautiful young woman dressed in a flowing, white silk gown. Her eyes focused on her trembling hands that carried a bouquet of white daisies. Her chin slightly pointed; nose, round; cheeks, perfectly smooth.

Sam tried to swallow but found a huge lump in his throat. *Dacee June, you look just like Mama! I had no idea. You're . . . you're so grown up. What are you doin' marryin' that . . . that kid?*

He watched her expression as she glanced over at the man by her side.

His hair was solid gray. His face, tan and wrinkled at the eyes. His chin, proud. His large mustache drooped. His tie was crooked. His eyes danced as they looked into hers.

"Daddy?" Sam blurted out.

Abigail flinched.

The crowd grew silent.

The organist continued to play.

The bride and her father searched the aisle.

Then Dacee June dropped her bouquet and her father's arm and shouted, "Sammy! I just knew you'd be here!" She ran down the aisle dragging her silk dress.

The crowd gasped.

The organ stopped.

She threw her arms around his neck and pressed her lips on his. For a minute she wouldn't let go. He could feel her warm tears flow down her cheek and mingle with his. When she pulled back, the crowd remained completely quiet.

With a voice that sounded more twelve than twenty-one, the groom called out, "Dacee June?"

She bounced on her toes and grinned when she looked around at the astonished crowd, "It's all right, everybody—this is my brother!"

The congregation burst into applause as Brazos walked over to Sam.

"Thanks for coming to li'l sis's wedding." Brazos offered his hand.

Sam grabbed it, and his father didn't let go.

"I'm glad you got the invitation," Brazos added.

"I . . . I didn't get an invitation. . . . I didn't even know it was today. . . . I didn't even know I was comin'," Sam mumbled.

"Didn't you get my package?"

HOME

"I got your carbine. There was no invitation, no note, no letter . . . just the gun."

Brazos nodded. His eyes pierced straight into Sam's heart. "That's all I sent."

"You just sent me the gun and expected me to show up?"

"Son, what could I say in a letter that I haven't said in twelve years? I just sent the gun."

"And you figured I would come to Deadwood?"

"I was right, wasn't I?"

"But . . . but . . . I . . . this is . . ."

Brazos still didn't let go—he pulled his son close and threw his arm around his shoulders.

Suddenly, two strong men grabbed Sam and pulled him aside.

"Just like you to get the first kiss from the bride!" Todd gibed.

"How did you get so old?" Sam prodded.

"Me? I've always been old, remember? How about you with all that gray hair?"

"It's all those nights worryin' about you two," Sam laughed.

"Us?" Robert countered. "We're all surprised that you're alive."

Sam lowered his eyes and murmured, "So am I, boys. So am I." He glanced up and put his hands on his little brother's shoulders. "General Fortune, you look mighty good in that uniform."

"Captain Fortune," Robert corrected.

"They sewed the uniform on him, and he can't take if off 'til he dies," Todd joshed. "Jamie Sue says he takes a bath with that thing on."

Robert continued to stand at near attention. "Can you believe it, Sammy, I'm thirty-one years old, and he still torments me like that?"

"If you boys have finished ruinin' li'l sis's wedding, we could at least get on with the vows," Brazos insisted.

Todd motioned for Sam to join them up front. "We'll squeeze over and make room for you."

Sam glanced back at Abigail Gordon, who nodded for him to go ahead.

"I'm fine right here, boys. You see, I brought Mrs. Gordon with me as my date, and I don't want to abandon her."

"Abby?" Todd laughed, "Sammy, how long have you been in town?"

"About two hours."

"And you already have a date with the most beautiful, eligible woman in town?"

"Two hours?" Robert grinned. "Todd, I do believe Sammy's slowing down with age!"

The brothers laughed.

The women cried.

The organ resumed.

The children squirmed.

The preacher said some important words.

The vows were said.

The ring was given.

And a very nervous twenty-one-year-old man kissed a smiling twenty-one-year-old woman on the cheek.

☞ ☞ ☞

A noisy reception at the ballroom of the Merchant's Hotel followed the wedding. After dancing with young Amber Gordon, Sam Fortune spent the first hour being introduced to his sisters-in-law, nephews, and nieces. Finally he walked Abigail and a very

HOME

tired Amber Gordon home, then toted Dacee June's wedding present back with him. After having the bride draped around his neck for a good thirty minutes, Sam scooted out to the front porch of the hotel where he spotted Todd sitting alone on the railing.

"You feelin' like the older brother in the prodigal story?" Sam asked.

Todd laughed light and easy. "Not me, Sammy. It has been a very good day. I haven't seen Daddy this relaxed since Brownsville. I don't know if he's happier to see you—or to let some other man take responsibility for li'l sis."

"I'm surprised he let her go."

"He'll be sixty-one his next birthday, Sam. She's a very enthusiastic young lady. I think he was getting a little worn out."

"I have to admit, it has been a great day," Sam confessed. "I didn't know what would be waitin' for me up here. The Lord has been good to me."

Todd studied Sam's eyes. "Do you mean that?"

"Yep."

Todd loosened his tie and unfastened the top button of his white shirt. "This day has turned out so good, it's fretful."

"I know what you mean, big brother. Let's enjoy it while we can."

Todd studied him head to toe. "You look good, Sam. I figured . . . you know, after you being in prison and all."

Sam Fortune pushed his hat back and rubbed the back of his neck. "You knew about that?"

"I heard you were in prison, but I didn't know which one . . . or which state."

"Did Daddy know?"

"I didn't tell him. We never talked about it. But I think he suspected as much."

"How did you find out?" Sam asked.

"After that dime novel about me came out, we had—"

"A what? You had a dime novel written about you?"

"It's mostly all lies, of course. I'll give you a copy so you can laugh about it."

"What's it called?"

"Now you're embarrassing me."

"I'll find out sooner or later."

"It's called *The Flying Fist of Deadwood Gulch*."

Samuel chuckled.

"Anyways, after it came out, we had a number of men come through claiming to be pards of yours down in the Territory."

"I reckon they all wanted handouts."

"Mostly."

"And what did Mr. Flying Fist do with them?"

"Daddy bought them all a meal, no matter how ridiculous the story."

Robert sauntered out on the porch. "What are you two planning?"

"Come sit a spell, General Fortune," Sam invited. "I just heard about big brother's dime novel."

Robert scooted up next to the rail, placing Sam in the middle. "He's an inspiration to us all."

"All right, you two. Hawthorne Miller said he would write the story whether I gave him any facts or not—I tried to explain things."

"Did I tell you I met Miller down in Arizona at Stuart Brannon's ranch?" Robert said.

"Brannon? You're a friend of Brannon's?" Sam questioned.

"Me and forty other soldiers met him one day."

"Is he a big man? I heard he's big man," Sam commented.

HOME

"He's about Todd's height—but stronger, of course. Todd's always been the weakling," Robert teased.

"Yeah, Bobby, but he does have the 'flying fist'! None of the rest of us have that," Sam joined.

"All right, you can both quit acting like—"

"Brothers?" Robert completed.

"Bobby," Sam said, "do you remember the time that Todd taught us the flyin' dismount?"

"Was that the time he taught us how to dig a ditch with our noses?" Robert recalled.

"Nope." Sam stood and threw an arm around the shoulders of each of his brothers. "I'm thinkin' about how he would organize us into a Texas Ranger posse, with him as captain, of course. He must have been about ten, and I was nine—"

"I must have been six," Robert calculated.

"We reined up next to the Garcia Barranca . . . and he tumbled right out of the saddle. He just picked himself up, brushed off his hat, and said, 'Now, that's the way to have a flying dismount, men.'"

Brazos Fortune strolled up while the three were still arm in arm. "Is this a private matter, or can an old man join in?"

"I'm glad you came along, Daddy. Your youngest sons were ganging up on me," Todd said.

Brazos stood next to his three sons and gazed out on the street. "Well, that's different. It seems to me most of the fights were when you and Bobby ganged up on Sammy."

"As I recall, I usually deserved it," Sam Fortune admitted.

Brazos surveyed the crowded ballroom. A lively fiddle orchestra played. "Li'l sis looks happy, doesn't she?"

"Maybe she'll stop tormenting Carty now," Todd added. Then he grinned, "Probably not."

"He's a brave man," Robert concurred. "Maybe a little naïve . . ."

"I'll tell you what's a tad naïve," Brazos said—"having Sam here own a telephone exchange. Hard to imagine you as a businessman."

"Me? How about you, Daddy? A prosperous store owner and enjoyin' it."

"I've prospered, but I've never enjoyed one day of it."

"You getting restless, Daddy?" Robert pressed.

"Maybe. . . . Somethin' about havin' an empty house after all these years. Not that I want to move. This is home. But maybe it's time for the four of us to saddle up and go huntin' for a day or two, providin' Mr. Telephone Exchange can spare the time."

"I'm ready," Sam replied. "You want to leave tonight or in the morning?"

"Whoa. I'll have to check with Jamie Sue and the kids," Robert cautioned. "I've only got another week before we all have to be back in Arizona."

"I can't get away. With Dacee June and Carty gone on a honeymoon, I'll have to be at the store," Todd explained. "Besides, Rebekah just told me she was expectin' again, so I can count on a sick mama for a while."

"When that lady made up her mind to have children, she didn't hesitate," Robert razzed.

Brazos shrugged. "That's good news. Keeps an old man lookin' forward. Maybe we can try it later in the year. Bobby, why don't you get up in the fall before it snows too much, and we'll do some elk huntin'. I was just thinkin' it would be nice for the four us to do something together."

"I doubt if I can get back up here before Christmas," Robert said.

HOME

A large, unshaven man rode a mule straight up on the wooden boardwalk in front of them. "Say, do any of you men know a Sam Fortune?" he bellowed.

"I'm Sam."

"There's an ol' boy from Dodge City down at the Piedmont Saloon. Said he was lookin' for ya and gave me two cash dollars to deliver the message. No one down there knew there was a 'Sam' Fortune. Anyways, if I were you, I wouldn't turn my back on him, if you get my drift. He looks like he's tryin' to rile himself up for a fight."

"Thanks," Sam tipped his Stetson. "I reckon I'll take a little hike down there and check this out. Where 'bouts is the Piedmont?"

"I think I'll come along," Robert offered.

"No reason to go. It's somethin' I have to deal with all the time."

"Not in my town, you don't. Think I'll go, too." Todd added, "You never know when you might need The Flying Fist of Deadwood Gulch."

"Well, shoot, boys—we're all goin'," Brazos announced. "I told you the four of us ought to do somethin' together."

CHAPTER SEVEN

Outside the Piedmont Saloon & Gambling Emporium, badlands district, Deadwood, D.T.

The cloud-draped sun had long disappeared behind Forest Hill. For a moment Deadwood was caught between pale gray and black. Even the steady breeze had died off, as if waiting for night to officially arrive. In the distance, the stamp mills of Lead rolled their dull thunder down Whitewood Gulch.

The four men walked shoulder to shoulder down the center of an almost deserted Main Street. "Sammy, do you know who we're lookin' for?"

"No, but I surmise I'll recognize him the moment I walk through the door." Sam pulled his Colt pistol out of his holster, checked the chambers, and reset the hammer on the empty one. The grip felt slick. The trigger cold. *It's been a month since I've drawn this pistol. That must be a record.* "Now, look, boys, the last thing I want is for you to go home to your mamas tonight carryin' a bullet because of your no account brother. I appreciate your offer to help, but don't

HOME

get in front of me. If I can't face down one ol' boy from Dodge—well, I need to know that right now."

Robert adjusted his dark blue, close-fitting double-breasted surtout coat that sported an insignia with two braids and a single knot. "We aren't about to let you come down here and ruin li'l sis's wedding day by getting yourself killed."

"You think the inside of the Piedmont is a good place to confront him?" Todd parked his hand on the .45 Colt tucked into his brown belt.

"This is where that famous Todd Fortune captured the nefarious Cigar Dubois single-handedly," Robert prodded.

"And I haven't been back since," Todd added.

"Whoever he is, I'd rather confront him inside a saloon than in some dark alley or wait until he shows up at li'l sis's party." *Lord, I certainly hope I know what I'm doin'. I've never had to worry so much about my partners before.*

Brazos pulled the massive hammer back on the Sharps carbine until it clicked once, then cradled it in his hand. The top button of his white shirt was still fastened, but the black wedding tie flagged on the railing back at the Merchant's Hotel. "Son, you aren't wanted for a crime and have bounty hunters sniffin' you out, do you?"

The four men stopped in the street in front of the Piedmont to watch an open stage from Sturgis pull up in front of the saloon. Sam shrugged, "That's always a possibility. Servin' time in prison doesn't always make everyone happy. I was supposed to stay in there ten years and got out in less than three. Some folks surmised I was in cahoots with the authorities by revealing information about them."

"If they thought you'd betray a friend, they don't know Fortunes very well," Brazos declared.

"I didn't do it, of course," Sam cleared. "Though I would hardly call some of them my friends."

"How did you get out so soon?" Robert asked as he threw his arm around his brother's shoulder. They were both a couple of inches taller than Brazos, but several inches shorter than Todd.

Sam glanced at his brothers. "Officially or unofficially?"

"Both," Robert pressed.

"Officially, I was listed as rehabilitated, the model prisoner. It's nice to find out I could do somethin' right."

"And unofficially?" Todd prompted.

"I got out because of the warden's wife."

Todd raised his eyebrows. "She pulled strings?"

"Nope. The warden pulled strings. Seems he didn't want me within fifty miles of his wife."

"But you were in prison," Robert protested.

"For some gals, that just doesn't make a difference."

"Some things never change," Todd gibed.

Sam rubbed street dust out of the creases of his eyes. "Well, I've changed now, boys. I'm not very proud of the way I've been livin'."

Brazos pointed past the Sturgis stage at the open front doors of the Piedmont. "Son, that saloon is a den of snakes. You can't never tell which direction they'll strike from. You aimin' to go through the back door, just to look things over first?"

Sam put his hand on his father's shoulder, grinned, then looked at his brothers. "Is Daddy tryin' to test me? A man in there wanted to see me, so I'm goin' through the front door. Never show any sign of weakness—you taught us all that."

Brazos brushed back his long drooping mustache with his fingertips. "I was younger then and didn't reckon there were exceptions to the rule."

HOME

Sam waved his arm in the still, Dakota twilight. "How about you and the general takin' the back door. Me and big brother will go through the front. With the legendary Todd Fortune and his flying fist of destruction at my side, I imagine they'll all cower down."

"The book was all fiction," Todd muttered.

"Where do you think fiction writers get their ideas? They steal 'em from the truth, that's where. Then they twist it around and disguise it as a story. Writers are all liars and thieves. It's the nature of their business." Sam nudged his father's shoulder. "Daddy, we'll wait about three minutes for you two to get around back."

Although the Piedmont Saloon had been rebuilt in brick after the 1883 fire, the masons had spent more time at the bar than at the wall. The mortar was mixed too sandy in many places. After only two years, bricks began to tumble on hapless patrons. This lead to the abandonment of the upstairs dance hall. Most figured the entire building would collapse someday. A fact that did not seem to worry citizens of the bad lands.

That was usually the least of their worries.

"Let me walk in first," Todd offered. "He's not looking for me. He doesn't even know me. At least I can see if he has an ambush set up."

"Nope. This is my life. I've got to face the consequences of my actions. Stay inside the doorway. I don't want someone sneakin' up and bushwhackin' me from behind." Sam pushed his suit coat behind his holstered revolver and positioned his right hand on the walnut grip.

Pipe and cigar smoke was so thick inside the saloon, Sam couldn't see the back door. But he sensed his father and Robert's presence. He strolled straight to the bar. Todd dropped back and stood, hands on his hips, by the front door.

With each step toward the bar, the banter and conversations died a little more. By the time he reached the brass footrail, the crowded room was quiet.

"Are you Sam Fortune?" the bartender asked as he broke off a hunk of obviously stale bread.

Sam turned his back to everyone in the room. *Lord, if it wasn't for Daddy, Todd, and Robert, I would never turn my back on this crowd.* "Yep. I hear someone is lookin' for me."

The bartender took the yank of bread and wiped a whiskey glass clean with it. "You related to them other Fortunes?"

Sam stared right at the man. "Yeah. I'm the mean, ornery one."

The bartender dropped the whiskey-soaked bread in a milk bucket half full of similar hunks. "I didn't think you was of the same family. Fortunes around here ain't known for bein' outlaws. If I'd known that, I wouldn't have let him send for you."

Sam tried to study the man's eyes, but the bartender examined the short glass, as if searching for imperfections.

"Fortune!" a man hollered from across the smoky room. "I want to talk to you!"

Even in the dimly lit room, Sam could spot the gold earrings that framed an unshaven, grimy face. "Mr. Burns, you're a long way from the alleys of Dodge City." Sam put his back against the bar. Several men, including the bartender, scurried away from him.

Burns sat alone at a round wooden table that was draped by a double-barreled shotgun. A wooden splint and dirty linen bandage girded his right wrist. His hair curled out from under his wide-brimmed, brown hat. His clothes were dirty. His eyes were amber-colored, like the whiskey bottle on the table before him. "Come over here, Fortune, I want to talk to you!"

197

"I'm here . . . talk."

"Ain't no need to shout. Come sit down. I'll buy you a drink."

"Are you too drunk to shoot straight this far, Burns? I'll stay right here. What do you want?"

Burns waved his shirt-clad arm at the empty chair across the table from him. "It ain't hospitable to shout across a room."

Sam now stood alone at the bar. All the other patrons shoved up against the walls near the front and back doors. "There's plenty of room over here," he challenged. "Come on over, and you can whisper for all I care. Where's your partner?"

Burns reached for the shotgun then pulled his hand back. "He's dead, and you're the cause of it," he hollered.

Sam tried to study the man's eyes, but the smoke in the room made it difficult. "He was alive when I left Dodge."

"Well, he ain't now. Gangrene set in that foot where you crippled him." Sweat coursed down the man's dirty forehead.

"Dodge City must have a dozen doctors, Burns. He was doctored in jail; I was there. If he died over that wound, he died because of stupidity."

Red-faced, Burns reached for the shotgun again but jerked back as Sam Fortune cocked his still holstered revolver. "Don't get too cheeky, Fortune. I've got friends in this room who will back my play."

Sam lowered the hammer back down to safety but left his hand on the walnut grip. "That's good, Burns. A man needs friends. Although, I don't understand why they would want to side with a man who kicks women when they're down."

"That' a lie," Burns screamed. "I didn't kick that woman! It was McDermitt that kicked her."

Sam surveyed the others in the bar. "At least I know what kind of friends you run with."

"Don't push it, Fortune, or there will be a dozen guns pointed at you."

With his finger pointed like a gun, Sam tilted his hat back with his left hand. "A dozen guns? Well, that should make it about even. Burns, you and me are new to Deadwood, but the rest of these boys probably already know that tall man at the door is my brother Todd. Some of you read about him in that Hawthorne Miller novel. Then, through the smoke, standin' at the back, is the Captain—little brother Robert is one of the army's best sharpshooters. He's been with General Crook down on the border lookin' for Geronimo. And, of course, you all know Daddy Brazos. That's a .50-caliber Sharps carbine in his hand. Did any of you ever see how big a hole that bullet makes in a man?"

"Only four of you? I told you, I've got a dozen men. So you better come over here, sit down, and listen to what I have to say," Burns raved.

"You ain't got me, Burns," a man at the back of the room called out. "I ain't goin' up against them Fortunes, no matter how many is on our side. I ain't that drunk."

"There's only four of them," Burns shouted.

"Four Fortunes is worth forty of any other breed," another man hollered.

"I ain't standin' with you either, Burns," a broad-shouldered man blustered, his face still smudged from a shift in the mine tunnels. "I got too many leads left to follow and too many trails left to ride. I ain't goin' to git in a fight I cain't win."

Burns paced behind the table like a lawyer pleading with the jury for a guilty verdict. "But he jumped me and my pard from behind in an alley!"

A heavy, dark-skinned man, missing a lower button on his soiled, blue shirt, ambled to the front door. "Maybe folks

HOME

believe that in Dodge City," he called out. "But in Deadwood, Fortunes face you straight up ever' time. Your story don't float with me. I'm goin' to drink somewhere I ain't so liabled to get killed."

Burns scurried around the table, the amber whiskey bottle in his left hand. "What's the matter with you? You lose your sand? You goin' to let this bunch run the town?"

The bartender, looping his thumbs in his soiled, white apron, blurted out from the corner, "I was behind the counter the night that tall Fortune by the front door came in here, buffaloed Cigar Dubois without a scratch, and held the rest of the saloon at bay. You multiply that by four and take 'em on by yourself—well, you'd be the biggest fool to ever set foot in the Piedmont. And believe me, we've had some fools."

"You better watch what you say," Burns screamed. "The last bartender that double-crossed me nearly got his head bashed in, down in Dodge City."

It was like a bolt of lightening hit Sam's neck and flashed to his toes. He took two steps toward the man behind the table. "What do you mean, 'the last bartender'?"

Burns spun around and plopped down in the chair, his back to the wall. "You come sit at my table, and I'll tell you an interestin' story about your old pal Talbert."

Sam stomped to the table. *Not Talbert . . . not with a wife and kids and a picket fence . . . Lord, I'll kill him right here in the chair if he . . .* "What about Talbert?"

Burns pointed to the empty chair across from him. "Sit down. I'm tired of yellin'."

"I'm not sittin' down in front of your shotgun barrel. Even a back-shootin' drunk couldn't miss at that range."

Burns motioned to the group of spectators in the corner. "Come get my shotgun and Fortune's revolver. We'll jist talk about this for a minute. I ain't totin' a side arm."

A gray-haired man with wrinkled face and eyes almost whiskied shut, shuffled over to the table and retrieved the shotgun. Sam pulled his revolver but tossed it to Todd, who continued his vigilance at the front door.

"You ain't very trustin' of nobody, are you?" Burns challenged.

"I've got three men in this room that I'd trust with my life any day of the week. How many do you have?"

Burns looked up and bit his lip. "You made a point with that, Fortune." He laced his fingers behind the back of his head. "Now, sit down, and I'll tell you about your pal Talbert. There ain't nobody in Dodge who will stick up for you again, that's for sure."

Sam studied the wild-eyed man for a moment. *Lord, I've already made up my mind to kill him if anything's happened to Talbert. I haven't even been in town a day, and everything's spinnin' out of control. Maybe it's good that Todd has my gun, providin' I don't beat Burns to death with a chair.*

"You goin' to sit down or not?" Burns demanded.

"I can hear fine right here."

"Well, I ain't talkin' unless you sit down and put your hands above the table. I ain't havin' you draw no sneakgun on me. Or maybe you don't care about how much Talbert's wife was bawlin' that day."

Sam fought the urge to lunge at Burns. Instead he threw himself into the wooden chair, ground his teeth, and folded his arms across his chest.

In unison, three shots blasted across the saloon.

One from the front door.

Two from the back door, one of which sounded like a canon.

All three ripped into the ceiling above Sam's head.

HOME

Startled, he shoved back.

The chair fell over.

He tumbled to the middle of the sticky floor.

A shotgun blasted from a peephole in the second floor.

The chair shredded.

Todd, Brazos, and Robert fired another round into the ceiling.

Someone upstairs screamed and cursed.

Burns reached to his boot.

Sam dove at the table and slammed it against the outlaw's neck, pinning him to the wall.

Todd tossed him his revolver then shouted, "You and Daddy take that one; me and Bobby will get the one upstairs!"

Gasping for breath when Sam released the table, Burns pleaded, "Don't let him kill me, boys. Don't let him kill me!"

Gray-white, acrid tasting gunsmoke drifted across the room in silent response.

"Give me my shotgun!" Burns screamed.

The gray-haired man dropped the shotgun at his own feet. "Come and get it. I ain't takin' sides."

"What's the matter with all of you?" Burns hollered. "He's goin' to shoot me down!"

"That's usually what happens when you try to ambush someone," the bartender said.

Sam took a step closer and aimed the revolver at Burns's head . He was only two feet away.

The bartender stepped over to the busted chair. "Fortune, do you mind takin' him out to the alley, so I don't have to scrub blood off the wall?"

Sam holstered his gun and clenched his fist. *Not today, Burns— I will not kill you today! This is li'l sis's day, and I'm not going to muddy it.*

☞ ☞ ☞

The shots fired into the abandoned second floor of the Piedmont had exploded the wood flooring into a barrage of flying chips. Doc Hetcher spent a half hour plucking splinters out of McDermitt's face and backside. Then, Sheriff Seth Bullock locked both outlaws in the Lawrence County Jail.

The clouds that lined the Gulch all day had drifted east. The stars blinked open one at a time like bears stretching after a long winter's hibernation. In a mostly clear Dakota night, all four Fortune men slipped back onto the porch of the Merchant's Hotel. Inside, the fiddle band played a waltz. Dacee June spied them first.

"All right, just where have you been? I felt like my family totally deserted me." She scurried over and slipped her arm in her father's, her waist-length, brown wavy hair was braided in white ribbons down her back.

Brazos peeked through the window into the ballroom. "Your family is a husband with a tight shirt collar and a wide grin, who happens to be dancin' with Thelma Speaker, bless his soul."

Dacee June stooped to glance through the white lace curtains then faced the men on the porch. "Well, I know when I've been kicked out of the nest." She feigned a pout.

"Did you ever know a girl who could curl her lip better than li'l sis?" Brazos teased.

"There are certainly some things I won't miss!" she declared.

"Does this mean we don't have to spoil her rotten anymore?" Todd laughed.

Dacee June folded her white silk-sleeved arms across her chest and prowled across the porch. "Spoiled, am I?"

HOME

"Don't take it personally," Robert said. "Spoiling always looked good on you, li'l sis. "But now, Carty can do the spoiling, and we don't have to."

"Well, Sammy is still spoilin' me!" she purred as she slipped over and kissed his cheek. "You should see the silk dressing gown he bought me. It cost thirty-five dollars and it makes me the most elegant woman in the Black Hills. Jamie Sue and Rebekah said so! Columbia said she has never seen a more luxurious gown—and she ought to know."

"Well, these rich, telephone exchange company men have more money to toss around than a simple army captain," Robert joshed.

"If you divide that over twelve years of missed birthdays and Christmases, it's mighty stingy." Sam slipped his arm around Dacee June's shoulder and held her tight. *I can't remember the last time I held a grown woman I wasn't makin' a pass at.* He sighed and shook his head. "Besides, I earned ever' penny of that thirty-five dollars. I sold a stallion that bucked me off fourteen times. That devil pinned me against the gate at the sale yard and bit my shoulder. I should have shot him right then and there. I shed blood for the money to buy that gown."

"It's the most beautiful gown in North America!" she boasted as she slipped her arm around Sam's waist. "Although, having Sammy here is the most wonderful gift I could have gotten. The gown is just an extra blessing. I can't believe you bought it for me. I never thought I'd ever own anything so majestically royal. I'm going to feel like a queen every time I wear it!"

"You are the queen," Todd asserted.

"Big brother's right," Robert added. "You'll always be queen of the Fortune clan, no matter what your last name."

Suddenly Dacee June swung around, buried her head in Sam's chest, and sobbed.

Robert stepped closer. "What did I say?" Brazos and Todd also huddled near her.

"Dacee June?" Sam asked as he rocked her back and forth, "What's the matter, sis?"

"I'm not the queen . . . I'm only the princess," she whimpered.

"What?" Todd said.

"Mama's the queen. She'll always be the queen . . . to Daddy . . . to you boys . . . to me." Tears streamed down her face. She peeked at her brothers. "I wish she could have been here at my wedding."

Brazos turned away from the others and shuffled down the steps toward the street.

"Oh Daddy, I'm sorry . . . ," Dacee June cried out. "I'm sorry. I didn't mean to make you melancholy."

Brazos Fortune turned back. Tears cut across his tanned, wrinkled cheeks. "Darlin', there ain't nothin' wrong with missin' your mama. And I don't want a one of you to ever stop missin' her. You know I never will. Dacee June, this has been the most beautiful wedding I've ever seen. But I think maybe I need to go up to the house for a while. I've had a big day. I'll expect to see you three boys at the store in the mornin'—and I don't expect to see you, young lady, for a week!"

"Good night, Daddy," she called out. "I love you."

Brazos nodded his head and wiped back a few more tears. "Good night, darlin'. I love you too. I'm goin' to miss that sweet voice of yours in the mornin'."

All four watched him shuffle across the street.

"It's tough to see him gettin' old," Todd mumbled.

Sam shook his head. "He didn't seem old down at the Piedmont."

"He lives for moments like those," Robert added.

HOME

"The Piedmont? What were you doing down in the badlands?" Dacee June pressed.

"Don't go blabbin' to Rebekah, but we visited with a couple old acquaintances of Sam's," Todd explained.

Dacee June's eyes grew wide. "Are they dead?"

"Nope," Robert answered, "but they are in jail."

"The four of you took them on? I should have been there!" Dacee June complained, "Why didn't you come get me? But, I don't have my gun. They said it was bad luck to carry a gun in your wedding dress. I could have stopped by the store and picked up the shotgun. Then I could have—" She glanced down at her long wedding dress, then looked up at the evening sky. "I'm twenty-one years old, and I still sound like a twelve-year-old, don't I?"

"You sound like our li'l sis," Todd said. "You'll never have to explain that to the three of us."

"I think I'm just nervous. That's why I'm so emotional."

"Everyone's nervous on their wedding day," Robert assured her. "You remember how I went for that long walk, and Todd had to come find me on my wedding day?"

"I'm more than nervous," Dacee June admitted. "I'm scared to death."

"About being married? Bein' on your own? Settin' up housekeepin'? Preparin' to have children some day—and all those things that happen after a couple marries?" Todd asked.

Dacee June bit her lip and stared down at the porch. "No. I'm scared to death about what will happen in bed tonight after we turn out the lantern."

Sam glanced over at his brothers then back at Dacee June. "Now we're all really missin' Mama, li'l sis."

Dacee June stepped to the rail and stared across the street at the gas light that illuminated the front of the hardware. "Not as much as Daddy does. This must be tough on him. I've got Carty now. Todd has Rebekah. Bobby has Jamie Sue. Sammy has Abby. But he doesn't have—"

"Wait, wait . . . wait! What do you mean, I have Abby? I just met the lady this afternoon. I don't even know her," Sam protested.

Dacee June brushed down the front of her white, silk dress. "Well, you like her, don't you?"

"I hardly know the woman." Sam could feel his neck get hot. "And she doesn't know me at all! Don't you start tryin' to control my life."

"Sammy, absolutely no one—including the Lord—ever controlled your life," Todd challenged.

Sam pushed his hat back and ran his hand through his sandy blond and gray hair. "That part is goin' to change."

"Well, it's too late for you to back out." Dacee June laced her fingers together and held them at her waist. Her eyes danced, "We have all decided you two should be together, and that's that."

"Oh? Who's we?" He eyed Robert and Todd. "Are you two in on this railroad?"

"Shoot, no," Robert grinned. "We tried to tell them that Abigail's too good for you, that she could do better. But they wouldn't listen to reason."

"Rebekah, Jamie Sue, and I decided you and Abby would make a perfect couple," Dacee June announced.

Sam rubbed the back of his neck. "Did you ask Abby about that?"

Dacee June held her nose high. "What difference does that make? I'm sure you two will see it our way, in time."

"If you remember," Sam insisted, "I never did cotton much to being manipulated."

HOME

"That's simply because you have never in your life had to deal with the strong wills of three women at the same time." She addressed her other brothers, "Todd, you and Robert be honest: If Rebekah, Jamie Sue, and I set our hearts on something, will it happen or not?"

Robert shook his head, "Sammy, you haven't got a chance in the world."

"Bobby's right," Todd concurred. "You can't even get out of this by shootin' yourself, because those three would pray you back from the dead."

"I can't believe this. I show up after twelve years of bein' gone and my family wants to marry me off the first day."

"How old are you, Sam Fortune?" Dacee June interrogated.

"I'm thirty-four. You all know that."

"Have you been, or are you now, married?"

"Of course not."

"Well, you obviously are not doing very well on your own and need all the help you can get," Dacee June said.

"I don't need all the help on the same day."

"We have to make up for lost time," she insisted. "We decided the relationship needs to be accelerated, or Daddy will never live long enough to see your children."

"Now you're gettin' personal."

"So, to help move things right along," Dacee June announced, "Mrs. Speaker is going to baby-sit Amber tonight so you and Abby can be together."

"What? Tonight? It's . . . it's late."

"Well, it's your own fault for wandering down to the badlands," Dacee June countered.

"Does Abby know about these plans?"

"Not yet." Dacee June pushed him toward the street. "we thought you should go down to her place to surprise her."

"But . . . but . . . I don't believe this!"

Todd threw his arm around Sam's shoulder and escorted him down to the street. "Welcome home, Sammy!"

☞ ☞ ☞

Abigail Gordon stood on the boardwalk in the night shadows when Sam Fortune drove the carriage up in front of the dress shop. He climbed down and offered her a hand.

"Good evenin', again, Mrs. Gordon."

"Good evening to you, Mr. Fortune." She climbed up into the black leather, one-horse carriage.

He climbed up beside her and lifted the lead lines, but he hesitated to drive off. "Abby, do you feel as awkward about this as I do?"

She had a black, lace shawl across the shoulders of her purple dress. "Awkward, and rather amused."

"If you don't want to go for a ride and supper this evenin', I'll understand completely. I had forgotten how pushy my family can be," he admitted.

Even in the night shadows he could see her dark eyebrows raise. "Sam Fortune, if you're looking for a way to get out of this, just say so. I will not be offended if—"

"Me? No, I'm not lookin' to back away. I just didn't want you to think that—"

"You don't have to explain a thing. Just nod and I'll go back to my apartment and . . ." She started to climb down.

He reached over and tugged on her arm. "Wait. Perhaps we should drive around for a short while, just to make them happy."

HOME

Abby sat back down. "Yes, well . . . Amber adores having Mrs. Speaker babysit. Ever since my mother moved back to Omaha, Thelma has taken over the grandmother chores."

Sam slapped the lead lines. The carriage lunged out into the street.

"Where are we headed, Mr. Fortune?" A pothole jarred the carriage, and she clutched Sam's arm.

"With this relationship or our carriage?" he probed.

"Both," she laughed.

"I hear there's a nice French restaurant in Central City. It's only three miles up the creek. Why don't we go there for a late supper?"

The street smoothed out, but she continued to clutch his arm. "That sounds delightful.

"A slow, French dinner will give us some time to talk. What are we going to discuss?" she asked.

When they rolled past the last street lamp he no longer saw her face, but he smelled her sweet rose perfume and felt the warmth of her shoulder pressing against his arm. "I think I should tell you about the two men who showed up at the Piedmont to kill me today and why there's liable to be a steady stream just like them in the days to come. As you can imagine, it makes for a precarious life." Sam fought the urge to slip his hand around her waist. "What would you like to talk about?"

"I think I should tell you how I took my daughter and deserted my doctor husband in Chattanooga to became an actress . . . and how I still have men show up at my door thinking I'm selling something besides dresses."

He peered through the dark at her green eyes, then grinned. "This is crazy, isn't it?"

"Totally insane," she concurred.

"Do you do insane things often?" he quizzed.

"Constantly."

"Are you nervous?" he asked.

"No. Should I be?"

"No, ma'am." He let out a long, slow breath. "Should I be nervous?"

"Perhaps, Samuel Fortune . . . perhaps you should."

☞ ☞ ☞

The sky was mine-shaft black, and stars canopied the Black Hills by the time they reached Central City. A round, Dakota moon ushered them into Zachary Jacque's. A short, bald waiter led them to the privacy of a back table.

The conversation remained light through the first three courses, but then Abigail drew her knife through her garlic-stuffed shrimp with white wine sauce. "I have another question for you, Sam Fortune."

"Yes, ma'am. I've pelted you with a million of them. I reckon I need to answer a few myself."

"You arrived in Deadwood right after noon, rented a room, then were the surprise guest at your sister's wedding. You reconciled with your father and brothers after a dozen years, then stood down two men who tried to ambush you. Now, you're up the Gulch having an expensive supper with a woman you never met before today—a woman whom your sister and sisters-in-law insist is the right one for you to marry."

Sam kept his eyes on his china plate, arrayed with young asparagus stocks smothered in cheese sauce. "Yep, I reckon that sums it up." Then he glanced straight into her eyes. "What's your point?"

"Is this a normal day for you, Sam Fortune?"

"Absolutely not."

HOME

"I'm glad to hear that." She popped a bite of shrimp into her mouth.

"Normally, I don't eat green slimy things for supper. But all the rest is about typical."

Abigail laughed. "My life, especially since I retired from the theater, has been quite routine. And I absolutely love it. I have a store to operate, a daughter to raise, a church to serve, and some dear friends—most of whom have the last name Fortune—to laugh and cry with. I have a past I'd like to forget and a future that's totally unknown, but in God's hands. One of the things that troubles me about you and me furthering our acquaintance is that you will be quite bored with my lifestyle. I know you've been on the prowl for years."

"That doesn't mean I don't want to quit." He forked a bite of asparagus, then returned it to his plate. "I told you about Mr. Rocklin, remember? Well, I made up my mind in Dodge City, that I would just settle down and spend the rest of my life on the ranch. I'm tired of sleepin' on the ground, havin' to listen ever' night for those creepin' up on me. I'm tired of sittin' against the back wall of a cafe, inspectin' ever'one who walks through the door. And I'm really tired of tryin' to push the Lord out of my life."

Abigail brushed a strand of her dark, curly hair from her eyes and leaned forward. "If you didn't tell me these things, who would you tell?"

"No one."

"That's why you're talking to me," Abigail insisted.

"But we haven't known each other but eight hours."

She glanced up at the Roman-numeraled clock that hung over the double doors that led from the dining room to the entry. "Ten hours and fifteen minutes," she corrected. "Sam, sometimes we need someone besides family to talk to. And you haven't even had family for years." She wiped her full lips with a white linen napkin then folded her hands in her lap. "I've been honest with you. I'm purposely trying to live a quiet, peaceful life. It might seem totally tedious to you. Now, it's your turn. What worries you most about allowing our relationship to deepen?"

He laid down his knife and fork and stared at his half-eaten walnut and honey stuffed pork chop.

Abby took a sip of water from a crystal goblet. "Did I ask the wrong question?" she finally probed.

He brushed a few croissant crumbs from his gray, wool vest. "No. I just don't know where to begin. I enjoy your company. I feel relaxed, like I don't have to hide my past or try to rationalize the sinful things I've done. I believe the Lord has forgiven me of my past and will help me live different in the future. But I also believe a man reaps what he sows . . . and I've got a lot of things in the past that will track me down and torment me for the rest of my life."

She sliced off a small bit of bacon-wrapped asparagus and dipped it in the white cheese sauce. "Like those two men this evening at the Piedmont Saloon?"

Sam glanced around the room as if expecting to see someone sneak up on him. "Abby, I've been here half a day, and they found me."

"If they were trailing you up from Cheyenne, I wonder why they didn't ambush you in the woods?"

"They rode up straight from Dodge City. As far as I can tell, they read about Todd in the dime novel and figured I might be related in some way. They were just fishin' about."

Abby ran her tongue across her teeth. "Do you think they'll come after you when they get out of jail?"

"I reckon. Takin' a shot at someone at the Piedmont and missin' him isn't a very serious crime around here. But, they aren't the smartest of men. If they can find me so soon, so will others."

"Everyone in Oklahoma can't hate you."

"Abby, it's a distorted world down in the Nation. Everyone wants to prove how tough they are."

"But you don't live there anymore. You aren't the toughest man down there. Why would they travel this far?"

"That's exactly what I'd like to know from Burns and McDermitt."

"So, you're saying: Stay away from me, Abby Gordon, because I'm liable to end up like Wild Bill Hickok?"

"Abby, do you know what really bothered me about those two at the Piedmont this evening? Todd, Robert, and Daddy's lives were in just as much jeopardy as mine. Can you imagine what it would have been like if Todd had gotten killed because of me? It's the most horrible thing I can think of. I'm a liability to my family. And what if you and me get . . . you know . . . real chummy."

"Chummy?" she cracked a grin and waved her empty silver fork at him. "I don't get chummy without a wedding ring, Mr. Fortune."

"Yes, ma'am—that's what I mean. What if we were married and some drifter comes up this way and decides to get famous by shootin' me, but he's so drunk he hits you . . . or Amber instead? It's so horrible I can't even think about it."

For several moments Abby O'Neill gazed across the nearly empty cafe. Then she took a deep breath and let it out slowly. "I appreciate your thinking of Amber and me. But, what does this all mean? What are your alternatives? Do you plan on moving to a cave and shooting anyone who approaches?"

"Abby, there's nothin' I can do to keep someone from sneakin' up and takin' a shot at me. But maybe if I act smart, I can keep them from shootin' others close to me. I've got to do that much."

"Does that mean you're leaving Deadwood?" she asked.

"It's crazy, isn't it? On the day I arrive and reconcile, I'm thinkin' about leavin'. My family would blindly ask me to stay. But I need an additional opinion. What do you think I ought to do?"

She unfastened the top button on the high collar of her dress and fanned herself. "Give it two weeks. Didn't you say you'd need at least that much time to canvass the area about a telephone exchange?"

"Yes. That project seems to have been shoved aside."

"Dacee June has gone on a honeymoon for a week. Robert and Jamie Sue and kids are headed back to Arizona. Rebekah and her brood are tucked safely up on Forest Hill. Todd's tied to the store, and your father . . . well, I just don't imagine Daddy Brazos will be highly concerned about saddle tramps and bushwhackers. Perhaps today was the aberration, not the rule."

"How about Mrs. Abigail Gordon and her precocious daughter? My presence in one of her rental rooms might present a dangerous threat."

"Why don't you ask her what she wants you to do?"

"Mrs. Gordon, what do you want me to do?"

She smiled slowly, dropped her chin, and batted her eyes. "I think I want you to move," she spoke very softly.

"You do?" Sam boomed.

She leaned across the table and whispered, "Yes, I think it would be safest for me and my daughter if you didn't live across the hall from us."

Sam felt his heart sink. He leaned across the table until their faces were only inches apart. "Yeah, that's what I was thinkin'. How far away do you think I should move?"

"Across the hall," she whispered.

"What?"

Abby sat up quickly and held her hands out between them. "But, unfortunately, there is no wedding ring on my finger, Mr. Sam Fortune, so you'll just have to stay put in your rental room for now."

"I can't believe you said that!" He felt sweat roll down the back of his flushed neck.

"My, you do have a lot to learn about me. I, too, am over thirty and see no need to be coy. What I'm saying is, stay right there in that rental room, do your telephone exchange work, and let's see what happens. Every day cannot be as exciting nor as threatening as today. I've spent a few hours with Samuel Fortune, brother-of-the-bride, member of a prominent Deadwood family, repentant sinner, and former horse thief. Now I'd like to get to know Samuel Fortune, the businessman."

"I'm afraid I don't know much about being a businessman. Up until now, it's been like playin' poker. I've been pretendin', but now my bluff's been called. I have to produce, and I'm . . ."

"Looking for a trail out of town?" Abby finished.

"Maybe."

"Don't sell yourself short. You obviously convinced Mr. Edgington in Cheyenne of your abilities."

"Actually, that was just kind of a fluke. They talked me into it. I happened to—"

"Would you quit changing the subject?" Abby insisted. "After I brought Amber home from the wedding, I gave this some thought. Have you decided where to establish the telephone exchange office?"

"Office?" Sam ran his fingers through the graying hair swept back over his ears. "I haven't even—"

"Did you know Todd and Rebekah own a vacant building a block down from the hardware? It used to be a hat shop, but the proprietress married a lawyer and they moved to Carson City, Nevada. I'm sure Todd will give you a good deal on rent."

Sam laid down his knife and fork. "The first thing I need to do—"

"Is to establish credibility. Yes, I know that. Having the name Fortune is a good start in Deadwood. Get your sign above the door made, and make sure your last name is prominent. You'll need some business furniture inside: desks, shelves, cabinets—things like that. Daddy Brazos's friend, Quiet Jim, sells furniture over at the lumber mill.

"Then you should set up a couple of sample telephones. You can hook up a short little demonstration line across the room, can't you?"

Sam tugged his tie completely loose and unfastened the top button of his white shirt. "Yeah, I think I can do that. Of course, I'd have to have it shipped up from Cheyenne."

"Have them send it on the stagecoach. The freight wagons are much too slow."

"But I was goin' to wait until I—"

She reached halfway across the table and tapped the thick, white linen tablecloth with her forefinger. "Then get yourself a dynamic office manager to run things while you—"

"Office manager?" he gasped. "I don't even have a company yet."

She sat back against the Genoa, maroon silk velvet of the mahogany-inlaid armchair. "'S. Houston Fortune, co-owner'" she triumphed. "That's the way you should put your name on the sign."

"How did you know my middle name was Houston?"

Her eyes seemed to dance in rhythm with her tongue. "My goodness, I've never known a Texican named Sam who didn't have the middle name of Houston. It's more businesslike. Besides, no old

HOME

outlaw acquaintances will be looking for S. Houston Fortune, businessman. Perhaps you should grow a full beard."

"Why?"

"Because no one from the Indian Territory will be looking for a full beard. Plus, that is what Mr. Bell has. I saw a photograph of him once when I was in St. Louis."

"Who's Mr. Bell?" he asked.

"The man who invented the telephone," she replied.

"Oh—that Mr. Bell. . . ."

She held her slightly clenched fists up in front of her chest as if to assist the words to come out more quickly. "Yes, yes. And then as you call on businesses and homes, you can give them a small printed card, a coupon that provides them with a telephone demonstration at no charge."

"I couldn't charge them for a demonstration, anyways."

"Yes, but they don't know that. Everyone will need a coupon."

"Why?"

"To promote interest, of course. It will make it seem like a special privilege. In fact, you should start passing out the coupons even before the office is open. Make them wait a little while before they get to try it out. Your office manager can take subscriptions as people sample the telephones. That way, when you are out calling on them, you're only asking them to stop by and check it out. It will keep you from seeming like a mere solicitor. If you have the right office manager, it will be quite effective."

"How can I hire an office manager when I don't even have a company yet?"

Abby rattled on as if Sam was not even there. "It will take a special person who is willing to sacrifice in order make the company go."

"Are you volunteering for the job?" he asked.

"Heavens no. I have a business to run. But I do know the perfect person."

"Who?" he asked.

A wide, easy grin broke across Abby's face. "Mrs. Toluca."

Sam's forehead curled. "Carty's mother?"

She shook her head in feigned resignation. "Carty's mother lives in Billings. I'm talking about young Mrs. Toluca, Carty's wife."

"Dacee June?" The name exploded from his lips like an easy word at a spelling bee. "You think li'l sis should be my office manager?"

"She'd be perfect. She knows everyone in the Black Hills on a first name basis, and she's also quite aware of who is related to whom."

"What if she doesn't want to work?" he asked.

"What if she does?"

"What if Todd needs her at the hardware?"

"What if he doesn't?" Abby kept up the pressure.

"But . . . but . . . I . . ." Sam shook his head but no words came out.

Abigail leaned back in her chair and stabbed a cold bite of pastry-encased salmon, baked in the shape of a butterfly. "Oh, of course," she blurted out, "I was just rambling. It's your turn. Now that we've established the fact you can't run away and hide, what are your plans for starting up the business? You have a strategy besides knocking on doors and asking for subscriptions, right?"

Sam stared across the table. *Lord, what am I doin' in this occupation? I don't have any idea what I'm doin'.* A big grin broke across his face. "I'll tell you what," he laughed: "You set up the telephone exchange, and I'll run the dress shop."

"Oh no you don't, S. Houston Fortune. So that's the reason for all of this backpedaling—you haven't been worried about getting shot in the back; you've been worried about starting a telephone business."

"Worried? Scared to death would be a better description."

"What's the worse you could do? Fail?"

"Fail in front of my very successful family," he said.

"Then I suggest you don't fail. I think you should call it the Black Hills Telephone Exchange, rather than Deadwood or Lead. That way, if you need to expand, the name will still be valid. The B.H.T.E. has a very good sound to it. You'll need a snappy little trademark. I know a set designer and mural artist in Omaha that could . . ." She stopped talking and laid her hands in her lap. "What are you staring at?"

Sam ran his fingers across his lips. "A very attractive and multi-talented lady."

"Mr. Fortune, you've never even seen me dance or heard me sing. Almost all people have more talents than they use. I mean, you're good at something besides stealing horses, aren't you?" A sly smile creased her wide, full lips.

"I'm a fair hand at robbin' a stage and specialize in banks. But I always thought kissing attractive women on the lips was one of my best specialties," he concluded.

She laughed until she had to cover her mouth with her hand. "You see, S. Houston Fortune, you are a multitalented man."

"Did you really used to be an actress?"

She raised her eyebrows. "Did you really used to be an outlaw?"

"This is a very strange friendship, Mrs. Gordon."

"Yes, and I believe it will be rather exciting, don't you?"

"I doubt we will be bored."

"Infuriated, angry, delirious, emotional—and wanton if we're not careful—but never bored," she confirmed. "Now, I suggest you get your office all equipped in the next couple days. Have the newspapers write stories about what you're going to do, and open the office the day Dacee June returns from her honeymoon."

"What if she doesn't want to work for me?"

"You don't know your sister very well, do you."

"I don't know any of my family very well, Abigail Katrina O'Neill Gordon."

"You know my full name? I'd say you've talked to Dacee June, too."

"You don't think we just hummed Strauss while we were out on the dance floor, do you?" he chided.

"Did she tell you about my first husband?" she probed.

"Yes, she did. It was quite noble of him to help Mr. Landers, even at the cost of his own life."

"It's the only known noble thing he ever did. Did Dacee June tell you about my second husband?"

Sam jerked back from the table. Then a wide grin broke over him. "Was that the old boy from the Indian Territory with broad shoulders and a devilishly smooth smile?"

"No. He had mostly gray hair and looked out of place in a suit."

"What ever happened to that hombre?" Sam quizzed.

"He went and hid in a cave and was buried by an avalanche."

"I'm sorry to hear that. Of course, I don't have time to go runnin' off to a cave myself—I have to get back to Deadwood and open a telephone exchange office."

"And hire a dynamic office manager?"

"Yes, ma'am."

"Why are you staring at me like that?"

"It just dawned on me that ever since my mother died, I have not had a woman controlling my life. Now, within one day, I have a sister, two sisters-in-law, and an attractive landlady volunteerin' for the job."

HOME

"Are you bragging or complaining, Mr. Fortune?"

"Neither—I'm just stunned. A few weeks ago I was sleepin' under a mesquite tree and wonderin' if there was any way to get a meal without committing a crime. Now look at me: I'm afraid I'm going to wake up from a good dream."

"Sam Fortune," Abigail insisted, "you just woke up from a bad dream . . . twelve years of a very bad dream."

CHAPTER EIGHT

In the office of the Black Hills Telephone Exchange, 675 Main Street, Deadwood, D.T., August 17, 1885, 10:35 A.M.

Dacee June glanced up from her desk as Sam strolled in. A light pink, ironed, linen handkerchief peeked out from the breast pocket of her shirt waist charcoal gray blouse of cotton shirting Cheviot. The cuffs, high collar, and belt were a pink and gray stripe. The puffed sleeves at the shoulder gave her waist an even narrower image as she stood up. "Daddy thinks this whole thing is really wild," she announced.

"That's my style, li'l sis. When did I ever do any thing like ever'one else?" Sam hung his Stetson on the mahogany hat rack near the door and ambled to the polished wood railing that separated his desk from hers.

She spun around to face him. "Daddy says that when you were little you'd watch Todd, then do just the opposite."

Sam leaned against the railing. "If I had my life to do over, it might be different."

HOME

"Would you copy Todd more?"

"Not necessarily." He stared out of the open doors to the street. "But just being contrary isn't a very smart way to live, either. A person needs to think through things. I spent a lot of years not usin' my brain very much."

She reached down and plucked a long, brown hair from the sleeve of her jacket. "How about the past few years?"

He tugged on his shirt collar and nodded. "Yeah, I needed to use my brain a lot—just to stay alive."

"Well, the last few weeks have been the best in my whole life." Still seated in her oak swivel chair, Dacee June turned her back to her brother and looked out the open doors. "I keep thinking it's too good to keep going."

Sam stepped up behind her and began to rub her shoulders and neck. "Which part is so good, li'l sis?"

She reached back and patted his hand. "All of it, Sammy. Did I tell you I really, really like being married?"

He squeezed her fingers. "I think you've mentioned it about ten times a day."

She dropped her chin and her voice, "Carty treats me so nice."

He spun her chair around so that they looked eye to eye. "He'd better, or he'll have some brothers to face."

"Carty's a lot like you three. That's why I picked him, of course. But it's not just being married that's a dream. It's having you show up on my wedding day . . . and now . . . coming down here every day and see you walk in, dressed all handsome-like in a suit and tie. I used to dream about you coming home all the time, but my dreams were never this good." Dacee June plucked up a lead pencil and twirled it in her fingers. "Daddy's right. The whole thing's wild."

"I'll tell you what's wild." Sam pointed over to the telephone units on the oak table next to the south wall. "We have one hundred and twelve telephone subscribers, and we haven't even installed the system yet. Mr. Edgington down in Cheyenne will be quite surprised."

Dacee June grabbed a form off her desk. "One hundred and thirteen. Mr. Wong came in this morning and subscribed."

Sam glanced down at the paper. "Which one is Mr. Wong?"

"Mr. Fee Lee Wong owns the Wing Tsue store and some others," she explained.

Sam brushed back his sandy blond and gray mustache with his fingers. "I thought that Wing Tsue was the man's name."

"No. Look," she pointed to the form, "his name is Fee Lee Wong."

"So, we'll have telephones in China Town?"

"At least one."

"That's good . . . Dacee June, that's the great thing about telephones. Everyone in town can have one—and anyone can talk to anybody, no matter what district you live in. There's total equality!"

Dacee June's mouth was large for the width of her cheeks, but even wider when she smiled, "Where do I sign up, Mr. S. Houston Fortune?"

Sam strolled across the office to a table where a telephone receiving unit was mounted. "I guess I'm gettin' more enthused, as this looks like it might actually work."

"Just a few more . . . critical details. I've been praying about all of it, Sammy."

"Me too, li'l sis. But I seem to keep gettin' into the same argument with the Lord. I keep debatin' whether I'm supposed to sit still and do nothin' or use the brain he gave me and make some decisions on my own."

Dacee June pulled a small hand mirror out of her center desk drawer. "Which side of the debate is right?"

Sam lifted the receiving unit and held it to his ear. There was no sound. "That's one of the things we'll find out soon enough."

"Here comes Professor and Mrs. Edwards!"

Sam turned and waited for the couple to enter the store.

"Morning, Dacee June . . . Sammy," Mr. Grass Edwards greeted as he waited for his wife to lead the way in.

"I believe we should start calling him, Houston," Louise Edwards corrected.

"I've known that boy since he was no taller than *Delphinium occidentale*," Grass answered. "It's going to be hard calling him something else."

"Maybe when all of this settles down, we can dispense with the name change," Sam offered.

"No," Edwards insisted, "change can be good. Look at me, Sammy. For years everyone called me Grass Edwards. But I wrote that book and now it's Professor Edwards. I get much more respect. Even porters on the Pullman cars give me a better berth when they see that word *Professor* on the train ticket."

"Well, Professor Edwards, at least you haven't changed your taste in clothing," Dacee June teased. "I don't know of any other man in the Black Hills that has a bright yellow shirt like that."

"It's not yellow. It's called 'mustard,'" he insisted. "Of course, to me it looks like *Sonchus arvensis*."

"I think he means a perennial sowthistle," Louise Driver Edwards explained.

"That shirt makes you stand out like an *Asteraceae* in a field of *Amaranthaceae*," Dacee June added.

Edward's eyes widened. "Like a sunflower in a field of pigweed? My word, Louise, a college-educated woman is a marvel to listen to!"

"I learned that from you, Mr. Edwards. Remember the time you, me, Yapper Jim, and Daddy got stuck in that tent north of Miles City until the Missouri River quit flooding? You kept us up until midnight for six days reciting that botany book."

He turned to his wife. "Are you sure we can't adopt this girl?"

"No need for that," Louise chided. "You and the others have been treating Dacee June like your own daughter for over twenty years."

"I reckon you're right about that. Well, come on, Louise darlin'," Grass pointed to the far wall. "I'll show you how these telephone receiver units work."

"She knows all about them," Dacee June insisted. "She helped me set up the whole office while you were speaking in Laramie City."

Grass Edwards threw up his hands and shrugged. "Then she can explain them to me. I figure if this is going to work we ought to look busy."

"Just help yourself, Professor," Sam said. "If you figure out how they cram a voice down that wire, maybe you can explain it to me." He retreated past the railing to his desk in the back of the office.

Rebekah wore a stylish black blazer with shawl collar; her vest was faced with Sicilian silk. She swaggered into the room followed by a hatless Todd Fortune.

"Good morning," Rebekah called out as she strolled up to Dacee June and wiped her gray gloves along the edge of the oak desk, then examined her fingertips. "Can I sweep and dust for you?"

"Oh, you don't need to . . . ," Dacee June protested. "I just cleaned everything last night."

HOME

Rebekah held the soiled glove in front of Dacee June. "Nonsense. I want to do something besides wait for the men to settle things." She and Dacee June scooted to the storeroom in the back. They emerged with a feather duster and a frayed cotton rag.

Sam held open the short wooden gate that opened to his desk. "Mornin', big brother."

"Mornin', Sammy." Todd sauntered through and plopped down in a leather side chair. "You ready for a big day?"

Sam sat in his oak swivel chair and reclined, placing his polished boots on the nearly clean desktop. "You know what I was thinkin' this mornin'? I tried to remember why it was I didn't come up here in '76 when I first heard about your movin' up here. And the truth is, Todd, I can't remember why I was so dead set against it."

"Still fightin' the war, maybe."

"I suppose Daddy was right. We couldn't win, and it only made things worse in Texas."

"Did you ever tell him that?" Todd challenged.

"No, but I will."

"I think that will be good for him to hear," Todd encouraged.

"I know I have a lot of things I ought to say. I'll have to trust the Lord will give me time to say them all."

"You worried?"

"The Lord's been so good to me over the past two months, Todd. Sometimes I feel guilty askin' him for anything else."

"Enjoy it," Todd encouraged. "Some days it's a struggle to get by. Other times it's kind of like blessings are 'good measure, pressed down, shaken together and running over.'"

"Amazing grace . . . ," Sam murmured, "amazing grace."

"Say, I got a letter from Bobby down in Arizona." Todd sat up and tugged his revolver from his vest holster. "Says that since you're here in the Black Hills, he and Jamie Sue are talking about getting mustered out after they round up Geronimo again, then moving up." He checked the chambers and then shoved the pistol back into his holster.

"That will make a lot of Fortunes in the Black Hills," Sam said. He slid open the two top drawers of the desk and scanned the walnut-gripped Colt .44s.

Todd slowly rubbed his long hawkish nose and nodded. "I don't know if Bobby wants to live right in Deadwood. There's some rim-rock country on the back road to Rapid City. If a man wanted a little solitude and a nice little spread, that would be the place to settle."

Sam kept a close watch on the front door of the store. "You figure Jamie Sue for a ranch girl?"

"No. But she's followed Robert from fort to fort. She's no more a ranch girl than Rebekah."

"Or Abigail?"

Todd rubbed his light brown goatee. "I don't suppose you've asked that lady to marry you?"

"Not until the dust settles. I don't want to sound dramatic, but there really are too many nightmares from the past following me."

Todd watched Rebekah and Dacee June as they flittered around cleaning the mostly empty office. "I figure that's Abby's decision."

"If it is, then she deserves to see the whole picture before she decides. Anyways, if things go bad today it won't matter much what I think, will it?"

Quiet Jim rolled his wheelchair through the big, double, glass and oak front doors that were propped open by two, black iron, miniature beaver statues. Behind him, toting his Sharps carbine, walked Brazos Fortune.

HOME

Sam stood up and strolled to the railing that separated his desk from Dacee June's. "Don't tell me you got tired of tellin' windy stories over at the hardware?" he teased the two gray-haired men.

"Is this lad castin' suspicion on the veracity of our past accounts?" Brazos replied as he leaned the carbine against the wall next to the front door then ambled toward his sons.

"It's a sad commentary on the present generation," Quiet Jim added as he rolled along beside Brazos. "The day will come when no one believes the truth, and they will rewrite the history of this land for their own benefit. But with any luck, Brazos, you and me won't be here to see it. Progress does not guarantee improvement."

"Whoa—this old man's beginnin' to sound like Yapper Jim," Brazos chided.

Quiet Jim's eyes blurred as he stared back over the years. His voice softened, "You know, I actually miss that loud mouth of his."

"I know what you mean." Brazos cracked a smile. "The world always seemed so quiet and peaceful when he stopped talkin'."

"Sort of like when the stamp mill shuts down for repairs and a man can hear his own heart beat," Quiet Jim added.

Brazos and Quiet Jim moseyed over to the telephone receiving equipment on the table against the south wall.

Todd sauntered up next to Sam. "Think I'll go over and show Grass how he can ring Daddy and Quiet Jim," he said.

Sam fixed his eyes on the older woman peeking in the front door. "Hard to imagine those old Texans usin' a telephone."

"Everything in Deadwood's different," Todd remarked. "Look at you and me, wearing store bought suits like prominent businessmen."

"You and Daddy are prominent businessmen," Sam said. "For the time being, I'm just a notorious businessman." He ambled to the front of the store. "Mrs. Speaker, that's a very charming hat you have on."

The gray-haired woman's hand went to her red-rouged cheek. "Oh, this old majorie with buttercup wreath? Well, yes, I do enjoy it, Samuel."

Sam peered into the wicker basket looped over her arm. "Have you been shopping?"

"Just apples. A man has a wagon full, down in front of city hall. He had them shipped all the way to Miles City by train, then he freighted them in." Thelma Speaker scooted past Sam and meandered over to Louise Edwards.

"Hello!" Grass shouted into the little, round, black receptacle. "Can you hear me?"

"I could hear you if you were up on Mount Moriah," Brazos hollered into the other unit on the other side of the room.

"Talk softly!" Sam instructed. "Try whispering." He pulled out a pocket watch and studied the gold hands. *OK, Lord. It's 11:00* A.M.

A triple-tandem freight wagon pulled by twelve mules was parked in the middle of Main Street. Mert Hart's fancy, closed carriage trotted by, pulled by a matching pair of coal black horses. A man with silk top hat and cane scurried by Sam. On the distant side of the street, Sheriff Bullock tipped his hat, then pointed back to the west—and kept riding.

☞ ☞ ☞

The top right drawer on Sam's uncluttered desk was open several inches and he was leaning back in the oak chair when Burns and McDermitt burst through the door, fired a pistol toward the ceiling, and shouted, "You're a dead man, Sam Fortune! We got the drop on you this time!"

HOME

Rebekah screamed.

Thelma Speaker dropped her basket of apples, which rolled across the floor like field mice scurrying for cover.

Louise Edwards fainted into the arms of her husband.

Brazos stalked toward his abandoned carbine.

Quiet Jim rolled his wheelchair back behind the telephone display.

Dacee June, seated in her chair when the two burst in, dove under her desk.

Todd slipped a hand inside his coat pocket.

"Don't try it!" With a face pack-marked from splintered wood, McDermitt screamed at Todd. "We ain't above shootin' the women as well as the men, so keep your hands out where we can see them." He spun around and pointed his gun at the approaching Brazos Fortune. "Stay right there, old man, or you'll be the first Fortune to die today!"

Sam stood and inched his fingers toward the top drawer of his desk. "You two on a lunch break from jail?" he called out.

Burns's round, gold earrings made his face look long. "Ain't no Deadwood jail goin' to keep us for long." He kept his revolver pointed at Sam Fortune.

Sam leaned forward slowly so he could lower his hand into the drawer. "You boys are only makin' it worse. You'll get another five years for bustin' out. I hear that prison over in Yankton is a sorry hole in the ground."

"They got to catch us first, and ain't no one will find us once we get back into the Indian Territory," Burns screamed.

"Then why are you wastin' time in this store?" Todd challenged. "Sheriff Bullock will stop you before you leave town. You'll be carrying lead before you cross the deadline."

"I don't think so. He'll be too busy investigatin' a murder." Burns rubbed his wide, flushed nose with the back of his free hand. He stalked toward Dacee June's desk while pointing his revolver at Sam Fortune. "You are goin' for a little walk out into the alley with us!"

"If you couldn't pull it off when you planned it down at the Piedmont, you certainly can't do it now. There are too many of us," Sam challenged. "This is insane." His hand slipped down into the drawer and surrounded the cold, polished walnut grip of the .44 revolver.

"Head to the alley, Fortune. That's where you like to bushwhack people, and that's where you're goin' to get what's comin' to you. But you're goin' to get an arm and a leg busted before you get a bullet in the brain." McDermitt, still nursing a limp, faltered toward Brazos.

Just as Burns drew even with the desk, Dacee June leaped up and jammed a pistol into his ribs. "Drop it, mister!"

He spun around and grabbed her wrist. The gun she held exploded, ripping splinters in the flooring near his feet.

Sam pulled out the revolver and pointed it at Burns.

Thelma Speaker clutched her breast and sank to her knees, "My heart . . . it's like a vise is squeezing it!"

Rebekah ran to her side.

McDermitt pointed his revolver at Todd.

Burns yanked Dacee June's hair out of its combs and spun her around between him and the others, his revolver jammed into her temple.

"Put those guns down, or this girl is dead!" he screamed.

"Both of you are goin' to die in this store unless you release li'l sis," Sam hollered. "That's a fact!"

HOME

"We won't be the only ones dead, Sam Fortune!" Burns yanked her hair back and shoved the barrel into her ear.

Dacee June began to sob, "Don't let them kill me, Sammy!"

"I mean it!" Burns hollered. "Put your guns down and back away."

Quiet Jim rolled his wheelchair out from behind the telephone equipment. He lifted a short-nosed revolver at the gunman holding Dacee June. He didn't hesitate to pull the trigger.

The bullet caught the brim of Burns's hat, and sailed it to the floor. McDermitt spun around and fired at Quiet Jim. His crippled body was flung so violently against the back of the chair, it toppled backward. His motionless body sprawled out on the floor.

Rebekah screamed.

Thelma Speaker, still clutching her heart, fell facedown on the floor.

Dacee June bawled.

Brazos lunged at McDermitt, but the armed gunman stepped aside. He grabbed Brazos's collar and shoved the barrel of his revolver into Brazos's back.

Todd and Sam, guns still drawn, stalked the two hostage-holding gunmen.

"You're both dead!" Sam yelled.

"There's going to be a roomful of dead if you don't put those guns down!" Burns screamed. "We ain't got nothin' to lose, Fortune. You do."

"Shoot 'em, boys," Brazos hollered. "Send them off to hades where they belong!"

"I don't want to die," Dacee June cried out. "I just got married. . . . I don't want to die, Daddy!"

"Grass, you got a gun?" Sam called out, not taking his eyes off Burns.

"In my hand," Edwards replied.

"If either of them is left standing after me and Todd pull our triggers, shoot them," Sam insisted.

"This ain't good, Burns," McDermitt mumbled.

"Stay right there!" Burns cried. "If you don't put those guns down, I swear the old man and the girl are dead. There ain't no way we're goin' to miss from this distance!"

"They already killed Quiet Jim. Shoot them! I'm ready to meet my Maker," Brazos prodded.

"I don't want to die, Sammy!" Dacee June sobbed. "Please . . . please don't let them shoot me!"

Sam Fortune glanced at Todd, then back at Dacee June. He dropped his revolver on the desk.

"What are you doin'?" Todd hollered at him.

"Put it down, Todd . . . ," Sam replied. "It's not workin' like I thought. Put it down."

"I'm not going to let them shoot you," Todd insisted.

"Better me than Daddy and Dacee June. It's all my fault, anyway."

"Shoot them, Todd," Brazos screamed. "Shoot them!"

"No!" Dacee June cried.

Todd dropped his weapon.

"And the one in the yellow shirt, too!" McDermitt called out.

Grass Edwards slid his gun across the wooden floor.

"I'm here . . . unarmed," Sam hollered. "Turn them loose, and shoot me."

"We got a meetin' in the alley!" Burns snarled. "You ain't dyin' until them bones is broken."

"Turn them loose, and I'll go," Sam insisted.

"You ain't got no say in it. Get goin'!" Burns pointed to the storeroom door.

HOME

"If you aren't goin' to turn loose of them, I might as well die right here!" Sam asserted.

"Then 'li'l sis' will die with you!"

Dacee June wailed.

"Wait!" Sam screamed. "I'm goin'. . . ."

Amber Gordon sprinted into the store and shouted, "Where's my mother? Have you seen my mother?"

"Amber, get out of here!" Rebekah shrieked.

Amber raced toward Dacee June's desk. "But I've got to find my mother!" she sobbed.

"Get her over by the wall," Burns yelled.

Rebekah motioned with her arms. "Come on, honey. Come over here by me!"

"No!" Amber cried. "My mama's in trouble. She drank a whole bunch of laudanum and said she was going to get even with that scoundrel, Sam Fortune."

"Out the back door, Fortune!" Burns shouted.

Rebekah slowly crossed the room and knelt down by Amber. "What do you mean, 'get even' with Sam?"

"I'm goin' out the door," Sam said. "Are you two comin', or are you goin' to let me run down the alley?"

"Mama said he grabbed her in the middle of the night and beat her up and compromised her . . . ," Amber sobbed. "What does *compromise* mean?"

Amber pulled away and started to run at Sam, but Rebekah lassoed her with her arms and held her as she kicked and screamed, "What did he do to my mother?"

"Don't worry, kid. We'll take care of him for you," Burns hollered as he stalked to the back of the room, pushing Dacee June ahead of him.

"Sam Fortune!" a woman at the front door screamed.

All, including the gunmen, spun around to see a barefoot Abigail Gordon stagger into the room. Her hair was matted. The flower-print dress was ripped. Dried blood was smeared across her arm and neck.

"Abby!" Rebekah cried and struggled to her feet. "What happened?"

"Sam Fortune can tell you what happened!" Abigail Gordon grabbed the Sharps carbine by the door and marched straight toward Dacee June's desk.

"Put down that gun, lady!" McDermitt demanded.

"Why? Are you going to shoot me? There are worse things. A lot worse things." Abby threw the carbine to her shoulder and pointed it at Sam Fortune.

"Shoot her!" Burns ordered McDermitt.

"She ain't pointin' it at me," McDermitt hollered.

"What's this all about, Sammy?" Brazos demanded.

"She didn't complain last night," Sam mumbled.

"You dastardly rogue!" Abigail shrieked, then cocked the massive trigger.

"Wait, lady!" Burns screamed.

"Mama, don't . . . ," Amber cried, breaking free from Rebekah and running toward her mother.

The blast of the .50-aliber carbine rattled the front windows of the telephone exchange.

Abigail Gordon stumbled back toward the open doorway.

Sam Fortune tumbled back over his desk chair, landing with a thud at the base of the blood-splattered wall.

Dacee June pulled away and sprinted to her brother's side, sobbing, "No! . . . No! . . . No!"

"She done killed him!" McDermitt released Brazos's collar.

HOME

Abigail let the heavy, single-shot gun fall to the floor and collapsed to her knees and cried, "Shoot me . . . for mercy sake . . . somebody kill me!"

"This is crazy," Burns shouted. "In ten minutes ever'one in the room will be dead!"

"I'm leavin', Burns!" McDermitt bolted through the back door.

As he sprinted to catch up, the gold-earringed Burns pointed his revolver at Sam's body. Dacee June dove out of the way, just as the shot exploded. "He's dead now—that's for sure!"

As if stunned into immobility, everyone in the room froze in place.

There was no movement.

No cries.

No moans.

Just the lingering cloud of gunsmoke.

Then, the stomp of boot heels at the door. Sheriff Seth Bullock poked his head into the building.

"Are you all done? I've got half the town lined up down the block wantin' to know what's goin' on!"

Brazos picked up his carbine and helped Abby to her feet. "Are those two bushwhackers out of town?"

The sheriff pushed his hat back and rubbed his long drooping, gray mustache. "They ought to be halfway to Sturgis by now. We tied fast horses in the alley. Someone owes the Montana Livery one hundred and ten dollars for them nags and saddles."

"It's a bargain," Brazos said.

Dacee June leaped up from Sam's side. "How did I do, Abby? I think I did the screaming and crying very well. But, I got my new blouse dirty when I crawled under the desk." She reached down her hand to her brother. "Did I do all right, Sammy?"

He sat up and studied the red substance on his hand and shirt. "What is this stuff, Abby? It sure makes a mess."

She walked toward the back of the room. "It's a combination of pureed tomatoes and beet juice. We used it often on the stage."

"Would someone give me a hand!" Quiet Jim called out from the far wall.

Brazos began to applaud. The others laughed and joined in the clapping.

"Very funny! That's not what I had in mind," Quiet Jim mumbled as the roar died down. "Help me back up to my chair."

"I do believe Quiet Jim's expert shooting and his tumbling backward in the wheelchair was the premiere act!" Rebekah informed. "At that point, we had believers out of both of them."

"You'll never know how tempted I was to move that over a few inches," Quiet Jim remarked.

"I wish I could have seen the first part," Amber pouted. "I wanted to peek in the window, but Mother said we had to stay out of sight."

"Some of us weren't given very big parts," Grass Edwards complained.

"And some, dear sister, added quite liberally to the script," Louise Edwards scolded as she brushed off her long, black skirt.

Thelma began to retrieve her apples. "I thought the fruit rolling across the floor and the heart attack added a little extra flair. And I've always been quite good at heart attacks."

"No one but intellectually deficit outlaws would have believed your performance," Louise said.

"Now, now, dear sister," Thelma soothed, "you and the professor did quite well. Remember, there are no small parts in a

HOME

successful drama. I thought Abigail's script was very good, very good indeed."

"And I think your costume was a little much," Sam complained as he walked over to Abby. "You were so convincing, I was ready to shoot myself for bein' such a villain."

Abby looked down at her ripped dress. "This was a little overboard, wasn't it," Abby admitted. "I suppose I've done too many melodramas."

"I think the whole thing was dangerous," Sheriff Bullock surmised. "I don't intend to let you do something this foolhardy again! What if they had checked those guns and put in real bullets instead of blanks?"

"Then plaster would have splattered from the ceiling on the first shot," Brazos reported. "Those two were too dumb to even look up."

"Well, Daddy Brazos's Sharps kicks a wallop, even with a blank," Abby complained, rubbing her shoulder. "I'll have a bruise for a week."

"Did I do all right, Mama?" Amber scooted over to her mother.

"You were wonderful, dear—but no, I'm not going to let you be an actress when you grow up."

"Not even in Dacee June's Christmas plays?"

"You can act in Dacee June's plays again, but that's all."

"You really think this will work?" Sheriff Bullock challenged.

"Within two weeks ever'one in the Indian Territory will know that Sam Fortune was killed by a wronged woman in Deadwood," Sam reported, then looked at the others in the room. "And I am ashamed to admit it; most folks down there will have a very easy time believing it."

Louise Edwards emerged from the back room and handed Sam a wet towel. "I don't know about the rest of you," she announced, "but I've had quite a morning. I think I'll adjourn to write in my journal."

"I'll be along shortly," Grass informed her.

"Professor Edwards, I expect you to walk me home—now!" she insisted.

"Eh . . . yes ma'am." Edwards adjusted his round hat and offered his arm.

"Listen, before ever'one leaves, I want to thank all of you. You put your safety in jeopardy for me, and I'm obliged to you," Sam announced.

"Yes, you are!" Rebekah concurred.

"Remember, as a way of sayin' thanks, I'm having a fancy dinner at 1:30 in the ballroom of the Merchant's Hotel. It's my treat . . . and I really would appreciate all of you bein' there."

"Oh, good," Dacee June giggled, "a cast party!"

☞ ☞ ☞

The single table in the middle of the large ballroom of the Merchant's Hotel was prepared for a private dinner of fourteen. Linens. Silver. Crystal. Fresh flowers in the center of the table. The place settings were La Reine in a colored spray pattern on a semiporcelain body, festoon plates, gold edges, knobs and handles.

Goldplated candelabras graced both ends of the table. The flicker of seven white candles in each provided the only light besides that which filtered through the lace-curtained window that peeked out on the expansive porch.

Samuel Houston Fortune paced the floor, stopping occasionally to peek out at the hotel veranda and the street. He pulled his gold watch from his vest and noticed that it was exactly sixty seconds later than the last time he looked at it.

HOME

What is this? It's almost 1:30 P.M. No one is here? No one is coming? This is strange—they all showed up to put their lives on the line for me, but they can't be here on time for dinner?

"Mr. Fortune?"

He spun around to see a thin waiter with starched white jacket, black bow tie, and receding hairline, standing at the open, ten-foot tall, carved oak door. "Mr. Fortune, Quiet Jim sends down his regrets. He said their housekeeper took sick, and Columbia doesn't want to leave the children alone, so they will not be able to make the banquet."

"Yes . . . well . . . Mr. Hobson, perhaps you'd rearrange the table setting."

"Twelve will give everyone a little more room, sir."

"I suppose so. At the moment there's plenty of room." Sam straightened his suit coat and tugged at the cuffs of his white shirt.

"Shall I bring in the chilled lemonade?" the waiter asked.

"Let's wait for the guests . . ." Sam circled the table. "They'll be along shortly."

"Certainly, sir." Hobson ambled back toward the hotel's main dining room. "Would you like this door left open?"

"Yes . . . eh, no . . . no, go ahead and close it," Sam instructed.

If I'm going to look nervous, I might as well be nervous by myself. Not that I have anything to be nervous about.

The heels of his polished black boots banged a repetitive signal as he continued to pace. Stooping low to peek out the window, he saw Sheriff Seth Bullock stroll up the boardwalk and disappear into the hotel entrance.

Sam met him at the ballroom door and motioned toward the table in the middle of the ballroom. "Glad you made it, Sheriff—"

"Sorry, Sam. I just stopped by to tell you I can't stay for dinner. I've got to scoot over to Cheyenne Crossing this afternoon. A dead body was found in Spearfish Creek, and they are mighty anxious for me to do something about it."

Mr. Hobson strolled back into the room just as the sheriff reached the exit. "Shall I remove another plate?" he queried.

"Better make that two," the sheriff reported. "Daddy Brazos is coming with me."

"Daddy? He knows this is an important dinner!" Sam chafed.

"I believe Mrs. Speaker is trailing after him again, and he prefers a little ride out of town. You know Brazos—he'd rather eat around a campfire than off a china plate."

"Two more removed?" Hobson questioned.

"Yes, I guess so," Sam mumbled. "That does narrow things."

The waiter paused at the door as he exited.

"Sorry I'm late," Abigail called as she entered the room. She wore an open front, reefer jacket made of fine, tan broadcloth, embroidered with tan and gold cording. "It took me a while to get all that dirt and stage blood washed out. Please forgive my damp hair." She stopped halfway across the room. "Where's the rest of the cast?"

"Some are late. Some made other plans."

"Oh dear. It would have been so fun for everyone to make it. You should hear the rumors around town about the gunshots at the telephone exchange."

"What are they saying?" Sam asked.

She slipped her arm in his, and they made their way to the table in the middle of the room. "Some say that Daddy Brazos declared the telephone receiver the work of the devil and blasted it with his .50-caliber Sharps."

Sam laughed. "If folks stay home to visit on the telephone instead of meetin' at the woodstove ever' mornin', he just might do it."

When they reached the table, Abby circled it, still attached to Sam's arm. "Some say that a jealous husband came lookin' for S. Houston Fortune, the man who stole his wife."

"But I've only been in town for a few weeks."

"Your reputation precedes you."

"I know I deserve comments like that. But it must pain the rest of the family. A black sheep is difficult for a good family to explain."

"A former black sheep."

"What else have you heard?" he asked.

"The one I like best is the rumor that Abby O'Neill is going to make a comeback in the theater and was secretly rehearsing a new play."

"Is that true?" Sam stopped walking, and Abby dropped his arm. "Is Miss O'Neill making a comeback?"

"Oh, I'm making a comeback all right. But it has absolutely nothing to do with the theater. It started about five years ago when I hiked up seventy-two steps to Forest Hill and first met Rebekah. My life has been one success after another ever since."

"You're not the only one that feels renewed in Deadwood." He walked with her to the front window and glanced out at Main Street. "Look at this town, Abby. A dirty, little, two-street village crammed in a gulch. It has seven times as many saloons as churches. There's not a night when gunshots aren't heard. Those stamp mills would drive other folks plumb distracted. And what kind of name is *Deadwood* anyways? Why wasn't it called Ponderosa City or somethin' else? The name itself is gloomy. And what's the most famous song about this area? 'The Dreary Black Hills.'"

She folded her arms across her chest. "And your point is? . . ."

"You found a fresh, new start here."

"Thanks to Rebekah."

"And I found a brand new direction here. What I'm sayin' is, Deadwood is a special place, not because of the gold . . . but because of what the Lord is doing here."

"You plan on staying?" she pressed.

"I have a goal that I haven't told anyone about," Sam announced. "I'd like to see at least two Christmases here."

"That's all?"

"That's as far as I can imagine. I haven't spent two months in the same location for over ten years, let alone two Christmases. How about you, Mrs. Abigail O'Neill Gordon? How long will you be in Deadwood?"

"As long as there's a Fortune in the Black Hills, Amber and I will be here."

"Say, where is that girl?" he asked.

"She wanted to go over to 'Grandma' Thelma's. The two of them are going to sing a duet in church, and they wanted to practice."

"That's quite an age spread."

"Yes, but don't tell them. They think they're the same age. Now, who does that leave for our little celebration?"

"Todd and Bekah, Dacee June and Carty . . ."

"How about Grass and Louise Edwards?"

Sam again peeked out the front window of the big ballroom. "Yep. That makes eight of us."

"That will be nice. We can visit better with only eight." Abby pointed out the street. "Look—here come the professor and Louise."

"Yes, but she's not getting out of the rig."

They arrived at the ballroom door just as Grass Edwards poked his head in. "Say, we're going to pass on dinner. I just got word from the commanding officer at Fort Meade. Said he discovered some noxious weeds making his horses sick. He wants me to identify

HOME

which ones and give a little talk to his officers about what to watch out for. Besides, Louise wanted some fresh air. All that gunsmoke plugged up her head like a nest in a chimney. We'll catch you all next time around."

"Have a nice ride," Abby called out.

"We'll be home late. Sammy, I'll see you at the hardware in the mornin'. I assume you'll be there with all the rest." Grass tipped his hat to both of them.

Mr. Hobson scooted in before the door closed. "Would you like me to begin serving yet?"

"Not yet . . . ," Sam reported. "Set the table for six. Looks like we're having a more private dinner than we planned."

"Dacee June and Carty, Rebekah and Todd . . . that will still be nice. I don't think we've all been together since the wedding," Abby noted. "I've never known a family that cared so much about each other and enjoyed being around each other as much as your family, Sam. Todd was in paradise having you and Bobby around for a week or two. He is so serious and businesslike all the time. Rebekah says he's even that way at home. But when you two were with him, he relaxed and even got jovial."

"I've missed Mama for years and will until my dyin' day. And Daddy? Well, hardly a day has passed when I didn't see somethin' that reminded me of him. But Todd, Bobby—and Dacee June—my, how I've missed them."

Abby sauntered back to the table and plucked up an empty fruit plate. "Aren't these dishes beautiful?" She set it back down and once again clutched his arm. They promenaded around the big empty room as if a full orchestra were playing a slow waltz.

"My family is so small," she said. "I'm an only child. Amber is an only child. Mama, me, and Amber . . . that's all there is."

"You're an adopted member of the Fortune family."

"And for that, I am grateful."

Hobson waited by the table when they circled back in that direction. "Can I pour you two some lemonade?" he asked.

"That would be nice," Abigail replied.

"I suppose we could sit down." Sam motioned to the well-spread table. "Hobson, the others will be along any moment now. Why don't you go ahead and bring out the food."

"Yes sir. I certainly will."

With crystal goblets of pulp-strained lemonade and winter froze ice, Sam and Abigail lingered near the front window until the waiter had completely unloaded the service cart and disappeared back into the main dining hall.

"Shall we sit at the ends and let the other couples sit next to each other?" she asked.

"If you promise not to whisper anything that I can't hear."

"Me?"

"You and Rebekah whisper and giggle more than any gals over twenty I've ever seen." He stopped pacing and stared intently at the food spread on the table.

"Thank you, kind sir, for that compliment," she curtsied.

He looped his thumbs in his vest pockets. "Compliment?"

"You could have said two gals over thirty."

Sam pointed to green, spiny blossoms, as big as his fist. "What do you suppose that is?"

Abby leaned low and examined the plate. "I believe they are artichokes."

"Are they edible or just for decoration?"

"They are quite edible, a very unusual vegetable."

Sam waved his hand. "Look at this table: sweet potatoes, corn, beans, turnips, and artichokes. That's more vegetables than I've seen in twelve years."

HOME

"Ham, venison, and pheasant . . . I believe we will have enough meat, too," she added. "Let's have Rebekah take the surplus home to her children. And another basket to Mrs. Speaker and Amber."

"They can have my share of artichokes. They look awful tough and woody. Maybe they waited too long to pick them. It's a cinch they didn't know how to cook them. I bet you're supposed to boil them."

"Hi, Sam; Abby!" Dacee June greeted as she slipped through the door. "Wow, this is really, really fancy! What are those?"

"Haven't you ever heard of artichokes?" Sam chided.

"I read about 'em once. When do they get ripe?"

"Eh . . . I think they're ripe now," Sam offered. "You're a tad late, li'l sis."

She slipped her arm around his waist and then looked Abby in the eyes. "Did I miss anything?"

"Not yet," Abby replied.

"Where's the newly-wed husband? I thought Todd gave him the afternoon off," Sam questioned.

Dacee June released Sam and rocked back on her gray, lace-up boots. "Carty is at the house. He . . . eh . . . well, this is kind of embarrassing."

"What?" Abigail pressed.

Dacee June rolled her eyes to the ceiling. "Well, he said that I look so nice today that he has no intention of sharing me with anyone else. He wants me to stay home and—"

Abigail raised her hands. "Enough said. We know exactly what you're talking about."

"You do? But you're not even married."

"We can imagine," Sam said.

"Yeah, well, I'm sorry. But all of this is sort of new to me."

Abby raised her thick, dark eyebrows. "But fun?"

"Oh, yes!" Dacee June giggled and scampered out, swinging the tall door behind her.

Abby locked her arms across her chest and smiled. "Now there is one happily married lady."

"Were you ever that young and giggly?" Sam challenged.

"I was that young, but I don't know if I ever had that much fun. How about you, Sam? Were you ever giggly?"

"Men don't giggle," he grumbled.

"Why is that?"

"Well, it's . . . it's . . . you know . . . sissylike."

"Oh, my a semanticist. Just what exactly do men do?"

"We chuckle, snicker, or guffaw . . . perhaps we even roar with laughter—but never giggle."

"Little boys giggle. I wonder why they stop?"

"Excuse me, Mr. Fortune?"

Hobson came through the door again. "There's a note here for you. It might have been at the registry for some time, but they forgot to tell me. I'm sorry for the delay."

Sam took the note, opened it, reading as he returned to Abigail's side.

"Who's it from?"

"Who's left to hear from?"

"Rebekah?"

"Listen to this:

'Dear Sam and Abby,

By now you have figured out there is a conspiracy afloat to abandon you two at dinner. If you are upset, get angry with me. It is all my idea. I thought you needed to spend more time alone. We didn't want you

HOME

to have any interruptions or distractions. So enjoy your meal and your visit. To help you have an interruption-free meal, we have instructed Mr. Hobson to lock the door after he delivers this letter.'"

"What?" Abby gasped.

"Let me finish . . ." Sam insisted.

"In fact, I am considering leaving the door locked until you two decide to marry. If you should so decide, you could slip a note under the door, and I'll fetch Rev. Colton within the hour. (Just teasing! You can't get married until Bobby and Jamie Sue get a chance to come back!)

Enjoy yourselves.

And remember, you have to tell me every single detail of what happens.

Love, Rebekah"

Abby stared at the big table covered with food. "Well, Sam Fortune, what are we going to do?"

"Right now, or in the future?"

"Both."

"Is the door really locked?" he asked.

Abby scurried across the empty ballroom and clutched the round, crystal doorknob. "Yes! It really is locked."

"Well, I have no intention of letting all this food be wasted."

"And I have no intention of us sitting at opposite ends of a twelve-foot table," she pointed to the full expanse of the table full of steaming food.

"I have an idea," Sam offered. "Help me slide the table to the window; then we'll both sit on this side."

Soon they sat side by side, facing the window, plates loaded with food.

"This is the strangest meal I've ever eaten," Sam admitted.

"I don't believe I've ever had a meal with this much food for only two people."

"Look at this: a huge empty ballroom . . . a spread fancy enough for the banquet feast of heaven . . . a beautiful lady . . . and one Sam Fortune. Even in my dreams, I could not imagine something like this."

"I do believe I won't soon forget this! Did you try the Chinese sweet and sour sauce on the pheasant? It might be the sweetest meat you will ever taste in your life." Abby stabbed a bite on her fork and held it over for him to sample.

Sam hesitated.

"Oh—don't you eat off someone else's fork?"

"No . . . no, I didn't mean to offend."

He surrounded the bite with his lips and slid the morsel into his mouth. After a moment of chewing, he smiled. "I could get spoiled with somethin' that delicious."

"Yes, but why did you hesitate?"

"I hesitated because no lady has offered me a bite off her fork since my mother died thirteen years ago. I was startled when I thought of how long it's been since I've been this close to a woman. I'm not talkin' about my virtue, but about how I feel in my heart. It just startled me; that's all."

"Now, everything's changed?"

"You can't imagine. A few weeks ago I was eatin' a bowl of cold beans with my knife. Oklahoma dust blew in my eyes, and a cocked carbine lay across my lap as I prayed for the cover of dark."

HOME

"When the Lord blesses, he blesses good." She leaned over and kissed his cheek.

He flinched. She sat straight up. "What are you scared of Sam Fortune? I presume your feelings for me aren't quite as intense as mine are for you."

"Abby, that's not it at all. Just the opposite."

She raised her eyebrows. "That doesn't always come across."

"That's because I'm so hesitant."

"Of me?"

"Of disappointin' you. I don't think you realize the burden I carry with me. I can't live a normal life like my brothers. For the rest of my life, someone like Burns or McDermitt will show up."

"I thought we took care of that this morning," she said.

"We took care of two of them. And I'm prayin' we slowed down the parade to Deadwood. But, I'll be lookin' over my shoulder . . . sittin' with my back to the wall . . . pullin' my pistol at ever' thump in the night—for the rest of my life."

Abby, slowly, let out a long breath. "I can learn to live with that."

"And ever' time some ol' gal from out of town strolls down the boardwalk and smiles at me, you're goin' to wonder if she was a friend of mine from the ol' days. Abby, sometimes she will be."

"But the Lord's forgiven you for all that."

"Yes, he has. But I have to live with the results. I'll tell you what else scares me. I'm afraid you're attracted to me because of Todd, Daddy, Bobby, and Dacee June. You have an idea what Fortunes are like. But I might not be able to live up to those standards. I never could when I was young."

"Did you try?" She speared another bite of pheasant, dipped it in the red sauce, and held it up for him to eat.

"Not really." He slid the morsel into his mouth. "I guess I've always had a streak of rebellion."

Abby wiped her lips with the linen napkin. "I'll make you a promise." She handed the napkin to Sam. "You never have to be like Todd, if I never have to be like Rebekah."

He wiped his lips and handed it back to her. "She intimidates you?" Sam stabbed a long piece of pickled okra with his fork.

"She's a dear friend, but she will always be one step—at least—beyond me. Socially, spiritually, culturally, and intellectually. Did you hear how we first met?"

"Something about you still being an actress?" He held the bite up to her lips, and she bit off the tip of the okra.

"I was playing the Gem Theater, and she sat royally up on the porch of that Forest Hill home, gazing down on the rest of town. I've never loved a woman more than I love Rebekah, but she'll always be the queen on the hill."

He leaned over and kissed her cheek.

This time, she flinched.

Sam sat back up. "What are you so scared of, Abigail Gordon? I presume your feelings for me aren't quite as intense as mine are for you."

"OK . . . I deserved that. We're not young anymore, so can I be real blunt with you?"

"Are you goin' to embarrass me?" he asked.

"I doubt if either one of us could be embarrassed by anything the other one said. I want you to know that my greatest battle in life has always been self-control. I know that is one of the fruit of the Spirit in the Bible. But it does not come easy, even after five years of trusting the Lord."

"How does that fit with my kiss on the cheek?" he pressed.

HOME

"After I left my husband, Dr. Gordon, I spent a number of years with little self-control. I went where I wanted, did what I pleased, chased all my whims and dreams, and dragged Amber around with me. If it felt good to me, I did it."

"And?"

"And you kissing my cheek, Sam Fortune, feels good. Really good."

"What's wrong that?"

"Because I won't want you to stop with the cheek! The next thing I know I'll want to kiss your lips, and then . . . well, you see what I'm talking about? I have no sense of moderation. I'm beginning to sound like Dacee June, aren't I?"

Sam slipped his hand into hers. "Do you yell when you get mad?"

"What?"

"When you get angry, do you stomp and yell?"

"What does that have to do with anything?"

"Answer my question," he insisted.

"Yes, I have a tendency to get loud and theatrical when I'm angry," she announced.

"Good, so do I."

"What's good about it?" she challenged.

"Then you'll understand that I can love you, even if I'm yelling at you. Some women don't understand that."

"Are you trying to say that you love me, Sam Fortune?"

"Of course I am."

"Good," she triumphed.

"Why?"

"Because I love you too. And since your family is going to force us to get married, it's nice that we love each other." She raised up their hands and brushed a kiss across his fingers.

"What are we goin' to do about the screamin' when we're angry?" he asked.

"I believe we should live on the edge of town."

"I think you're right. How about a place along Whitewood Gulch, beyond Ingleside?"

"That might be a long walk to get to Rebekah's. I need to talk to her every day."

"You can call her on the telephone," Sam suggested.

"There will be telephones up Whitewood Gulch?"

"There will be telephones anywhere I want them to be. Of course, I don't have the money to build such a place for a while."

"We can wait," Abigail assured him. "In the meantime, we could live above my store."

"Yes, that's nice." He raised her hand and mashed a kiss into her fingers. "I can have my own room."

"When we're married, you do not get your own room, Mr. Fortune. You'll have to share."

"But, I hear you're self-centered."

"Too bad." She lowered their hands to the top of her thigh.

"Will we rent out my room to someone else?"

"No, we'll combine the entire second floor for an apartment, until we build a place on Whitewood Creek."

"I trust we won't have to wait very long." He slipped his hand from hers and ran it out to her knee, then squeezed gently.

"For the marriage or for a house?" She put her hand on his knee and squeezed tight.

Sam chewed on his tongue. "Both."

"Well, I don't think Bobby and Jamie Sue will be coming back until Christmas." Abigail ran her tongue across her top lip.

"That will work. It's the logical thing to do." Sam tugged his tie loose. "We can get to know each other better . . . make some

HOME

plans . . . save up some money . . . get this phone exchange company up and running . . . and then have a Christmas Eve wedding
service."

Abby took a linen napkin and wiped the perspiration off her
forehead. "Oh, that sounds wonderful! Romantic! Sounds like
something Dacee June or Rebekah would do, doesn't it?"

"It certainly does."

"I suppose we can tell everyone we're engaged." She reached up
and unfastened the top button on the high, lace collar of her
blouse.

"Yes, that should satisfy them for a while." He took the napkin
from her hand and wiped the back of his neck.

"I think Dacee June would spend all fall planning the wedding
for us." Abby reached over and unfastened the top button of his
stiff, white shirt collar.

"Undoubtedly." Sam searched the food scattered around on the
table. "There's not a scrap of paper anywhere on this table, is there?"

"No . . . I don't see anything. I suppose you could use one of
these linen napkins."

He leaned closer to her and slipped his arm around her waist.
"The hotel might frown on that."

"How about that paper doily under the candelabra?"

Sam hugged her tight then released her. "Yes, that would work."

Abby pulled out a lace-edged, round paper doily, folded it in
half, then handed it to him. "Do you have a pencil?" she asked.

"Yes. It's a legacy from being a businessman. Dacee June makes
sure I carry a sharpened pencil at all times." He cleared a spot on
the table, took the folded doily, then began to write.

"I'm grateful to Dacee June for that. She seems to really enjoy
working at the telephone company." Her left hand remained on his
right knee.

Sam finished up the note and folded it in half again. "Yes, she does, but I figure she'll tire of that once she begins havin' children."

Abby stood and plucked the note from his hand. "And when do you think that will be?"

Sam stood, pulled off his suit coat, and hung it on the back of his chair. "I'd say about nine months from today, wouldn't you?"

"I think you're right about that." Abby sashayed across the empty ballroom and slid the folded doily note under the door. She watched as it was immediately tugged through from the other side.

She waltzed back over and slipped her hand into Sam's. "Well, Mr. S. Houston Fortune, how soon will it be before Rebekah brings Rev. Colton?" she quizzed.

"I told her she needed to bring Amber, a marriage license, and Rev. Colton within an hour, or we're all goin' to be in big trouble," Sam reported.

Sam held her arm tight and began to stroll the big empty ballroom.

"And just what are we going to do for a whole hour, Sam Fortune?"

He could feel her soft, warm fingers laced into his thick, calloused ones. He raised them to his lips and brushed them with a kiss. "I think, Abigail O'Neill Gordon, that we'd better keep walking!"

Look for Robert Fortune's story in

Book Four of the

Fortunes of the Black Hills Series

HEAD FOR THE HILLS

WITH THE OTHER TWO TITLES IN THE FORTUNES OF THE BLACK HILLS SERIES.

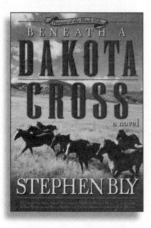

If you enjoyed *The Long Trail Home*, pick up the first two titles in the Fortunes of the Black Hills series---*Beneath a Dakota Cross* and *Shadow of Legends*. The series traces the lives of the Fortune family as they struggle to survive during the Dakota Territory gold rush of the 1870s. Best-selling author Stephen Bly brings this authentic western saga to life with strong, moral characters and a storyline that weaves issues of the west with important spiritual lessons. The result of his powerful prose is a rich tapestry of drama, intrigue, adventure, and romance set in the Old West.

Book 1, *BENEATH A DAKOTA CROSS*
0-8054-1659-5, tp, $12.99

Book 2, *SHADOW OF LEGENDS*
0-8054-2174-2, tp, $12.99

Available wherever fine books are sold, or call 1-800-448-8403 to order.

BROADMAN
&HOLMAN
PUBLISHERS